Men Among Sirens

Jennifer Olmstead

ISBN: 1-4392-3684-4
ISBN-13: 9781439236840
LCCN: 2009904613

To order additional copies, please contact us.
BookSurge
www.booksurge.com
1-866-308-6235
orders@booksurge.com

I want to thank my family and friends, whose support made the completion of this book possible: Walter, Patrick, Jill Arnone, Patty Holmes, Teri Lanning, Alana Tarvin, Kim Powis, Lanie Deans, Betty Freeman, Jane Plante, Sherri Furchenicht and Judy Cowling; my brother David and sister Mary Ann, who filled in the blanks where my own memory of childhood visits to the Upper Peninsula failed me, and contributed countless hours of editorial assistance; Professor Cummings, whose advice I should have heeded in 1978; and lastly, my parents Joseph and Mary Ann.

Forgotten is Forgiven.

—*F. Scott Fitzgerald*

chapter I

AINSLEY BOHAN'S FOOTSTEPS echoed through the cavernous entrance hall of 313 Water's Edge Lane. It was a scorching Wednesday in June, just shy of eight in the morning and humid enough to leave you breathless, but the Victorian home's foot-thick walls held fast against the onslaught of another southern Virginia summer. Through the front door's leaded-glass window, Ainsley saw three young women, crammed together against the threshold, each of them clutching a large object to their chest. They reminded her of restless racehorses gamboling in a closed starting gate in the final seconds leading up to a race.

"Good morning, ladies." She spoke quickly and stepped aside, clearing their path toward her daughter.

"Good morning, Mrs. Bohan," they answered back.

Individual voices were indistinguishable as the trio sprinted by her, chattering, and began scaling the thick oak steps of the foyer's massive spiral staircase. Sage green bridesmaid dresses, sheathed in plastic and dangling from hangers, sailed along behind them.

"Hurry up guys," twenty-one year-old Ruby Bohan called down the stairwell. "We only have an hour this morning. Got a family breakfast thing at nine." Barefoot and dressed in a gauzy white skirt and pink cotton top, Ruby precariously balanced her upper body over the second-floor balustrade. Long, straight, toffee-colored hair fell past her shoulders and framed her heart-shaped face. With the sun streaming onto her from a window above, she looked ethereal.

The siren gene—that's what Ruby's maternal grandfather, Don Plante, called it. He coined the phrase for his wife, Julie, the first of three generations of women with the same voluptuous build, impervious to any amount of weight training or dieting, gossamer brown hair, and pale blue eyes. The women were a living testament to the power of heredity. And, heredity dealt them one wildcard: well proportioned, almost elegant noses—except for a small but noticeable bump in the middle. A veteran lawyer, Don maintained a pragmatic yet philosophical stance on their shared flaw. "Something had to give—to keep you humble," he reasoned. "Otherwise, you'd be too perfect. You'd lack character."

Three short days and a lengthy list of unfinished tasks remained until Ruby's Saturday wedding, throwing the entire Bohan household into varying degrees of chaos. Fortunately, 313 Water's Edge Lane provided more than enough room for all the necessary wedding preparations and revelry. Ainsley had converted the home's now dormant playroom and her adjoining dressing room into a pre-bridal salon for Ruby's hair, makeup and wardrobe, as well as storage for a steadily growing mound of wedding gifts. Seven spare bedrooms stood ready to accommodate out-of-town family and any friends who celebrated more heartily than anticipated. Following an afternoon church ceremony, the reception would take place under tents in the Bohan's expansive side yard, the same location as Ainsley's wedding reception, twenty-four years before.

By nine o'clock, Ruby's bridal party huddle was complete. She trailed behind her friends as they clattered down the stairs and out the front door. "Final fitting tomorrow morning, guys—then it's spa day. Don't be late!" she called to them before wheeling around and running down the hall to find her mother.

"My God, Ruby, you're...effervescent!" Ainsley said, amused by her daughter's unbridled giddiness.

"I know, Mom. Here I am embarking on the most adult of journeys, and I'm acting like a kid. But, I'm just so happy!"

Ainsley sensed an emotional outpouring on the horizon. Ruby obliged.

"Mom, I want to thank you for all the help you've given me with the wedding," she told Ainsley. "I know you and Dad—well, you mostly—are worried about me being only twenty-one, and Rob and I making this huge commitment. When you married Dad, you were only one year older than I am now, and look at your marriage. All these years together, what you've been through—Uncle John's death, Dad's accident." Her voice wavered with sentiment. "I've learned so much from you two. We're ready to do this, and we'll make it work. Mom, I'll be in D.C.—only three short hours away." She took a breath, sniffled, and wiped her nose.

Ainsley smiled with reassurance, unwilling to spoil Ruby's vision of her parents' marriage days before the start of her own. It was her daughter's right to feel a sense of joy and endless possibilities the week of her wedding. "Ruby," Ainsley began, "if any two people belong together—"

A sudden, deafening roar drowned out her words. The thunderous boom escalated to earsplitting decibels with each passing second, as a pair of FA-18 Hornets breached the airspace over the house, producing a high-pitched hum in dozens of century-old windows, forcing glass panes to rattle in their frames. Flyovers were a daily occurrence in Virginia Beach, typically at eight or nine in the morning, noon and four o'clock, drawing phone calls, arguments, church services, weddings, and funerals throughout the city to a simultaneous, minute-long halt. *I Love Jet Noise* stickers adorned tens of thousands of vehicles and storefronts alike, reminders of the military's integral presence in the community.

Ruby locked eyes with Ainsley. "I know, Mom," she said, looking upward, "Uncle Johnny." She'd never met Ainsley's brother, USN Captain John "Johnny Angel" Plante of Oceana Naval Air Station's Heavin' Bulldogs Squadron. His jet took a fatal dive into the Atlantic Ocean just shy of a year before Ruby was born. Vestiges of John lingered in the house: photographs; stories her parents and grandparents shared on birthdays and holidays; the personal effects that she browsed in his third floor bedroom, which remained much as he left it when he joined the Navy in 1982.

"Speaking of uncles," Ainsley said, shaking off an old, stubborn wave of sadness, "have you seen your dad or your Uncle Blaine this morning?"

"I think Dad is in the kitchen having coffee with Rob...and Grandma and Grandpa." As she spoke, Ruby made several futile attempts to tie her straight, slippery hair into a knot. "I don't know about Uncle Blaine."

Ainsley took a turn at smoothing Ruby's hair and managed to fashion it into a spiky, twisted bun. "Would you find him and tell him we're ready to go to breakfast?" she asked.

"Sure," Ruby replied. "When we get back, can we drop the others off here and hit those stores we talked about? I need help picking out a bathing suit for Fiji."

"Absolutely," Ainsley agreed.

Ruby ascended the stairs, straight-backed, her chin upturned, clearly practicing for Saturday's trip down the aisle. Once she vanished from view, Ainsley went into the downstairs guest bath to freshen up and comb her hair. Confronting her reflection in the mirror, she had to acknowledge that time was finding its way onto her face. A fine line at the corner of each eye. Slight deepening in the contours of her cheeks. That inexpressible trace of grief behind her smile. World-weary but still pretty, for what it was worth. What *was* it worth in an unfulfilled life? An occasional stare, or glare, depending on the situation and the gender of the observer? Maybe the waning of physical beauty—however subtle or graceful—served as a stark visual record of how much in life cannot be recaptured, a cruel mapping of the loss of youth. Hers was falling away behind her, and she feared growing old and regretting not only her mistakes—her sins—but also those things she should have found the courage to do, and couldn't name or define. That reflection was too painful to confront right now. She turned off the bathroom light.

Upstairs, Ruby floated by her bedroom, pale blue with white draperies and bed linens, bathed in sunlight from a floor-to-ceiling bay window. She passed the hall bathroom, the linen closet, and a small alcove on the way to her Uncle Blaine's room, the same room he used each time he visited from Michigan. The room's heavy door had drifted open several inches, its untrustworthy old latch once again failing to hold without the skeleton key engaged. As she pulled her hand back to knock, Ruby caught him standing in front of a full-length mirror, wearing black paisley boxers and an open white shirt. She didn't mean to look; it was startling to see him half-dressed for the first time in her life. He secured two small collar buttons and buttoned his cuffs, then moved in the open shirt and rolled his shoulders, exposing a tight, smooth abdomen. Ruby didn't know of any other fifty-year-old man as fit as he was, especially in his line of work. She stood in place, curious, watching him as he buttoned the shirt's placket. That's when she saw it—a small, burgundy spot, not much larger than a mole, inside his right hipbone. She froze, locking in on the mark as though it was a target.

"Oh, my God!" she shrieked, jerking back her hand. She ran to her room, slamming and locking the door behind her.

Alarmed by Ruby's screams, Blaine went to the staircase landing, still barefoot and in his boxers. "Ainsley! Ainsley!" he shouted into the stairwell as he ran to Ruby's door. "Something's wrong with Ruby!"

Ainsley grabbed the staircase railing and rushed up the stairs, all thirty-two of them, to the second floor. "Ruby," she gasped, winded from the climb, "are you hurt?" She elbowed Blaine out of the way and pounded on Ruby's bedroom door. No answer. She tried the doorknob. "Ruby, please!"

Through the thick door, Blaine and Ainsley heard muffled crying and creaking floorboards as footsteps came in their direction. Seconds passed, a key turned in the lock, and the doorknob crawled sideways.

"I think 'someday' is here now," Ainsley said, motioning Blaine away as the door began to open. He stayed in place. "Please, Blaine," she whispered, "go downstairs with the others. Take them to breakfast—now. Keep them there while I find out what's going on."

"Are you sure you'll be all right?" he asked, placing a hand on her shoulder.

"What are you doing?" she snapped, rebuffing the gesture.

He hurried to his room to finish dressing.

Several inches of daylight separated the dark mahogany door from its doorway, and Ruby's red, tear-stained face filled the space. "I hate you," she seethed.

Ainsley was frantic. "For God's sake, let me in! What is going on?"

Ruby cracked the door wide enough for Ainsley to squeeze through, closing it tight after her. "I don't want *him* in here."

Ainsley tried once more to reason with her daughter. "Is it the wedding?" she asked, praying that her suspicions were wrong and Ruby's outburst was a simple case of cold feet. "Are you having second thoughts? Because, that's normal, you know—"

"No!" Ruby shouted, tears rolling down her chin and onto the front of her t-shirt. "What's 'normal' about this?" She pushed up the shirt and shoved her skirt down past her hip. "Look familiar, Mom?" She collapsed onto the bed, sobbing.

Ainsley sat down next to her. "I'm sorry," she said, her voice trembling.

"Sorry!" Ruby roared back. She dropped her head onto a pillow and stared at the wall, absorbing the shock of her revelation. "I feel... dirty," she said, and then shot up from the bed and began hurling questions. "What kind of person are you? How could you do this to me—and our family? With Uncle Blaine? That's sick!"

"Ruby, please...keep your voice down," Ainsley pleaded. "I wanted to—to shield you."

"Shield me?" Ruby paced the floor with clenched fists. "I do need to be shielded—from you! My whole life, I thought you were a good person. I idolized you. I wanted to be you! I thought that you loved Dad. Oh, God. Dad." A look of disgust washed over her. "What's been going on here, in our house, and up in Michigan, all of these years?"

"I never meant to hurt you—or your father," Ainsley insisted.

The faint sound of multiple footsteps and Chris Bohan's motorized wheelchair rolling along the porch floorboards below indicated that Blaine had been successful in herding the others off to breakfast, leaving the two women with the house to themselves for several hours.

"We'll go downstairs," Ainsley said, as she opened the bedroom door. "I'll make some coffee." It sounded absurd; she had no idea why she suggested it.

"Coffee?" Ruby was incredulous. "I don't want coffee!" She stormed past Ainsley and out of the room.

Five minutes later, Ruby reunited with her mother in the kitchen. Despondency had replaced her anger. She wore a glazed expression as she sat on the fireplace hearth, her arms wrapped around her knees, holding herself tightly. "It's true, isn't it?" she asked. "Who knows about this—aside from you and...Blaine?" Her lip curled in repulsion as she said his name. She looked as though she was about to be sick. "Who else, Mom?" she demanded. "Surely...not Dad?"

"No one else knows, Ruby. I've lived a very...careful life."

"You mean a lie, don't you?" Ruby corrected her. "You've lived a very careful lie. You and Blaine."

Ainsley pulled a chair up to the kitchen's long, rectangular table, host to countless school projects, holiday baking marathons, late night talks, and even a tryst or two when she and Chris were newlyweds. "Ruby, it's a lot," she said, exhausted from the confrontation, and from guarding the secret of her past for more than two decades. Her finger traced the letter "A," permanently etched into the table's surface, a relic from her own childhood. "How much of the story do you want to hear?" she asked.

Ruby let out a weighty, miserable sigh, wiped tears from her face with her hands, and fused her brows together in a frown. "All of it," she said coldly. "I want you to tell me all of it."

chapter 2

As she stood in her laundry room, in the middle of a pile of clothes, Ainsley's entire body shook with rage. She was in clear sight of her husband Chris, who leaned his slim hips against the kitchen counter, engrossed in the process of popping the cap off a bottle of imported beer. Pale blonde curls fell across his forehead, covering one of his eyes, which were the color of a forest green crayon. Dark brown lashes and light brown eyebrows, just visible enough to reflect his frequently changing expression, framed them. His hair dripped into ringlets when he let it grow long, which was most of the time, unless he was nagged into shearing it by his parents, who considered it unbefitting of a future attorney to resemble a rock star. Ainsley never got around to asking him to cut it because she loved it so much. Right now, though, she detested it, along with everything else about him.

She wrung the leg of a pair of his jeans in her hands. "Goddamn it, Chris, not again. We've been married less than two years! If you don't want to do this, I'll let you go."

Chris put down his beer. "What are you talking about?" he asked, wide-eyed.

"I'm talking about this!" she yelled, pulling a torn condom wrapper out of the jeans' pocket. Without thinking, he had tossed the pants in the laundry the day before. She had somehow managed to keep silent about her discovery overnight, waiting for the right time to confront him. There would be no right time, she realized. "Should I be grateful that you used a condom?" she screamed, casting the jeans at him. "Or, maybe I'm infected with something already?"

Her eyes brimmed with angry tears, but she refused to let him see her cry. "You're disgusting!"

"Let me explain…." Chris shook his head as he spoke, and his curls bounced and then redistributed themselves around his face. He filled his cheeks with a long swig of beer and swallowed.

"Explain? Explain how?" Ainsley's shouting woke up her three-month-old Mastiff puppy, Attila, who ran to her and sat at her feet. "No explanation. No excuses, Chris. I've already heard them all."

"She meant nothing to me, Ains."

"Then, why? Why do it? Aren't I—isn't our life together—enough for you?"

He stared at the floor, shuffling some non-existent object between his feet, a remorseful child. "It was a mistake. I drank too much."

"You always drink too much now, Chris, and your tactics aren't working. They dragged John's body out of the Atlantic Ocean two weeks ago. You told me the day of his funeral that his death made you realize how precious life is, our marriage is. You were going to re-prioritize, remember? Now this? Fuck you!" She bolted from the room. Attila trailed behind her, struggling to keep up.

"Ains, wait." Chris followed her up the oval staircase to their second-floor bedroom.

"Wait?" she bellowed back. "I'm tired of waiting for you…to grow up…to decide what you want. You're twenty-six. I'm twenty-four. How much longer is it going to take?" She pulled her suitcases from the closet. "I'm taking John's ashes to Michigan alone," she said, and then corrected herself, "with Attila." Turning her back to him, she packed blind, haphazardly stuffing three seasons of clothes into two giant suitcases, since the spring weather on Michigan's Upper Peninsula was unpredictable. May wasn't too late for freezing weather to blow in after a seventy-degree day, and the selection of clothing stores in the area was sparse. Most Upper Peninsula residents did their shopping through the Sears Roebuck catalogue.

Chris stood in the bedroom doorway until Ainsley's silence froze him out, and he shrank down the stairs to drink alone, behind closed doors, in the library.

She finished loading her new blue-and-white Ford Bronco in two trips. "I'll be gone until June twenty-eighth," she shouted to Chris through the closed library door.

"June twenty-eighth?" he called back. "That's a whole month—and our anniversary!"

"Our anniversary? Are you serious?" She snorted in disgust. "You should have thought about that before you went out dicking around again."

"Ains, please," he begged.

"No more chances, Chris. No more of this. Give anyone who calls for me the number at the Makwa Point house. Or, have them call Jill. She knows where I'll be if anything comes up."

Chris opened the library door. "Jill? She knows more about this trip than I do."

"That's because I see Jill more than I see you, Chris," Ainsley fumed. It was a true statement.

At the end of Bohan's block-long yard, over the thick wall of Forsythia, sat a neat, red-brick ranch bordered by pink azaleas. When its original owners died, Jill and Bill Horner made it their first home. He was a Navy SEAL, gone most of the year. She was an elementary school teacher, now working part-time and caring for their new baby. The day Ainsley met Jill—delivering an armful of roses from her garden to Jill as a housewarming gift—she knew they would be friends.

"You know what, Chris? Don't bring Jill into this. It's about us." Ainsley gathered up Attila's heavy, wrinkled bulk, and carried her to the car. The puppy studied her with sleepy eyes.

Why did I believe him? she thought, driving away from her towering house. She and Chris had fallen in love as teenagers, and married after her third year of college and his first year of law school. Long commutes to Williamsburg for late-night study groups presented him with temptations he claimed he couldn't resist, in the form of female law students with steaming libidos and no expectation of significant, long-term relationships. When she and Chris moved back into her family home, Ainsley envisioned a fresh start, the two of them filling it with their own memories, of children and happy noise. Instead, its three stories resonated with pain and betrayal. Coping with her brother's sudden death left her no reserve of sympathy or pity for Chris' serial infidelity—only regret that she hadn't learned the truth sooner. Her priority now was honoring John's request that his ashes be scattered on Lake Michigan.

Ainsley made her way through Virginia Beach toward Interstate 64. It was eleven in the morning. With twelve straight hours of driving and an overnight in Ohio, she could make it to her family's summer house by early evening the next day. She adjusted her rearview mirror and caught a glimpse of the urn containing John's ashes protruding from a cardboard box on the backseat.

Like everyone in his family, Ainsley's brother John loved the water. Almost as much as he loved flying airplanes. His first time airborne was helping to throw bubble gum and chocolate eggs onto the Virginia Beach Country Club's golf course on Easter Sunday 1970, when he was ten and Ainsley was eight. The two of them accompanied their father, Don, and Don's friend Bill Sanders, who owned a small Piper aircraft, on the annual mission. A bumpy takeoff from the grass runway of the Virginia Beach Municipal Airport signaled the start of Ainsley's terrifying, maiden flight. She clutched Don's arm for most of the one-hour trip, her face ashen. John was oblivious to the plane's bumps and dips, talking non-stop to Bill, asking about altitude, controls, and take-off and landing.

"What's wrong honey?" Don asked his daughter as she dug her fingers into the armrests of her seat. "Don't you want to help Johnny throw some candy onto the golf course?"

"I feel sick, Daddy. My stomach hurts." She started to cry.

"You're just anxious, Ainsley. Everything's okay. Trust me. We'll be on the ground soon." They were, but it took Ainsley a solid hour to calm down.

"Well, we know you won't be a flight attendant, dear," Don said, laughing.

"It's okay, Ainsley," John told her. "When we grow up, I'll fly you where you need to go, and I'll go real slow. I'm gonna be a pilot," he said, smiling. John always looked out for her, was always there for her. They were best friends—until he died.

The telephone call came at three in the morning on May 4, 1986. Ainsley fumbled for the phone in the dark.

"Honey, were you asleep?" It was her father. She barely recognized his voice.

"That's okay, Dad. What's wrong?" she asked, steeling herself for bad news. "Is it Mom?"

"Honey, you'd better sit up and turn on a light...if you haven't yet."

She heard her mother whispering in the background, and felt a pulse of relief. It quickly evaporated. "Dad, you're scaring me," she said, certain that she would remember the phone call for the rest of her life.

"Ainsley," his voice faltered, "it's about Johnny." He began to sob into the phone and Ainsley did too, knowing her brother was gone.

The call roused Chris from sleep, and he sat up in bed. "What's going on?" he asked, disoriented.

Ainsley didn't hear him. "No, Dad," she whimpered. "How?"

"His jet—it went down—over Kitty Hawk. They're out there now, retrieving his body—and his aircraft." Don's voice was hoarse, his words almost indiscernible.

"Maybe he got out," she said. As she spoke, weakness swept over her.

Listening to her half of the conversation, Chris pieced together the story.

"No, honey," Don muttered, "he didn't eject. They would have known."

"What about Mom?"

Now Don's voice was high and weak. "She's here with me. We're leaving on the next flight out, but it'll take us a day or two to get there. You might get some calls from John's commanding officer at Oceana. We gave him your number...since we'll be in flight."

"I understand, Dad." She took a breath, digging deep for some strength, for her parents' sake. "Give me your flight information."

She squeezed her eyes shut for a moment to stop crying. "I'll be waiting for you and Mom at the airport."

The next morning, Don and Julie boarded the once-daily commuter plane from Fiji, the first phase of their forty-hour journey home to Virginia Beach.

Their unexpected relocation to the South Pacific began as a two-week, once-in-a-lifetime vacation to Taveuni Island in 1985. Talking with some Fijian locals one day while boating to an outlying island to snorkel, they were stunned to learn the island's low cost of living. Then they stumbled onto the grounds of an abandoned copra farm while hiking to a scenic mountaintop lookout area. There, on the lush, green hillside overlooking the Pacific Ocean, eating chicken roti sandwiches and sipping wine of some little-known provenance, Don and Julie had a joint epiphany. After obtaining permission from the village chief to buy the plantation, a necessary prerequisite for foreigners, they returned home and announced their intentions to their astounded children.

"Dad, you're forty-nine!" John said, as he and Ainsley sat with them in a booth at the Ready Room Diner, located steps away from the gates of Oceana Naval Base. "Is this a joke?"

"We love it there!" Julie's face lit up as she spoke. "It's paradise. Unspoiled, pristine and safe. It's a chance to bring that gorgeous old plantation back to life as an Inn!"

John rolled his hazel eyes. "Oh, shit, it's the old 'fix it up' routine, like the house," he said, plunking a combat boot onto his parents' seat. He brushed through his black crew cut with his hand and gulped sugary coffee, trying to stay awake. "And, you're still fuc—futzing around with that."

"But your career, Mom," Ainsley protested. "You put it on hold to raise us, and you've just gotten it going again."

"Just gotten it going?" Julie challenged. "Ten years is a respectable career span, Ainsley, and I'm positive that the world will survive with one less real estate attorney. Besides, both of you know that your dad has always been more important to me than my career."

Ainsley knew they had made up their minds. "You'll be a world away from us, literally," she lamented.

"Don't worry. We'll get it up and running, and then move back home," Julie vowed, pushing her breakfast around her plate. "You know how we are. Dad and I will make it successful and probably sell it as soon as one of you has a grandchild for us to baby-sit. We really don't see ourselves staying there forever. You two have made your own lives at such a young age, we have the chance to do one last foolish thing—yes, Johnny—like when we bought Water's Edge Lane and restored it."

"And, a change of scene will do us good, especially after that whole cancer scare I went through," Don said.

"How will we see you?" Ainsley asked, dejected.

"Well, for John it's easy...sort of." Julie turned to her son. "You can hop a MAC to the closest allied base. Ainsley, all you and Chris need is airfare, because you won't have to worry about rent anymore."

"What do you mean, Mom?" Ainsley asked.

"Well, I'm sorry Chris isn't with us to hear this firsthand, but your dad and I figure, as long as you keep half of the third floor reserved for us when we're stateside, you and Chris will have our house. Make it your own."

Ainsley almost choked on her food. "Mom!" she gasped. She loved the house more than anyone should, hoping to call part of it hers someday, in the far-off future, after her parents were gone. Their offer to her today, to let her take a turn at running the household, was overwhelming.

313 Water's Edge Lane began its life in 1867 as the home of Forrest Keach, sole heir to a Norfolk railroad baron's fortune. He designed the twelve-thousand-square-foot, Second Empire French Victorian mansion as a duplex, reserving one side to share with his wife, Anne, and offering the other to his ailing, elderly mother. The house sat on a manicured, two-acre lot on the southern edge of Princess Anne County, Virginia, later known as Virginia Beach.

Intent upon impressing their social circle and putting the devastation of the Civil War behind them, Forrest and Anne spared no expense on the bones of the house, its elaborate façade or its interior details. Its two, three-story units were almost identical save some small variances in staircase design, window placement, and room layout. Guests who braved the journey from Norfolk out to the far reaches of the county were rewarded with long weekends of horseback riding, lawn tennis, lavish dinner parties and strolls through Anne's spectacular rose garden. A childless couple, the Keach's deaths sparked the grand home's decline. Over the next fifty years, it passed from owner to owner, each one less able than their predecessor to afford its proper maintenance.

By the time Julie Plante stumbled upon the ramshackle monstrosity, which locals dubbed "The Psycho House," it was a cold November day in 1960. She passed it on her way to a local farm market in search of fresh gourds and pumpkins for her Thanksgiving dinner table. Eight months pregnant and eager to create a family nest, she backed up her car and pulled into the overgrown driveway, punted open solid oak front entry doors, whose hinges were frozen with rust, and gingerly crept across the first floor of the abandoned residence, dodging broken glass, dead birds and rotting floor boards. The project spelled challenge. And Julie loved a challenge. She and Don bought the house for twenty thousand dollars, cash, since no bank would approve financing the dilapidated structure, knocked down the common divider wall on all three floors, and vowed to restore it beyond its former grandeur.

"Let's do a dark red roof and porch floor with cream siding," Julie suggested, as she and Don stood in the front yard of their new home, gazing at weathered, gray siding and broken roof tiles. It was Christmas week, and their first child was due any day. Both of them were exhausted from a weekend of moving.

"Are you crazy? How gaudy!" Don boomed. He saw the hurt look on her face and wanted to kick himself for his thoughtlessness. He tried for a quick recovery. "I mean...honey...it'll stick out like a sore thumb."

"And it doesn't now?" she shot back at him, fuming.

"You have a point, dear." He was still on thin ice and knew it.

"Why be afraid to make it beautiful?" she said, near tears, a common state as she approached her due date. "Let's give it life again,

Don. It'll always be out of place here. But if people are going to look at it anyway, why not make it something worth seeing?"

"Okay, you win." He put his arm around her. "I'll call the roofer and the painter tomorrow."

She leaned into his shoulder.

"Today," he conceded, "I'll call today."

Julie's instincts were right. In time, 313 Water's Edge Lane traded its reputation as a vermin-filled eyesore for that of a local point of interest, even garnering a feature article in the regional newspaper's house and garden section. After living there for twenty years, she still considered the house a work in progress, always finding some little thing to improve or rearrange.

"Well, Ainsley?" Julie asked.

Ainsley looked from her father to her mother. "Mom, Dad, are you sure about this?"

"It's a lot of work, Ainsley, and I can't throw Margie into the deal," Julie said. "She told me that she's retiring for good this time. Are you sure you're up to taking care of it on your own? You just started your first real job."

"I'll find a way. Don't worry about that. I know how to clean a house. Chris will take care of the repairs and maintenance." She was ecstatic at the prospect of returning to the house, even if she had to spend half her time cleaning it.

"And John, there's plenty of room, if you want to use it as a... crash pad," Julie said. "Isn't that what you call it? Ainsley, you and Chris won't mind if John uses it as a home base, too, will you?"

"I'm good with the Oceana BOQ right now," John answered politely. "Otherwise your home will become another 'Animal House.'"

Julie baulked.

"Sorry Mom, but we do get a little loco sometimes—after we've protected the planet from certain doom for days on end."

"Well, I think we have a deal, dear," Julie told Ainsley, smiling. "Maybe you can finally restore that old rose garden. I never did get around to working on that thing."

One month later, Julie and Don moved to the other side of the globe, leaving John to circle the free world in his FA-18, and Ainsley and Chris, married for one short year, to abandon their three-room apartment for her childhood home, all twenty-five rooms of it. Ainsley tried to be optimistic about a change in venue triggering a change in Chris' behavior. He'd been unfaithful twice—that she knew of. Both times, it meant nothing, he declared. Both times, he was under the influence of alcohol, he said. Both times, she died a little inside. Ainsley never told her family about either incident, and agreed to give him one more chance.

When John died a year later, she was devastated, crippled by grief. Chris uncharacteristically stepped up and helped Julie and Don with final arrangements. He even coaxed Margie out of retirement to clean the entire house and manage the post-memorial reception. It was as though the death of someone his age shook him into maturity. The night following John's memorial service, after her parents left for the airport, Chris made a promise to Ainsley: "I'll make you, and our life together, my priority. I don't deserve you, but I'm going to change that—starting now. It's time for us to take a look at our own family's future."

"What do you mean by that?" she asked him, drained from the long, heartbreaking week.

"I think we should fill some of these empty rooms."

She was taken aback. "Now? Start a family now?"

He pushed her onto their bed and crouched on top of her. "Come on, baby," he crooned. "Throw out that diaphragm thing of yours and let nature take its course. No pressure. We'll see what happens."

"I'm not sure that you understand the ramifications of this decision. It will be a big, permanent change in our lifestyle."

"Exactly. I've been thinking, and I've concluded that it's what I need—what we need. To breathe some life back into this old house. Especially after what happened to John."

Once again alone in the house, they made love, sadly at first, and then with abandon, excited by total freedom from preparation or preventative measures.

A week later, Julie's voice faltered as she spoke to her daughter over the phone from Fiji. "Listen Ainsley, if you're not sure about this—taking care of John's ashes, I mean—your dad and I will come back over to Virginia." She muffled her sobs. "We'll take Johnny's ashes up to the lake."

"No, Mom," Ainsley told her. "He loved Michigan. It's what he wanted, and I want to do this for him."

"Honey, I don't know if I want you making that trip alone."

Ainsley collected herself. "I'm okay. And, Mom, Chris is coming with me. It'll be good for us to get away together. He likes it up there, too."

"If you're sure, Ainsley," she said. "You know, I think John's watching over you now. I do."

"Is he?" Ainsley asked. She felt no sense of her brother's presence at all—only a dark, sickening void.

"What was that, honey?" Julie asked.

Ainsley was glad Julie hadn't heard her. It was a stupid, childish thing to say to a mother trying to survive burying her son. "I said, 'I love you,' Mom. Now, go outside with Dad and eat some mangos for me, right off of the tree."

"Be careful, Ainsley," Julie said, her voice quivering. "You're all we have now."

A putrid smell jolted Ainsley back to the reality of driving. It was noon, and she had already passed through the Hampton Roads Bridge-Tunnel and was in Newport News without remembering how she got there. She took her foot off the accelerator and drifted into the right lane. "Oh, no, Attila," she groaned, "you didn't."

The puppy looked at her from the passenger seat with soulful eyes as she sat in a pile of her own excrement, her copious drooling foreboding a bout of vomiting. Ainsley found a wide piece of asphalt road shoulder and pulled over. Using half a canister of baby wipes and wads of paper towel, she cleaned up both the seat and Attila, and then wrestled a motion sickness pill down the dog's throat. "Let's try this again, Attila," she said, pulling back onto the interstate. With one hour of driving behind them, and seventeen more to go, it was going to be a long trip.

chapter 3

AS SHE MERGED into the exit lane leading to the Mackinac Bridge, Ainsley gripped the steering wheel of her Bronco with damp palms, took a deep breath and focused straight ahead. For her, the ten-minute crossing was both exhilarating and somewhat frightening, a worthwhile payoff for the grueling, boring drive through Ohio and southern Michigan. Five dedicated men lost their lives working on the soaring suspension bridge, the world's third largest, which opened to traffic in 1957. Its five-mile straddle of Lake Michigan and Lake Huron began with a gradual ascent from the beaches of Mackinac City, culminating minutes later in a two-hundred-foot-high grid roadway overlooking the teal blue waters of the conjoined Great Lakes. Every trip was the same, whether Ainsley was a passenger or the driver. Only after the vehicle that she occupied had safely climbed to the bridge's halfway point and begun its slow descent to the safety of land, did her anxiety subside enough for her to enjoy the scenic, panoramic view of the Upper Peninsula beyond.

Traffic on the bridge was light, making Ainsley's passage to northern Michigan fast and uneventful. St. Ignace's clustered tourist restaurants and gift shops thinned out to none, and another world opened up ahead. On the south side of U.S. Highway 2, lapping waves kissed the sand or crashed into lighthouse breakwaters. Deep primordial woods rose high above the road's north shoulder, sheltering black bears, foxes, porcupines, deer and moose. Flocks of wild turkeys and Sandhill Cranes picked at vegetation along utility easements and at the edges of seasonal swamps. Even road kill was different here. Drivers found themselves swerving to avoid lynx or bobcat, mortally wounded the previous night as they crossed the highway to the beach for Lake Michigan's fresh water. The elusive, beautiful animals now looked as though they were asleep on the edge of the pavement. Miniscule towns with a lone, blinking light offered smoked fish, fresh-picked berries and other local cuisine to enthusiastic tourists and hard-core hunters seduced by the rustic, formidable beauty of the place.

Centuries before Longfellow contemplated penning *The Song of Hiawatha*, the native Ojibwa people thrived in Mishigami, or Michigan, their word for "big lake." They had the region to themselves until European colonization began with the French in the late 1600's, and continued with waves of English, Finnish and Norwegian settlers, who infiltrated the territory to trap fur, mine copper and iron ore, and log. The melding of immigrant and native traditions in the remote, rural area produced a distinct regional identity and culture. No one who spent time in the Upper Peninsula, or "U.P.", seemed neutral about the place. They either loved it or couldn't wait to leave. Several generations of Ainsley's family loved it.

Each summer, weeks prior to making the annual Michigan trek, Ainsley would search out Don's old, hard-shell suitcase and fill it with items she deemed essential for the expedition: bathing suits, flip flops, crayons, a sailor hat, her windbreaker, a minnow net. Julie's favorite picture of Ainsley showed her, age three, grinning ear to ear, wearing a pink nightgown and straw hat, and lugging the suitcase by her side. Julie kept one framed copy of the photo on her dresser at the Virginia Beach house, and another in her Fiji home.

Like daughter, like mother, Julie displayed her own signs of readiness for the Plante's Michigan vacation, adopting a uniform comprised of a crisp cotton shirt tied at the waist, pedal pushers, and beaded moccasins, worn until the heels of her feet eroded their deerskin soles. She replaced them each year with a fresh pair purchased from Totem Village, a small U.P. souvenir store. It was a family tradition.

With two hours of driving left until she reached Makwa Point, Ainsley surrendered to her craving for a pasty, and pulled into Lehto's Pasties for lunch. A handmade brown-and-white wooden sign, unchanged since she could remember, and probably since the stand opened in 1947, boasted one large word: Pasties. Lehto's square, one-story building, dark green with a thick, white horizontal stripe through its middle, had no seats, only a long white counter with room for up to twenty eager customers to stand and wait for their pasties to be wrapped and bagged, fresh from the oven. Unless it was a sell-out day. On those days, the Lehto family might have some uncooked pasties available for customers to purchase and bake later. Those would sell out, too. Like many establishments in the U.P., Lehto's accepted no checks or credit cards. They didn't have to. If they were open for business, cars and campers filled the parking lot. From a young age, Ainsley's mother warned her to beware of other pasties.

"They're a waste of money," Julie lectured. "Lehto's are the best. If they're closed, keep going and wait until the drive back home."

A simple, paper wrapper held a short-flour crust, molded and pinched into a half-moon shape, bursting with a fistful of ground sirloin, potatoes, onions, secret seasonings, and—rutabaga. Ainsley never met anyone who had tried the odd, yet mouth-watering mixture and didn't love it. She thought about the dozens of times she and John sat in the same parking lot, sand from a quick stop at the Mackinac City beach still coating their bare feet and legs, wolfing down pasties and Vernor's Ginger Ale, another local favorite. She missed those days. She missed her brother.

"Nice day, eh?" a friendly older man said, as he came out from the kitchen area behind Lehto's front counter.

"Beautiful," Ainsley answered back, the squeaky screen door clapping shut behind her. "I'll take six pasties, please."

"Where ya headed?"

"Garden Peninsula, Makwa Point."

"Heard they've seen some moose and black bear up that way. Be careful now, eh?"

"I will. Thanks." She paid and took her brown paper bag of pasties to the car, where Attila slept, curled up on the floor of the front seat. The fragrance of the pasties roused her briefly, but then she surrendered once again to a deep sleep.

Back on the road, things were quiet. The sealed urn containing John's ashes remained in place, lashed into the right back passenger seat with the seat belt. Having the ashes provided Ainsley with an odd comfort. True grief would hit when they were gone from her possession forever, surrendered to the lake as he'd requested of her years before, when he was a newly commissioned officer, cocky as hell, and death was a concept, not a reality. She turned her eyes to the road, flipped on the radio and unwrapped a pasty.

Just as Ainsley crossed the Pointe Aux Chenes River, Attila woke up panting and whining, signaling that she needed a pit stop. Ainsley parked the Bronco on the deserted landside road shoulder and clipped on her dog's leash. "Come on, girl, let's go," she said, leading Attila away from the highway pavement to the sandy base of a mile-long line of dunes that rose to heights of thirty feet, held in place by spiky beach grass and Indian Paintbrush, a bright orange wildflower that bloomed through the summer. The dry breeze flowing between the dunes carried the scent of sweet grass and cedar.

Waddling back and forth along the roadside, Attila sniffed and examined each clump of grass until she came to a makeshift roadside memorial. Ainsley hated the shrines. To her, they were a morbid distraction, their placement signifying bloody and brutal death scenes, not memorials of peaceful, eternal rest. This one had a wooden cross and some potted silk flowers. Stapled to the cross were a photo and a typed message sealed in laminated plastic. The message read:

Mark MacGearailt 1959-1985
I look for you every night. Wait for me.
Rest easy, my love.
—Maureen

"God, how tacky," Ainsley said, circling the shrine. Then she thought about losing John, and how this dead man left behind a family like hers—without warning—and questioned her sanctimonious reaction. Someone lived on, less able to trust, hope, or make sense of the world because Mark MacGearailt had departed it. She leaned in for a closer look at the fading photo. He was handsome, with short, brown hair and brown eyes. A sensuous, curvy mouth balanced his strong jaw and straight nose. Maybe even her type—in another, single life.

Attila yanked on her leash and Ainsley looked up to find her sitting a yard or so away from the shrine in a mound of sandy soil, next to what turned out to be a man's silver diving watch. Ainsley picked it up, horrified by the thought that it belonged to the dead man and became separated from him in whatever violent collision shattered his body and took his life. She took the watch with her to the Bronco, wrote down the name on the memorial and continued on to Makwa Point.

Makwa is the Ojibwa word for "bear." Makwa Point sat inside the tip of Lake Michigan's Big Bay de Noc, halfway between the towns of Manistique and Escanaba, with a predominantly elderly population that fluctuated between forty and one hundred people, the highest numbers attained during Christmas, July Fourth and spring wedding season, or less jubilantly, a funeral. Inland from a string of old beach cottages, the five-street town claimed sixty houses, a post office, bank and general store, two churches, and a railway station, all of them, except for the post office, now defunct. In its heyday, most of Makwa Point's townspeople collected their paychecks from SchoolGrounds Incorporated, a manufacturer of wood seesaws and swing components for schools across the United States. The SchoolGrounds plant blew its final, four o'clock, end-of-workday whistle on Friday, June 27, 1976. From that point on, jobs, schools, gas and groceries were a minimum of five miles away.

Four streets intersected Main Street, where the town's row of boarded-up businesses once thrived. Ainsley turned onto the last of them, Bay Street, and headed to her family's vacation home, a turn-of-the-century, five-room schoolhouse that her grandparents had converted into their retirement home when they were still young enough to withstand the ferocious U.P. winters. Nowadays, Ray and Mary Spencer lived in a seniors' neighborhood in Florida, forced southward prematurely by Ray's two strokes, making Virginia Beach their northernmost destination.

From the outside, the house appeared unchanged since Ainsley's visit the previous summer. She slowed down to turn into the drive, catching sight of her neighbor, Janice Mercer, pattering across the street. When she spotted Ainsley's Bronco, Janice broke into a scurry.

"Ainsley, dear, so sorry about John," she began as soon as Ainsley's car came to a stop. "It broke our hearts when we heard. Well, now, everything's okey-dokey with the place. No busted pipes this winter, thank goodness." Janice smoothed her baby blue, stretch pantsuit and patted her short, gray hair into place. "Yah, I think there's a skunk messing around back by the garbage cans lately. Even though yours are empty, Ren's got 'em locked tight with bungees." She sucked loudly on a piece of hard candy. "She's probably got some babies back there she's trying to feed."

Ainsley spoke quickly while she had the chance. "Thanks for looking in on the house," she said as she got out of the Bronco. "Janice, I don't know what we'd do without you and Ren."

Janice's husband Ren was a bear of a man, as wide as he was tall, with muscular forearms the size of small hams. Always bronzed from the sun, even in the dead of winter, he was never without a peeling, soggy cigar in his mouth. He was by far the nicest person Ainsley had ever met. When Ainsley's grandparents left Makwa Point, Julie and Don struck a deal with the Mercers: Janice and Ren would collect bills and first-class mail and send them to Ainsley's family in Virginia Beach, monitor the home's thermostat, roof and windows, and keep the town's few teenagers from vandalizing the property. In return, Ainsley's family would pay them three hundred dollars a year, which Janice referred to as their Christmas club. The arrangement had lasted ten trouble-free years so far.

"Everything's fine with the place," Janice reiterated. "I'll let you get settled. Come and get me if you need anything. Ren spotted a bear back along the old railroad tracks. Careful now, going out after dark, eh?" She peered into the dark car. "Honey, where is that husband of yours this trip?"

"Janice, he couldn't make it this time," Ainsley said politely. She clucked for Attila to get out of the car.

"Oh, what a shame—" Janice hopped backwards as the dog bounded out of the car. "Jesus, Mary and Joseph!" she gasped, holding her hand to her throat. The puppy galloped by her, oblivious, and crossed the grassy yard. "Well," she said, flustered, "that husband of yours, he's such a handsome boy—I mean, man, and always in a good mood. He's something, eh?"

"He certainly is," Ainsley said, her exasperated tone escaping Janice's ears.

"Well, honey," Janice said, as she turned to leave, "I'd better scoot."

"See you later." Ainsley lingered outside for a moment, steeping herself in the sweet, clean fragrance of an early lilac season.

Once she secured Attila inside the house, Ainsley started to unpack for her month-long stay. Concerned about the puppy's lack of coordination, she carried John's urn into the guest bedroom and closed the door behind it. On one of her trips to the car, she noticed the watch from the roadside memorial. She reached for it, but then changed her mind and walked, empty-handed, across the street to the Mercer's tidy, asbestos-shingled house.

Janice answered Ainsley's knock with a smile, decades of a simple, predictable, unhurried life reflected in her serene face. "Hi, honey, what do ya need?" she asked, wiping her hands on her red cotton apron. The aroma of roasting meat and potatoes slinked its way to the front door.

"Janice, do you remember hearing about an accident on U.S. 2?" Ainsley asked. "Someone named MacGearailt?"

"Oh yah, that's the young man who was hit by the logging truck last year. Terrible. Not much left of him after a hit like that—" She stopped herself, mortified at drawing any comparison to Ainsley's brother John. Red-faced, she tried to recover. "He, uh, has some family in Manistique, I think they said. Why ya asking?"

"Oh, I saw the memorial on my way here. It kind of got to me." Ainsley wasn't sure why she stopped short of mentioning the watch. "I guess with John and everything...."

"I know, honey. It's probably all you think about, but it will get better with time. It's so fresh right now, so raw. You want to come in?" Janice offered softly.

Ainsley nodded "no" and waved. Talking, at this point, would have led to crying, and she was tired of crying.

"Take care now, won't ya?" Janice called out from the doorway. "You want some supper to take back over with ya?"

"Thanks, I'm good," Ainsley said quickly. She stopped back at the Bronco and retrieved the watch before returning to the house.

Having an early dinner left Ainsley with enough time and energy to start the annual house opening ritual she learned from her parents and grandparents. It began with a thorough vacuuming to erase a year's worth of dust and mildew from the furniture and rugs. Next, she found a utility knife in the kitchen, hauled an aluminum ladder out of the garage, and made her rounds outside, freeing the home's wood-frame windows from their suffocating Visqueen sheaths. When she finished that, she raised several windows in the main part of the house, creating open channels to the pine-scented breeze that blew off the lake, a half-mile away.

By nine o'clock, she had settled into the front bedroom with Attila, who stretched out at the foot of the bed, immobilized by a full belly and a long day of the freshest air she'd ever inhaled. *Making the trip for John is the right thing to do,* Ainsley thought, lying between the clean, cool sheets, counting the lavender rosettes on the wallpaper. *He would have done it for me*. She counted sixty-seven rosettes and asked herself what John would say about Chris' selfish, destructive behavior. She knew the answer: "Get out of the marriage now, Ainsley. Walk away." She made up her mind. When she got home, Chris had to move out. She started counting again. At ninety-three rosettes, she turned off the light, and slept surprisingly well.

The next morning, bed sheets that had doubled as furniture covers were washed and hanging on the clothesline, billowing against the silvery blue sky, like giant white flags. Braided area rugs hung over the back porch railing, airing out. Ainsley opened the thin, 1986 *Upper Peninsula Phonebook* that Janice had left on the kitchen counter some time over the winter months. Inside, she found one listing for "MacGearailt" in Manistique, a town of a few thousand people, twenty miles away. She dialed the avocado green rotary phone that hung on the kitchen wall. It rang eight times. She was about to hang up when a man answered.

"Hello?" he asked.

"Hi. I'm looking for a member of the MacGearailt family," Ainsley said gently, mindful of his loss.

"This is Blaine MacGearailt," he answered. She guessed he was the dead man's father.

"Mr. MacGearailt, I'm trying to locate a relative of Mark MacGearailt." With no sound on the other end of the phone, she was unsure of what to do next. "Hello?" she asked.

"Yes?"

Ainsley thought her call might be causing more harm than good. "Mr. MacGearailt, I don't want to upset you, but I think I may have found a personal item belonging to...Mark."

"Really? Okaaay...." He sounded skeptical.

"Do you know of anything of his that's...missing?"

"Hmmm, let's see. I suppose you found something of his and want a reward?"

The sarcasm in his voice pushed her. "Look, my name is Ainsley Bohan, I'm from Virginia, and my family has a summer house over in Makwa Point. My brother just died—and I'm trying to do a good deed." She was near tears. "If you don't believe me...screw it!"

After a long pause, the man spoke. "I'm so sorry—for your loss and my behavior. Mark is—was—my brother. I've had some crank calls lately, from kids. I guess they got the name from the memorial Mark's girlfriend put up where they found him—where he had the accident. I don't know...."

"That's horrible. Why would they do that?"

"It's some new teenage prank. The high school seniors are out for the summer, and there's not a whole lot for kids to do around here—"

"I understand. I come up here every year."

"Well, I apologize again for my rudeness."

"I apologize for my...expletive. I'm really struggling with my brother's recent death."

"Why don't we start again?"

"Good idea. I—my dog—found a diving watch along U.S. 2, west of Pointe Aux Chenes."

"It sounds like his. Is it a stainless Seiko?"

"Yes. Engraved. The back reads: Mac #2."

"That's incredible—that you found it," Blaine said. "I can come by and get it. How long are you here?"

"Until late June."

"Well, it won't take me a month to get over there. How about today?"

"Sure. No problem. Let me tell you where my house is." She gave him the address. "I plan to be home, but if I'm not, I'll leave it inside the front porch door."

"Thanks a lot. Most people would have kept it. Obviously, you're not like most people. Thanks again." He hung up.

Ainsley felt a small sense of normality by returning the watch, a break from her own grief, borne from the simple act of helping someone else with the mourning process. She put the watch on the entry table inside the screened front porch.

❦

Before she could scatter John's ashes in the bay, Ainsley had to inspect the family boat and ready it for a brief voyage. In the afternoon, she went out to the side yard and climbed onto a stack of concrete blocks serving as the red motorboat's makeshift dry dock. She got a firm grasp on the boat's old canvas cover and tugged hard.

Christened the "Queen Mary," the boat was a dream fulfilled by Ray Spencer for his grandchildren. Ejecting his wife Mary's brand new station wagon from its rightful place in the garage, he set up a workshop, bought a rolling caddy and filled it with simple tools, and built her completely by hand, over the first three years he lived in Makwa Point. As a concession to his wife, he named it after her and painted it the same schoolhouse red as their house.

Year after year, John and Ainsley cruised the waters of Lake Michigan with Grandpa Ray, fishing for Northern Pike and perch, or jumping overboard to swim in shallow lagoons tucked away inside the bay. Sometimes, Ray would take them along when he visited friends to talk about boating and fishing, or to pretend to complain about his wife. The lake was everywhere—at the end of every road, behind every stand of trees—so Ainsley and John would swim, catch minnows and fish from the beach while Ray and the other grownups reclined on woven-plaid picnic chairs, smoking pipes or cigarettes, and dunking crisp, cinnamon-dusted Trenary Toast in mugs of black coffee.

Today, as Ainsley unwrapped her from her tarp, the Queen Mary looked old and downtrodden, no longer seaworthy. Small holes in the canvas had allowed rain and snow to leak into the boat for just short of a year. Oily water pooled in the bottom of the hull, and rust coated the lines and cables running from the rear outboard engine to the steering wheel. The only part of the boat in mint condition was its carefully stenciled name, painted in white script.

"Shit," Ainsley said, thoroughly frustrated.

"That bad?" The voice came from behind her.

She turned and almost fell off the blocks. Looking back at her was the same face she'd seen on the memorial photo. She tried to speak but couldn't.

The man reached his hand up to her. "Blaine MacGearailt—but you've probably figured that out by now." Physically stunned by her looks, he forced himself not to stare.

"Twins?" she asked, and then answered her own question. "You're—you were—twins." She wiped her hands on her jeans and extended her hand down to him. "Ainsley Bohan."

He returned a strong handshake. "Yes, and we still are twins. Merely separated—for now." Her heart leapt into her throat at his response; she fought back tears.

"Is the...Queen Mary...giving you trouble?" he asked, looking into the boat's flooded hull.

"I have to take my brother—my brother's ashes—onto the lake, and I don't think my boat's going to cooperate."

"Well, maybe I can help you with that. Return your kindness."

"Let's go get your watch. This can wait." She jumped down from the pedestal of blocks and led the way to the house, where Attila greeted them.

"Who's this?" Blaine asked, squatting down to pet her.

"This is my traveling companion, Attila," Ainsley answered, "who's supposed to bark at strangers."

The puppy wagged her thick tail, the size of a kielbasa sausage, and the same circumference as her legs.

"I owe you a thank you, boy, " Blaine said, scratching Attila's neck. She sat down in front of him waiting for more.

"Uh, it's a she," Ainsley said.

"Oh." Blaine was confused. "The name...."

"I know. I liked the name. Hopefully, I haven't created an identity crisis."

He looked at Attila. "I think it suits her. How old?"

"Three months."

Ainsley left him with Attila and got the watch. "I hope this is his," she said, as she held it up in front of him.

"That's it." Blaine took the watch and pulled up his shirtsleeve, revealing an identical timepiece. "Our parents gave us matching diving watches when we got our certification years ago." He saw fragility in Ainsley's face and wanted to help her. "Now, about your boat. If you don't want to bother messing around with it, I'll volunteer mine, and my piloting skills as well."

She wasn't sure whether she wanted a stranger to be part of so intimate and painful a passage. He could be a lunatic for all she knew. "It's very nice of you to offer," she said.

He wouldn't give up. "We've gone through the same thing—except that I'm a bit farther along than you are," he explained, as though he had given it some thought. "A year now, Mark's been gone." He could tell from her expression that she was about to cry but trying not to.

"Ainsley," he said, louder, "I'll even conduct an informal blessing of the ashes, before you scatter them."

The last sentence brought her back to him. "Sorry—excuse me?" she asked.

"I said that I can conduct an informal blessing of the ashes for you." He smiled, showing Chiclet-white teeth. "I'm a Catholic priest. I think God will forgive me if I vary from doctrine in this instance, you know, overlook the *scattering* aspect of the ritual."

She was flabbergasted. Assessing his open manner, along with his jeans, topsiders, and cream Henley, she was unsuccessful in matching the man in front of her to the words he had spoken.

"Would it be an understatement to say that you're surprised?" he asked.

"I'm...sorry. I guess I think of priests as older, fatherly types." She stumbled over the words. "I mean, well, we have one woman priest in our church. You're so young, and your clothes...."

He put his hands in his pockets. "Well, we have to start somewhere. We aren't born old men in collars and black habits. Incidentally, I only wear mine when I'm forced to."

"Right." She laughed for the first time in days, still uncertain about how to relate to him. "Are you from here?" she asked quickly. He had no detectable U.P. accent, but more of a flat midwestern edge to his A's.

"No, Chicago. I attended seminary there, and I was ordained there early last year."

"How on earth did you wind up here?"

"It was my choice. They wanted me to start out in Chicago, but I didn't want to be a member of the corporate clergy, you know, attend cocktail parties and count money from overstuffed collection plates. I wanted a real grass roots experience, to help people on the front lines. Here I'll cover four towns, working mostly with older adults. People who don't have anyone else. It makes me feel as though I'm making a tangible difference in their lives every day. No one else wanted the assignment. They thought it was a waste of time, a little hopeless." He took a breath. "Well, that's probably more than you wanted to know."

"Your brother...did he live here with you—before he died?" she asked.

"No, he stayed in Chicago after school, and worked for my dad's company. Not much choice in the matter. Anyway, he was on his way to meet his girlfriend at the Grand Hotel on Mackinac Island the night of the accident. Looking back, we couldn't have known...what was going to happen. I'm glad—grateful—he stopped off here to stay with me for couple of days."

"God—gosh, I'm sorry. And his girlfriend's name was Maureen?"

"Yes. You saw it on the memorial? Is it still intact?"

"Yeah, it looks like someone is maintaining it."

"It's Maureen. She drives up from Detroit every month or so to visit it. She says it gives her some sense of comfort—closure." He looked at his brother's watch again. "Praise God, it still works." He tossed the watch in the air as though it was a peanut before enclosing it in his fist. "Listen, I've got a Mass to give over in Manistique in two hours, so I'd better hit the road. Think about my offer. I'm happy to help." He moved toward the back door. "God's peace."

"And you. Thanks." She smiled. "It was very nice meeting you... Father."

"Blaine to you. I left my name and number on that notepad on the kitchen counter in case you need it—although my handwriting's so bad, you may not be able to decipher it!"

Ainsley walked with him to the back porch and watched him get into his funereal black sedan. *No doubt diocesan-issue*, she thought. He didn't strike her as the black sedan sort. The front passenger window lowered automatically and Blaine waved goodbye.

"Wait," she called out to him. "I'm going up to Fayette tomorrow. Have you ever been?"

"Where? What's Fayette?"

"It's a park—a historic place. Everyone ought to see it once. You're welcome to join me."

"I have to say, I'm intrigued. What time are you leaving?"

"We could meet here at ten? The whole trip will take about four hours."

He thought for a moment. "Why not? Sure. My day tomorrow is slow. Unless I get an eleventh-hour call to deliver last rites or something, I will. Thanks for asking me." He waved again as he drove off.

The next morning, an old, green Ford pickup idled in the driveway.

"Two cars?" Ainsley asked, sticking her head in the open passenger window. "Your parish must be wealthier than I thought."

"No," Blaine said, noting that her blue blouse matched her eyes. "This is my truck, free and clear. And, I'm not giving it up. I don't think anyone could consider this old heap an accumulation of worldly wealth."

"I think you're safe there. Do you mind if I bring my dog?"

"Not at all. She's the hero of the hour, right? Finding Mark's lost watch?"

"Right. I'll go get her."

Blaine watched Ainsley walk to the house, the lines of her body accentuated by the lightweight material of her clothes. He found it a fine, challenging line to walk—welcoming closeness to people but keeping a distance, acknowledging beauty but not responding to it. Times like this made striking a balance difficult. He turned his attention to the truck's dashboard and fiddled with the radio.

Suddenly, she was back with Attila. The dog bounded into the truck and onto the center of the bench seat, leaving a thin slice of it empty for Ainsley.

"Okay, folks," Blaine said, cheerfully, "here we go. Uh, where in the heck am I going?"

The long, rural road along the Garden Peninsula was hilly and progressively rocky. Here and there, abandoned homesteads, summer cabins, and small farms erupted from grassy, boulder-littered terrain.

Right about the time it seemed that the road would never end, a non-descript sign appeared, marking the entrance to Fayette State Park. Blaine followed the drive to a hillside parking lot lined with birch, cedar, and spruce. Below that, in the center of a green ravine, was a non-descript, brick visitor center.

Blaine parked the truck. "This is interesting," he said. "What did you say this place is?"

"A ghost town now. It was created a century ago—specifically for processing iron."

He looked baffled. "Where's the town part?"

She let him wonder for a moment. "Okay, let's get going," she said, getting out of the truck.

"What about your dog?"

"Attila needs to stay in the car for the first part of the visit."

They walked past the visitor center and down a fine gravel lane, their shadows blending into the dimness of thick, deciduous woods. The lane forked and Ainsley led them to the left for another fifty feet or so until the landscape opened up, revealing what resembled a precisely executed museum diorama. A dozen or so wood-sided buildings of various sizes, weathered and bleached a striated brown, rose from short, wooly grass the color of celery. From foundation to window trim, each one of them was immaculately preserved.

"This is surreal," he said. "It really is a ghost town?"

She nodded.

They passed a pair of towering stone blast furnaces, teeming with pigeons and sea gulls. As the startled birds took flight, their frenetic wing beats created a haunting echo through the empty furnace chimneys. Seconds later, the birds alighted on the roof of the town's hotel, an enormous three-story structure with a simple porch running the full length of its façade. Six tall, rectangular windows spanned the building's first two floors, and two chimneys and three dormer windows peered down over its entrance, watchful sentries of any activity below. A lone whitetail doe emerged from the woods and walked confidently across the grass behind the hotel, unafraid of the smattering of people gawking, awestruck, at her graceful beauty.

"Ainsley, this looks like a beautiful home on Cape Cod—except that it's empty," Blaine said as they walked inside. While he surveyed the hotel's staircase and lobby, Ainsley stood in the space, breathing in the still, aged air.

"I love the smell of old wood," she said, smiling. "It's familiar. It reminds me of home, my parents' house—my house."

They toured Fayette's music hall, school, accounting office and several homes, all displaying period furniture and decor, ready for the bustling events of a day that would never come.

Blaine threw up his hands. "I give. Tell me the story of the town."

"It was built around the iron ore business following the Civil War. Everything happened in a span of about twenty-four years. Several hundred people left Canada and Britain to work and live in the town—start a new life here. A couple of decades later, it was all over. The method of processing ore became obsolete, and the town died."

He looked unconvinced. "They all left—abandoned the town? Are you pulling my leg?"

"Trust me. I've been told the story from the time I was a baby. You'll find it all in the park brochure. From beginning to end, the town thrived for twenty-four years. All of this work, all the dreams and expectations—lost. I think it parallels my life right now. And, I'm even twenty-four." She smiled dryly.

"You sound disillusioned about your life. What besides your brother's passing has happened?" He waited for her to confirm his observation. She didn't respond. "It's just...that comment," he said. "Do you want to talk about it?"

"I don't know why I said that," she answered. "I don't think I want to be counseled. Not right now."

"I didn't mean to pry," he said. "Forgive me. It goes with the territory—occupational hazard."

"No problem. I brought it up," she shrugged. "Let's explore the park. There's more to see."

Until now, the ghost town's pristine beauty and the beach serving as its backdrop obscured the true jewel of the site—ancient, chalky cliffs rising out of the bay. The towering white limestone bluffs jutted straight up from the sapphire water, their tops frosted with dark evergreens and birches, which dribbled down at various points as warm frosting does, coating the cliff faces with streams of green.

"I'm speechless," Blaine said, leaning against an old anchor in front of the blast furnace, the same one Ainsley and John had climbed on as children. Over the years, Julie had taken dozens of pictures of the two of them on and next to it.

"I know what you're thinking, Blaine. This place should be somewhere else."

"Well, yeah. I mean, why aren't people flocking here?"

"Blaine, how do you get back and forth from Chicago?"

"I drive to Escanaba, take the bus to Green Bay, get a commuter flight to Milwaukee, and then fly to—"

"Exactly!" she interrupted. "It's too remote, thank God. At least for right now. I'm sure someday, that will change."

They walked the park's slag beach, thick with ancient pebbles and chunks of ore but no sand, all the while observed by a line of gulls sunning themselves on a patio-sized slab of rock.

"Here, take my hand," he said as he reached out for her.

She grabbed his hand and hopped across a slippery rock. "There's one other feature of Fayette...I hesitate to tell you," she said.

"What is it?"

She pointed up at the cliffs. "The Overlook Trail."

"What's the story with that? Not worth the hike?"

"It's that...I'm...uuugh...I hate heights!" she almost shouted, embarrassed. "Anything higher than the third floor of my house—forget it!" she waved her hands dismissively.

"No big deal," he said. "Everyone has a weakness, a vulnerability, Ainsley. Some are simply more obvious than others, that's all. We don't have to go up there."

"You *should* see it. It's okay, I'll have Attila to protect me." She forced a laugh, scared to death and trying to hide it. "I'll get her from the car. We have to go past the parking area to get to the other trail anyway."

Ainsley walked several miles of the trail with Blaine, her legs like rubber every time the vertical drop of a cliff face came into view through the trees.

"I've got to come back here," Blaine said, as he leaned against the stone overlook wall, gazing down at Fayette and the bay. "This place is like therapy."

"If you really enjoyed it, you might want to see some more of the U.P., you know, the insider's tour," Ainsley said, tired from their hike, but sorry that the day was ending. "Do you have any free time in the next few days?"

"I'm not sure—yet. I'll take a look at my schedule. I don't have everything memorized—meetings and visits. You know, priestly obligations. The parish secretary keeps adding new things to my list."

"I understand. Just let me know."

"I should be able to work something out."

They were back at the truck. "So what's your weakness, Blaine?" Ainsley asked. "What are you afraid of?"

"Doubt."

His answer caught her off-guard. "Doubt?"

"Yes. Doubting myself, some of the decisions I've made. Lately, I'm not sure that I know myself as well as I should."

chapter 4

THE GREEN-AND-white sign read: Kitch-iti-kipi 8 miles.

"I always wondered what Kitch-iti-kipi meant," Blaine said, as they cruised along the wooded highway in Ainsley's Bronco. "I pass this way when I have services at Cooks Church."

"I haven't been here for a year. I'm assuming it hasn't changed much."

They wound through the park's entrance and followed the directional signs to the spring.

"I'm sure there's a story, some folklore associated with the place," Blaine said.

"Every place here has a story," Ainsley answered, amused. "The legend is that a young Indian chief—"

"Let me guess, Hiawatha?" he interrupted.

"Oh, so close, but that's another story. The local legend is that Kitch-iti-kipi, an Indian chief, canoed into the spring to prove his love for a woman, but his canoe tipped over and he drowned. His tribe named the spring for him in his honor—posthumously, of course."

"Of course. Very star-crossed and tragically romantic," Blaine said.

"Absolutely," Ainsley agreed, enjoying the banter. "The name also means "big spring," so there may have been some embroidery of the story—the whole canoe incident part. Personally, I've always preferred the canoe-Indian chief version."

They were the park's sole visitors that morning. The short footpath they walked through the woods ended abruptly at the edge of a glassy pool, two hundred feet wide and forty feet deep. Ancient shards of dead spruce and cedar trunks, long ago fallen, spiked up from the frigid emerald water. A suspension cable running the length of the spring kept a square raft, which resembled a floating picnic shelter on pontoons, aligned with a wooden, gated dock. Once onboard, passengers took turns cranking a simple ship's wheel that winched the raft along the cable, propelling it, at a creeping pace, across the spring.

Blaine assessed the curious contraption with trepidation. "Are you sure this thing is safe?" he asked.

"Be brave, step on, and we'll go," Ainsley said as she took the wheel and started turning. The tethered raft cut through the spring's surface, stalked by fearless trout, who glided by before circling back for food dropped from its center viewing hole or over its sides. White calcium silt boiled up onto the spring floor. Except for the metal cable's occasional creaking whine, the raft was quiet.

Blaine broke into the silence. "I probably sound like a complete chauvinist, but I'm surprised that you drive a truck and, um, came up here alone. The drive has to be punishing." He kept talking as he took over the wheel. "Am I prying again?"

"No. First of all, I need this truck, with my dog, and all of the things I do at home."

"What kind of things?"

"Well, my house is over a hundred years old, and something is always broken. I should own stock in a hardware store chain. And, I spend my free time biking and gardening. I love flowers, especially roses."

"And, you work, too?"

"My...husband's still in law school, so someone has to pay the bills. I write grants for a consulting firm—full time. We help non-profits keep their doors open."

"Do you like it?"

"I love working with my clients. I could live without the office politics, though. My goal is to have my own small firm, deal directly with the non-profits...someday."

"That's a good goal." He looked contemplative. "Wouldn't it be easier to fly up here? Safer—for a woman like you?"

Ainsley wasn't sure what he meant. "A woman like me?" she asked.

"Uh, you know, traveling alone, " he said. She seemed to him to be unaware of her beauty, and its effect on other people.

"Flying. I hate it. Always have. I can make this trip in my sleep, I've done it so many times."

He stared at the rings on her left hand. "Your husband—was he unable to take off time from school to come along and help you?"

She bit her lip before answering. "My husband? I don't hold out hope where my marriage is concerned. I'm planning to separate from him when I get home." Her words hung in the air. "So, here I am, your unofficial tour guide of the Catholic Diocese of...Marquette?"

"That's right." He stopped turning the wheel. "I'm sorry about your husband. Is there no other option? It's seems so soon—you're so young."

His probing put her on the defensive. "Look," she said, annoyed, "I know Catholics don't believe in divorce."

"I don't think anyone really *believes* in it, do they? I have divorced relatives, and my parents probably should have parted ways years ago, for the sake of everyone around them, but that's another story. It's true, we do consider the marriage vows sacred—"

"And, so do we, in my church and in my family. I took my marriage vows intending to honor them for the rest of my life. But, what about a marriage where one partner does...honor their vows, and the other flagrantly breaks them?"

"Of course, we would prefer the couple try counseling—"

She resented his apparent one-size-fits-all solution. "My husband can't—no—won't stop screwing other women. He's an alcoholic—I'm sure of it—and he doesn't believe in counseling." The words kept coming. "He says that there's nothing a therapist can tell him about himself that he doesn't already know. Tell me, where does that leave me? What options do I have?"

Her outburst startled him. "In that case," he said earnestly, "if your husband's unwilling to accept help, or work on your problems, perhaps you don't have much choice. You should do what you must to live a safe, healthy life." He'd known her less than a week, but couldn't stand the thought of her mistreated or unhappy. "He doesn't abuse you—hit you—does he?"

"No, nothing like that. I think he's wholly devoted to destroying himself, and I'm his victim of circumstance." She leaned over the railing and tossed some fish pellets into the water, her fine, brown hair falling like a sheet over her shoulder, and glistening red in the clear sunlight. "I promised myself that I wouldn't enter into this territory during my trip. I'm here for my brother." She flashed a bittersweet smile. "It's your turn. What about you? Why did you become a priest?"

"Let's see, I'm Catholic, so there's a predisposition," he joked. "No, really, like other clergy, I received God's calling and I answered."

"That's it? You just knew?"

"Yes and no. I went through a process of discovery. The decision wasn't quick or simple. It involved most of my family, too, especially my father."

"Your father? What did he have to do with it?"

"Well, not working for the family business was frowned upon—"

"You make the family business sound a little like the mob."

"Not quite, but close," he said.

"What exactly is the family business?"

"Oh, cleaning stuff."

"Cleaning stuff? What sort of cleaning stuff?"

"Have you heard of MJS?"

"As in Mac & Janssen Soaps?" she gaped. "As in Windoworx Glass Cleaner?"

"The very one."

"Well, in that case, I can see where there might be some pressure to carry on the family dynasty."

"Yes, but as a Catholic, being a clergyman is always an acceptable alternative." He couldn't believe he had said the words. "Most importantly, of course, I was answering God's call."

She took the raft's wheel again. "So, what's the calling like?"

"I can only speak for myself, Ainsley. It started as a sort of...internal dialogue that I attributed to my conscience. Eventually, there came a point when I felt the presence of God with me, washing over me, more and more of the time. I fought it for a while, but in the end, I gave myself up to it." He clasped his hands and played with a gold signet ring on his right ring finger. "I transitioned from one life to another. Oh, I don't think I've described it very well."

"You knew that meant, specifically, that you should be a priest?"

"Well, I talked to my uncle about it. He's a priest. He had a similar experience, and found peace through answering the call. That's how I knew it had to be the right decision. That was my sign."

"How old were you?"

"Oh, seventeen, eighteen, I think. It took a few more years for me to commit to the seminary."

"That's young," she said, "to make a decision that takes you away from so many of the things that are an inherent part of youth. On the other hand, it must be fulfilling to know precisely what path your life will take."

"Knowing what your path is doesn't guarantee you'll know how to get there, or that the journey won't be painful," he reflected. "I struggle everyday with the issue of how to design my life in the priesthood. How to follow the rules, but remain an individual. I'm sure you know that the Catholic Church is a place overflowing with differences of opinion these days. Many people on the outside see us as dinosaurs and our doctrines as archaic. My greatest fear is not meeting the true needs of my parishioners, not knowing how to help them in the best way possible. These people are placing their trust in me. I have to be worthy of that trust."

"I think someone as dedicated as you are to working through those issues has to succeed—in the holy life."

"That remains to be seen," Blaine said. "I'm a neophyte." The raft bumped up against the dock. "Looks like our stop." He checked the time. "I'd better call it a day. This would be a great place for a parishioner retreat. Or a field trip for the parish kids—the handful of them that we have up here."

Ainsley felt an unexpected tinge of disappointment at his hint of sharing the place she'd introduced him to with other people. It was a childish and inappropriate reaction—she knew it. "Yes," she agreed. "It would. They'd love it. Let's get going."

"Okay, then, we've hit all of the best places up here?"

"I'm headed up to Marquette sometime next week. It's a good place to explore." She had a destination in mind.

"That's one place I've actually been," he said. "I go up there every month to meet with the Bishop."

"Been there, done that?" she asked.

"Yes, I appreciate you thinking of me, though. It's been fun."

A voice inside her head told her not to push for anything more. "Well, then," she said, "back to real life."

chapter 5

"BIRTH, MARRIAGE AND death. Those simple passages frame people's lives up here," Ainsley said, glancing over at Blaine as they drove out of Manistique. The wind pelted his short hair through the open passenger window, shifting its part each time he moved his head. He looked more youthful and less priest-like each she saw him. Today he was downright boyish.

"It's the same everywhere, isn't it?" he asked, talking above the road noise.

"Not when you think about it," she answered, relieved he had decided at the last minute to accompany her to Marquette.

"What's home for you, Ainsley?"

"Home? It's my house. The ocean. Working in my rose garden. Picking up *The New York Times* on Sunday mornings, some days meeting friends for coffee." Her face fell. "It used to be a lot about Chris—until this last...incident. Spending time with John and his girlfriend. And, of, course, the monster in the back seat—Attila."

"That sounds good," he said.

"Yeah, but it's also deadlines, pressure, and too many things, too much stuff, that clouds the simple beauty of life. The need to escape to somewhere or something else," she said. "In the U.P., there's no big business or high fashion. Family, friendship, and the outdoors—everything revolves around that. It's the overwhelming largeness of the place, the quiet, the color of it all. Where you and I come from, you invite someone to dinner and they show up trying to impress you with an expensive bottle of wine. Up here, someone comes to supper toting wild strawberries, blueberry muffins, a string of perch or a beautiful piece of driftwood. No amount of money can buy that. People here depend on each other, trust each other. They have to—to survive. I've got to get my fix of this place, at least once a year, to balance the rest of my life. Otherwise I feel empty." She looked his way. "It's John, too. All of the memories of us—summers here, when we were growing up. I want to keep that alive...."

"But, as much as you love it, you wouldn't live here fulltime."

"I've thought about it, especially with my parents so far away now, my marriage over, my brother's death...." She sighed. "I don't know. I'm torn between the two worlds. I can't choose. I suppose I'm simply another fair-weather Yooper."

"A fair-weather what?"

"Yooper! You really are green, aren't you? The "U-P," Yoopers, get it?"

"Ah-hah," he said, reaching back to the seat behind him to pet Attila. "It's definitely a change from Chicago. My parents could never handle living up here. They barely survive an occasional, brief visit."

"They're certified city types?"

"There's more to it than that. They don't do well with any length of unstructured time for reflection or introspection. They need distractions from one another. There aren't many of those up here."

"I still don't understand how you managed to steer clear of the family dynasty."

"It had to be divine intervention!" He picked up Ainsley's clunky car phone handset and changed the subject. "So, is this thing really worth it?" he asked. "My dad just got one."

"I hope so. My parents got it for me because I'm on my own a lot of the time. It's good for emergencies. Of course, I can't get a signal in most locations up here. And it's very expensive to make a call. I doubt that these things will ever be a part of everyday life."

A little over an hour later, they made their way past the quaint, hillside storefronts of Front Street to the other end of Marquette, stopping at Togo's, the city's local and legendary sub shop popular with Northern Michigan University students, and just about everyone else. They took their sandwiches to Presque Isle Park, a wooded three-hundred-acre peninsula at the north end of the town. To reach the island park, they passed Marquette's monolithic ore docks, which were still in daily use. Glimpses of the steep drop to Lake Superior appeared as Ainsley's Bronco climbed Presque Isle's entrance hill. She found a familiar pullover leading to a steep embankment trail and stopped the car. "We'll keep Attila safe in the car while we walk on the rocks, and come back to get her before we leave."

"I can hold her. It's no trouble," he offered.

She returned a stern look. "You have no idea what's down there, Blaine. Trust me, it's not safe."

He wondered if she was exaggerating—until they set out on the unstable trail, dodging drop-offs and hanging on to the trunks of small spruce and birch trees for balance. The trees shot out of cracks in craggy red cliffs and peninsulas, undercut in some areas from millions of years of relentless, pounding surf. The red-rock island washed black as crashing sapphire waves collided with it, sending freezing cold water in all directions. Ainsley held her breath as a familiar pebble-strewn cove appeared, a straight forty-foot drop below the trail. Smooth green, brown and white stones, the size of baking potatoes, formed the cove's floor. She exhaled in short, deliberate puffs, a trick she used to fend off panic attacks whenever she had to travel by airplane.

"Whoa!" Blaine shouted, trying to keep from sliding off the trail. "Now I understand the "Danger" signs everywhere."

"Don't acknowledge fear. It will freak me out," Ainsley said nervously. "And, for God's sake—I mean—be careful and hold on to something as you go."

Eventually, they picked their way across a smooth slab of rock ten feet above the beach.

"Watch your hands," Ainsley warned, surveying the rocky coastline.

"My hands? Why?"

"The iron."

"What?" Blaine turned up his palms, now stained a henna color from bracing against the flaky red rocks that crumbled in his hands like crisp phyllo. He shrugged his shoulders. "You know what they say about Lake Superior never giving up her dead?" he asked. "Is that true, or was it fabricated for the song about the Edmund Fitzgerald—that horrible shipwreck?"

"It's true that the water's cold enough to preserve what lies beneath," Ainsley answered, doing her best to look menacing. They came to a stop on the flat top of the rock bluff. "Seriously, Blaine, most of the dead stay on the bottom nearly frozen, although some are permanently encased in ice."

She sat down and stretched out her upper body flat on the rock, feet together, arms splayed, gazing up at the cloudless, pale blue sky. Off in the distance, the sound of a motorboat's hum mixed in with the cries of laughing gulls. A steady line of waves smacked against the face of the headland. The air smelled of cedar, clean wind, and the slightest bit of iron from the rocks. "God could take me now," she said.

Blaine sat next to her, his khaki pants now smeared with rust-colored dust that had leached from the rocks. "I think it's safe to assume that you've reached nirvana."

"I told you, I have to get my fix of the place. Take it all in. It's in my blood. To me, it's spiritual."

"I'm all for anything that brings people closer to God," he said. "I appreciate you showing me around the area. It was completely unexpected, but exactly what I needed. During the past year, I haven't done most of the things I enjoy."

"Because of your church schedule?" she asked, sitting up. "Or, because of your brother's death?"

"Yes, to both of those, but some of it falls back on me. I've begun a life that by design is consumed by other people's needs—and that's as it should be. But, sometimes, I have to remind myself that I'm twenty-nine years old. I do miss being with people my own age, discussing politics or the state of the world. Or, sitting in front of a Cezanne or a pre-Christian artifact and just staring at it! I know that's the tradeoff for coming up here. When my brother Mark was alive, I kept a strong connection to my old life in Chicago. I do miss that."

"Maybe this isn't the place for you. Could you go back to Chicago?"

"I wouldn't even consider going back—not now. The places we've visited, the things we've talked about—I've learned more about life up here in the week I've known you than I've learned in the last year. I have a better understanding of why I'm here. I can't thank you enough for that."

"You're welcome, Blaine. Showing you around helped me, too—to get outside of my own grief, even though I know I have a long way to go, and a lot to confront when I get home."

Blaine threw some rock shards into the water. "The other day, I hope I didn't sound sanctimonious or judgmental, about your marriage. It's not my place to counsel you, unless you ask me to. You're a friend, not part of my flock."

"What's the difference, Blaine?"

"That's a good question," he answered. "To which I don't have an answer. I think my inexperience is showing again."

"About that conversation we had at Kitch-iti-kipi...I was childish and rude. I said those things about Chris to make you back off. To be honest, I haven't even begun to deal with that situation."

"But, what you told me is true?"

"Yes, it's true. It's ironic. I hoped Chris and I would have a relationship like the one my parents have. Ours couldn't be farther from it."

"Your parents' marriage sounds very special."

"It is," she said. "Other people only wish for a life like theirs. It's been that way since they met. Maybe their love is simply too rare to aspire to. Too rare to expect."

While the depth and breadth of Don and Julie Plante's feelings for one another were unquestionably resolute, their first meeting *was* unexpected. They discovered one another in a sweltering Norfolk, Virginia courtroom in July of 1957. Six-four, broad-shouldered and slim, Don cut a quiet, commanding figure. Quick, hazel eyes pierced his surroundings, immediately processing everything under their gaze. A long, slightly aquiline nose and square chin balanced a high, wide forehead and straight, dark brows, giving him the look of being immersed in deep thought even when he wasn't. He trained his shock of straight, black hair into place every morning with a light dressing of Murray's Pomade, touching it up with his fingers throughout the day. The trace residue kept his large, square hands unusually soft, and smelling as if he'd just unwrapped a coconut bonbon. His low, melodic voice lent itself perfectly to a profession dependent upon swaying others through the spoken word.

"What's her story?" Don asked his colleague, Scott Leighton, as they stood outside United States District Courtroom #5, waiting out a brief recess, hoping for enough time to grab a smoke and strategize about their joint case. Julie Spencer politely glided between the two men on her way to the restroom, her hourglass figure locked into a gray linen suit. She wore her dark brown hair in a French twist, exposing several strands of pearls draped around her long neck. She met Don's gaze and flashed him an open, blinding smile. He was smitten.

"You can forget about Miss Julie Spencer," Scott advised, lighting their cigarettes. "She came here from Detroit a few weeks ago. Replaced that Tiffany so and so for three months. They say she's got a four-year degree, but wants to spend some real time in the courtroom to decide if she wants to go on to law school—you know, try her hand at moving around in a *man's* world. Geez," he hissed.

Don exhaled a forceful stream of blue-gray smoke. "I don't know. I think that's pretty gutsy of her," he said, his eyes riveted to the Ladies' Room door.

"Oh, no." Scott shook his head back and forth mournfully as he spoke. "Not you, too. I know what you're thinking. Don't bother, friend. We all tried and struck out with her—royally. Besides, she'll be gone by fall."

"We'll see," Don said, with an air of confidence.

Don lost his concentration more than once during closing arguments, wholly infatuated after studying Julie for eight hours a day, five days a week. While everyone else in the courtroom mopped sweat from their faces and adjusted damp clothes, she stayed as cool as her ice blue eyes. On the last day of the trial, he summoned the nerve to ask her out on a date. Two months after that, he and Julie announced their engagement.

Scott was incredulous when he heard they were an item. "My Lord, how'd you do it, Don?"

"I walked up to her and invited her to church and Sunday brunch. I figured since I was going to marry her anyway, we might as well get used to doing those things—right from the start." He did marry her, and thirty years on, they were still together.

"For them, Blaine, it's ridiculously simple," Ainsley said. "They love and respect one another, above all else. My father openly worships my mother. He once told me that after years of being with her, he doesn't remember how it feels to want anything. And, my mother thinks my father is the most honorable man on the planet. They give so much to each other, that there's no room left in their marriage for resentment or selfishness. They fight. I've witnessed some whoppers, trust me. But it's always about the thing, not about each other. Now that my brother's gone, they're suffering—more than I am—but neither will allow the other to hurt so much that they can't still see hope—the good in life. I've always wanted what they have—to the point of seeing qualities in Chris that weren't really there."

"I think that happens a lot, Ainsley. We want something so much that our wish for it skews our perspective on what's real."

"Yes," she said. "Chris pursued me relentlessly, and I interpreted that as love, when it was selfishness. To him, I was a conquest, a goal to attain. Well, he got me. Now I'm old news, and he has other goals in sight."

"Do you love him?"

"I did love him, very much. The pain he's caused me, the damage...it's irreparable at this point. I can't go back. He's a time bomb, a disaster waiting for the right opportunity. I don't want to be there when he self-destructs."

"Have you thought about what you'll do when you get home?"

"Clean up the mess," she said glumly. "Try to start over."

They climbed down the rocks and into Lake Superior up to their knees, wading until they couldn't stand the cold any longer, and then hiked back onto the rocks.

"I meant to ask you if you and your brother Mark were twins who were alike, or if you tried to be different from one another, independent."

"I'd say we were complementary. We were best friends, and we kept each other entertained. We didn't always dress alike, but we were mistaken for each other a lot, since we had the same haircut." He picked at some moss in the crevice of a rock. "We pulled all kinds of tricks, like taking each other's classes, playing practical jokes on each other's girlfriends, but nothing seriously unethical, like taking each other's exams. I would say that I'm definitely the more sensible of the two of us."

"I guess I'll have to take your word."

"I have proof—anecdotal evidence."

"Such as?"

"Such as, one summer vacation we were traveling by car to Kentucky to see my Uncle Gordon—the other priest in the family. Of course, our parents relegated Mark and me to the back seat of the car, and we were bored senseless. We both had braces, and Mark was goofing around with the rubber bands on his, shooting them at me, stuff like that. Well, he decided to put one on the end of his nose, you know, clowning around. I kept telling him that his nose was getting red, and that he should take it off. He didn't listen. We stopped for gas about twenty minutes later. By that time, the end of his nose was a perfectly round, purple circle. He tried rubbing it, putting ice on it—nothing worked. It was already bruised."

"Oh, no," Ainsley said. "That's awful! Did it go away?"

"Yes, more than a week later. For our whole trip, it was purple. No one had any trouble telling us apart for that week. When people saw us—the people we knew in our Uncle's parish and town—my parents introduced Mark as Rudolph. It was a riot, at least to my nine-year-old brain. In every picture of the trip, his nose was like a bull's-eye. He'll never—I mean he never—lived it down."

"I do that, too," she said, understanding his slip. "Well, my brother John was a junior scientist. He liked figuring out how things work, everything, including his own anatomy."

"Do I want to hear the rest?"

"Oh, it's pretty good. When John was about seven—I would have been about five—he started experimenting with physics. He decided to see if every time he peed out of his third-floor bedroom window, the pee would fall in the same place. So, I—his gullible little sister—would go down to the yard with a handful of cocktail toothpicks that I found in the kitchen and mark the spot where the pee landed. That was my official job. Well, one day my mother saw me out there squatting down, sticking toothpicks in the ground. She asked me what I was doing—"

Blaine burst out laughing. "I'm sorry—the visual—and, you tell it so matter-of-factly."

"Is it really funny?" she said, deadpan.

"Yes!" he said as he lay back on the rocks. "Sorry. So you're squatting on the ground, examining the toothpicks...."

"Right."

He was smiling, waiting for the punch line. "Did you tell on John?"

"Well, first my mom thought that I couldn't hold it and I was out there in the yard...you know, going to the bathroom—"

He started laughing again. "Keep going."

"I was too young to lie, and I didn't think John would get in trouble, so I told her what I was doing. I showed her the toothpicks."

"What happened?" he asked, trying to keep a straight face. "Did she punish you?"

"No! She told me to carry on. What I didn't know was that while I was outside, she was on her way upstairs. She waited outside John's room until he went to the window."

"Then what?"

"Then she surprised him and scared the pee out of him, literally—and humiliated him to death. Needless to say, he never did it again." Ainsley repositioned herself on the inflexible rock's surface, taking on a serious expression. “Blaine, did you know, or sense, that something had happened to Mark when he died?”

“Yes and no. The night he died, I was at home. Not the rectory at St. John’s—it’s small, outdated—in use only in the summer. I only stay there when I have to. My folks bought a house up here so they could visit me comfortably. Anyway, I woke up in the middle of the night for no reason, and I felt a mild spark, like when you get static electricity on carpeting and then touch someone. That’s the only way I can describe it. I looked at my clock radio; it was ten minutes after one.”

“Was that the time of the accident?”

“No, that was the time he died, give or take a minute. He hung on for half an hour.” Blaine looked at her intently. “1:10 in the morning—that was his final heartbeat. He was letting me know he was leaving the world, moving on. I felt a brief sense of peace, calm. At the time, I had no idea why. The phone rang hours later, and things changed. Whenever I’m struggling with grief over Mark, I try to go back to that initial feeling of peace. It’s what he wanted to leave me with.”

“That’s an incredible gift...that he gave you.” Her eyes welled up.

“I’ve found nothing to convince me it could be anything else. And, it’s incredible that I’ve never told anyone this—not even my parents—and I told you.”

“I think the fact that you knew when he died means he’s still with you. I wish I could get a sign from John that he’s in a good place.” She wiped a tear from her cheek. “Every time I hear a jet fly overhead, I feel sick. Not because he died while he was flying, but because I don’t feel anything. It’s like a dead space inside me. We were so close, I want a sign, some indication of...peace, closure. I should have that, shouldn’t I?”

“Oh, I don’t know that I have an answer for that. It’s different for everyone, Ainsley. Over the years, I’ve heard of many different manifestations of a loved one letting a survivor know they’re in Heaven, or have passed on to whatever spiritual state they believed in during their natural life. With your brother John—it’s been less than a month. I do think that placing his remains in their final resting place may move that process along for you. And prayer. Don't underestimate its power."

She stood on the rock, looking out at the endless blue lake. "You know, John always said he felt closer to God when he flew. Well, I feel closer to God when I'm up here." She was comfortable with Blaine now. "Is your offer still good, Blaine? To help me with John's ashes?"

chapter 6

"THIS IS A yacht, not a boat," Ainsley declared three days later, as she walked tentatively up the floating dock at the Manistique Marina, where Blaine's fifty-foot cabin cruiser, "Great White," stood at anchor, dwarfing the surrounding sailboats.

"Not really," he answered. "Well, close, I guess. It's a family heirloom. On long-term loan, if you know what I mean. We priests aren't supposed to acquire a store of worldly goods, and there was a priest up here some years ago...he owned a farm, a bunch of rental properties, and rumor had it, he ingratiated himself with the elderly parishioners, trying to secure a place in their wills. It didn't reflect well on the diocese."

"I see." She dropped her tote bag onto the deck and returned to the car for the urn. She carried it with halting steps, like a water glass she had filled too full. Blaine held out a hand to steady her as she stepped from dock to boat.

"Are you ready to cast off?" he asked.

"Yes," she answered deliberately, relieved to be with someone accustomed to witnessing every human emotion out on full display, and capable of dealing with the best and worst of them. It also helped that he had personally been where she was right now.

"I was thinking about going out to the breakwater at the Manistique Lighthouse, and heading south from there," Blaine said, looking at his watch. "With the weather the way it is today, I don't want to go much farther than that. We should plan to be back by dark. Does that sound okay?"

"That sounds right—like the right place," she said. She felt shaky again, afraid she might break down.

"Ainsley, there's no one out here judging you," he said, jotting something down in a small burgundy ship's log. "It's okay if you lose it—fall apart. There's no right or wrong way to grieve."

"One minute I'm numb—the next I feel emotionally raw—I don't know how I'm going to feel five minutes from now—"

"Why don't we go upstairs to the bridge?" Blaine suggested, leading her through a sliding glass door into the large main cabin, and then up a set of stairs to the glassed-in upper helm. "In this weather I think I'd like to see exactly where we're going."

They reached the lighthouse area and headed south about a quarter of a mile in mildly choppy seas. Ainsley left her seat to go downstairs to the main deck, and felt a slap of unexpectedly cold air on her face. It was time to say goodbye to her brother for the last time.

Blaine dropped anchor and the Great White drifted until it reached the end of its tether, bobbing in the waves. Ainsley waited while he went into the cabin and down to the lower berth. She heard him moving around, opening and closing drawers. Her heart pounded as she imagined John's last minutes. Had he known what was happening to him? Was he conscious and terrified or accepting of his fate? When the Navy recovered his jet, there was no evidence of an attempted ejection; what was left of him remained strapped inside. Investigators concluded that he experienced a sudden loss of consciousness, which left him incapable of communicating any details about his situation. She prayed that was the case. John deserved to end his life with no pain, no fear. She found it ironic that he died while flying, and then came to rest in the water.

Blaine emerged from the lower cabin and came out onto the deck through the sliding door. "Okay, I've got what I need. Ainsley, are you ready to do this?" he asked.

"I'm ready," she answered, pointing at her tote bag, which now contained the funerary urn. "Should I—"

"Yes," he said. In his left hand, Blaine clutched a black prayer book, a stark contrast to his white Vans, jeans and navy windbreaker. Ainsley picked up the urn and held it to her chest.

She didn't hear much of the prayers he recited, only words like "soul," "almighty," and "eternal," here and there through silent, nauseating tears. He finished with Psalm 23, John's favorite. After she made the sign of the cross, Blaine took her by the elbow and led her to the boat's deck railing. She pulled at the urn's adhesive seal with shaking hands. He took the tape and put it in his pocket, never letting his eyes leave hers, steadying her with his gaze, with her through every step. She opened up the urn, handed him the lid and began to release the ashes overboard. Tears turned into wracking sobs, and her nose started to run. She let the urn follow the ashes into the water. Blaine held the lid over the rail and let it slip into the water.

"You did it," he said. "You did what he asked you to do." He offered her a pat on the shoulder and a pressed, gray handkerchief from his pocket, then stepped back from her so she could dry her face.

"I'm so sorry. I'll—wash it for you," she croaked.

"Don't worry about it. That thing's seen a lot of action." He cringed at his double entendre. "That came out all wrong. I meant, I'm in the business of helping people in times like this."

Ainsley forced a smile.

"Hey, you know what many people do after they inter or release ashes?" he asked her.

She blew her nose. "What?"

"They drink a toast to their loved one—a send-off, with some kind words. It's sort of an informal wake."

"Well," she sniffed, "I don't have anything to toast with. That was the last thing on my mind this afternoon."

"I might," he said. "Let me check the galley and see what I can find. Be right back."

Ainsley sat down on the bench seat and zipped up her jacket against the damp air. Her teeth chattered as she watched the unsettled water churn and swallow the last remnants of John's ashes, sending them to the bottom of the lake.

Blaine came back from the cabin with an open, nearly full bottle of red wine, two glasses in a basket, and two wool throws. "This bottle was already open. It's from my parents' last visit two months ago. It may be awful...."

Ainsley wrapped herself tightly in one of the wool throws and took her glass of wine, facing the cloudy sunset. "To John...and, to your brother, Mark," she said, touching Blaine's glass. The wine warmed her empty stomach and calmed her raw nerves. They drank several more toasts, and talked more about their families.

"I have to say, Blaine, that I expected you to be somehow suspended between heaven and earth, distant and unapproachable, not as open as you are."

"Like a doctor?" he joked.

"Very funny," she said, before turning serious. "No, really. I love Father Thompson, the rector at our church. He's a family man with two children, a father figure. But, as a Protestant, I've always thought of Catholic priests as cold and detached, distant, I suppose because they—you—don't participate in most of the common, life rituals that the rest of us long for. But, I feel as if I've known you forever." She finished her wine. "Listen to me. I guess everyone feels that way with you. That's your gift. That's why you're a priest."

"Are you hungry?" Blaine asked. "Should I try to find some food?"

"Umm, sure. If it's no trouble."

He disappeared into the cabin again. Ainsley stayed on the deck until she couldn't stand it any more. She stuck her head in the sliding door, where Blaine stood in the galley, arranging cheese and crackers on a plate. "More leftovers," he said.

Ainsley had a pained look on her face. "I'm praying, and assuming, that you've got a head on this boat?"

"Past me and straight down there." He pointed behind him to a set of steps, and then crossed the cabin to the main helm. "I'm going to check on the weather again."

She smiled and started down the stairs toward the head, dizzy from no food and bitter red wine. On her way back through the galley, she underestimated the narrowness of the passageway, and as she shuffled sideways trying to squeeze by Blaine, she found herself pressing against him. "Sorry," she said, looking up and waiting for him to back away so she could pass.

He put a hand on her shoulder, shifted his weight to one side, and then kissed her firmly on the lips. She started to push him away, but stopped, letting her head fall back against the wall. His tongue reached into her mouth like warm butter, drinking in her taste. They clawed at each other's clothes and fumbled their way to the sofa without speaking. She dragged him onto her, desperate to feel him inside of her, forcing his face toward her breasts, along her body. Naked, they rocked together on the sofa until she lost herself, forgot her surroundings. Overcome by emotion, she started to cry. The sound shocked him, and he pulled out and away from her violently.

"My God, what have I done?" he said, crawling to the edge of the sofa. Distraught, painfully aware of their nakedness, he shoved one of the throws in her direction. "I'm sorry, so sorry." He stared straight ahead, tears in his eyes. "My training, counseling, my commitment...gone. I'm a statistic, another priest who's abused trust—trust that should be freely given to me."

"No, Blaine," Ainsley said, wrapping herself in the throw, "it was...a mistake. A mistake that no one has to know about. No one."

The boat listed and Ainsley's stomach turned.

Blaine put his hands to his head. "Things like this...can't happen in my life. I...have to get us back to shore," he muttered, turning from her as he dressed. "I heard over the radio—that storm—it's rolling in."

Ainsley took her clothes and went into the bathroom to dress, barely able to look at herself in the mirror. *Could I have stopped it?* she wondered. *Why didn't I try?* She made her way back to the deck, where Blaine was pulling up anchor.

"I did this, Ainsley," he said, his voice heavy with regret. "It was my fall from grace."

They looked past each other into the growing dusk as they spoke.

"Was this—the first time?" she asked.

"I—I—can't talk about this—with you," he said, shaking his head. He started up a set of stairs to the boat's flying bridge. She followed behind him.

"This is...inexcusable, Ainsley. I should have prevented it. I saw it coming."

Her shame turned to confusion. "What? How could you know?"

"Because I'm not in control of my emotions when I'm with you. It's been that way since we met." He was talking more to himself than to her. "I shouldn't have spent so much time with you. I felt us getting too close. I thought I could somehow control it. That I could be a—friend to you—a decent man in your life, and stop it at that. You blinded me to things—things I knew were dangerous. I knew the consequences, but I couldn't stay away. I wanted to be with you."

A cold, misty drizzle began to fall. She pulled her jacket up around her face. "Are you blaming me for this?" she asked.

"I'm around women all of the time and nothing close to this has ever happened," Blaine said, standing stoically at the helm. "I hardly know you, and yet I turned my back on the church, my vows. I don't understand how this happened to me."

"To *you*? Nothing happened to you. It happened between us. We're both grieving. People do...extraordinary things...in extraordinary situations. This is one of those situations."

"No, no," he said. "That's where you're wrong, Ainsley. I'm not like other people. I'm a Catholic priest." He turned the steering wheel, staring straight ahead. "There's no excuse for what I did. I can't be trusted."

They sailed back to shore in painful, guilty silence. Blaine deposited Ainsley's belongings onto the dock as the misty rain that had been falling transformed into a heavy downpour. "It will take me some time to secure the boat," he mumbled. "You should go, before the storm hits."

"Yes, all right," she half-whispered. "Goodnight." She left him on the dock and ran to her car, cold rain mixing with the tears rolling down her face.

Ainsley heard the phone before she got through the front door. Attila was waiting for her in the entry, trembling and traumatized by its incessant, shrill ring.

"Come on, girl," she said, soaked to her shoes, dripping rainwater onto the floor. The puppy ran to her trailing a stream of nervous pee. Ainsley picked her up and stroked her, and then put her in her dog bed. The phone started ringing again. There was no time to think about what happened with Blaine.

"Hello?" she asked, expecting to hear Chris' repentant, drunken voice on the other end of the line, asking her to come home. She grabbed a clean dishtowel from the kitchen counter to dry her face. "Hello?" she repeated.

It was Jill. "Ainsley?" Her voice sounded odd.

"Jill, what's going on? Are you the one who's been calling?"

"Ainsley, it's about Chris. There's been a...car accident. You have to come home."

Ainsley slid down the kitchen wall onto the floor, right where she had been standing. "Jill," she said, hearing her own words in slow motion, "is he...dead?"

"No, he's alive. He's in the hospital. Try to stay calm, and get here when you can."

"How bad is it?" Ainsley asked, as Attila wandered into the room and plopped down next to her on the floor. "I want to know."

After a pause, Jill responded. "I don't know much. I can't see him because I'm not family. But, it's bad, Ainsley, really bad. The police came to the house looking for family. When they got no answer at your place, they came next door to our house."

"Is he conscious? Talking?"

"No. Ainsley, he's not. Just come home safely. I'll stay with him until you get here, in case anything...changes."

"Listen, I'm calling Chris' parents when I hang up, but if I give you their phone number, would you please pass it along to the hospital staff for me?"

"Sure. Whatever you need me to do. I'm so sorry to have to tell you this after everything else that's happened."

"It's okay, Jill. I'll leave as soon as I can...and drive most of the night. I'll have to stop midway. I'd fly, but by the time I get a flight out tomorrow, I think it will end up taking me as long as it will if I drive."

"Be careful, Ainsley. I'll keep in touch with you on your car phone."

Ainsley hung up the phone. Chris lay in the hospital, comatose, attached to lifesaving machines, possibly disabled or disfigured—Jill hadn't given details. The scene on the boat with Blaine replayed itself—more senseless damage. She was leaving Michigan the way she came: broken, confused, with questions but no answers. *What have we done to ourselves, Chris?* she thought, rushing to her room to pack for the trip home.

chapter 7

AT FIVE A.M., two calendar days after leaving Michigan and Blaine behind, Ainsley pulled into the driveway at Water's Edge Lane. A string of missed calls and condensed messages from Jill and Chris' family while she was on the road gave her, at best, a partial indication of his condition. The part she knew wasn't good. After showering and changing clothes, she drove to Atlantic Coast Medical Center. Jill was waiting for her when she found her way to the hospital's intensive care unit.

"How are you?" Jill asked, smiling sympathetically through huge brown eyes and looking more tired than Ainsley did.

"Exhausted, like you," Ainsley answered. "Where is he?" She started walking down one of the unit corridors. A waifish five-feet, two inches, Jill had to run to catch up with her before grabbing her by the arm.

"Ainsley, I don't know how to tell you this—I want you to hear it from me."

"What is it?"

Jill looked uncomfortable. "Chris...wasn't driving."

"I don't understand." Ainsley said, frowning. "On the phone, you said it was a car accident."

"Uh...." Jill hesitated. "Someone else was driving his car." She averted her eyes. "A woman, Ainsley. They were together. Alcohol was involved."

Ainsley's face fell. "Jesus, Jill. Who is he? I don't know him anymore."

"There's more to it, Ainsley. The woman he was with—she didn't make it."

"My God." Ainsley leaned against the hallway's thick chair rail. A wave of panic rose in her. "Have the police been here? They could charge him. He could go to jail."

"The woman was well over the legal limit, and there was no question that she was driving, if that's what you mean. I don't know that the police even asked about Chris' alcohol level in the emergency room."

"How did she—the woman—die?"

"I heard the paramedics talking to one of the nurses when they brought Chris in. The Mustang is completely gone. She was dead at the scene. No seatbelt. Massive head and neck injuries. They probably wouldn't have found either of them for some time, if it wasn't for the music."

"Music? What music?"

"From Chris' car. Some kids bike riding on Ironbound Road heard noise in the woods, and thought it was weird that people were partying back there, in the middle of nowhere. The stereo was at full volume—blasting. Then they noticed headlights, at an odd angle. The car was on its side, it turns out. They knew something was wrong, so they biked to a convenience store and called the police."

"What about the woman? How old was she? Who was she?"

"Do you really want to know?"

"Yes, I do."

"She was a twenty-two-year-old senior pre-law student. Karen Knight was her name. That's all I know."

"Twenty-two," Ainsley said as the two women stood together. "Jill, you've done so much for Chris—and for me," Ainsley said, hugging her. "Thank you. Now, why don't you go home to that baby of yours and get some rest?"

"Did you hear what you said?" Jill asked, injecting some humor into the depressing situation. "Go home to a baby—and get some rest? That's not possible."

"Okay, go home to Robin and *try* to get some rest."

"If you're sure you're okay...."

"Yeah, I'm okay."

Jill pointed down another hallway. "His room's down there—on the right." She looked worried. "Ainsley?"

"Yeah?"

"Prepare yourself, okay? Before you go in there."

"Okay," Ainsley agreed, walking away.

"May I see him?" Ainsley asked from outside the curtained, glass-walled ICU room, not much larger than a closet. "I'm his wife."

"Yes," the nurse answered, as she fiddled with an intravenous line by Chris' bed. Her large body blocked Ainsley's view of everything but the outline of Chris' legs and feet, which were covered by a thin blanket. "Five minutes only, please—until he's more stable." She produced the jaded smiled of someone who had witnessed the same scene too many times. "I'm right outside if you need anything."

Chris looked dead. His beautiful curls were gone, shorn to the scalp in order to treat his extensive head wounds. His face, swollen beyond recognition, oozed a brownish, bloody fluid from beneath several gauze dressings. Vital sign monitors beeped, attached to the few places on his body not covered by bandages or blankets. Ainsley gagged. Her impulse was to turn around and run. Away from him and everything that the last two weeks brought into her life—except maybe meeting Blaine. No, that was a mistake, too. Weighing everything Chris had done, she had every right to leave. She knew that. She just couldn't bring herself to do it—not yet.

A man walked into the room. He turned out to be Chris' physician, miraculously making rounds during her brief visit. His name was Robert Kanter. Ainsley fixed her eyes on his blue and white nametag, and then studied the white braided buttons on his lab coat, trying to recover from her first look at her husband. Dr. Kanter took her hand in his and delivered three forceful, evenly spaced pumps before launching into his assessment.

"Mrs. Bohan, it's only fair to tell you that while we think your husband stands a good chance of survival, his level of improvement—beyond where he is right now—is questionable, due to the extensive spinal cord and brain injuries he's sustained." The doctor crossed his arms.

"Will he regain consciousness?" she asked. "His parents didn't know when I talked to them."

"He has severe head trauma—there's a substantial amount of fluid and swelling in and around the brain. It'll take time for that to subside. The other challenge, er, issue is his spinal cord. He has a T-3 spinal cord injury." It was obvious by Ainsley's vacant expression that she didn't comprehend the meaning of his last statement. "Has anyone explained the spinal cord injury scale to you, Mrs. Bohan?"

"No, Dr. Kanter, not yet," she answered. "And, no one mentioned a—a—spinal cord injury." Things seemed to be spinning out of control.

He held a clenched fist to his mouth for a moment, retrieved a pen from his lab coat pocket and began writing on his clipboard. "Basically, if you look at the spine from bottom to top, injuries at the bottom compromise lower body function," he explained, producing a drawing that resembled a vertical set of railroad tracks with corresponding letters and numbers. "As we travel up the spine, we add in more and higher body functions to those lower functions that are compromised." He kept talking. Ainsley latched onto the term "compromised functions." She wondered if it meant difficulty functioning or inability to function.

"Mrs. Bohan? Mrs. Bohan?" Dr. Kanter waved his labeled drawing in front of her face.

"Yes," Ainsley answered. "I'm sorry."

"I was saying that the letters S, L, T and C correspond bottom to top."

"So, T is second highest on the spine and function scale...." Her words trailed off.

"Yes, and that region's vertebrae number from twelve to one, twelve being at the bottom, and one being the top."

"And, he's near the top at number three. What do you think he'll be able to do—for himself?"

"If I base my prognosis on where we are in medicine right now, he'll never walk again, at least not in the way you or I can."

Ainsley's own legs felt as though they couldn't support her. "No," she rasped.

Dr. Kanter took her by the elbow. "Mrs. Bohan, with medical breakthroughs in mobility devices—there's a lot out there that they're working on...."

"What else?" Ainsley found it hard to find her voice.

"He may not have full use of his arms or hands. There may be breathing problems, and cardiac complications are common in these cases. Now, other bodily functions...uh, involving daily routines, digestion, the possibility of children...well, we'll address those as we go along. Of course, all of this depends on the extent of his brain injury, how far he comes back if—when—he wakes up. Do you have any questions for me?"

She stood there, silent.

"Mrs. Bohan, I know this is a lot to take in. Right now, we're focused on waking him up. We'll know more when that happens. Take care." He excused himself.

The nurse waved at Ainsley and pointed at the clock outside Chris' cubicle. Her five minutes were up.

Ruby squinted into the mid-morning sun that blazed through the Bohan's kitchen windows. "Obviously, Mom, that story Dad told me when I was younger, about him losing control of his car the night of the accident because he was overly tired from exams, helping out a friend, that was—"

"That was a way of protecting you from things you were too young to understand," Ainsley cut in. "Telling you about his affairs, the circumstances of his accident, would have served no real purpose. He couldn't even remember what he'd done. Those things were part of the past, and I was trying to concentrate on the future—his and yours. It was hard work, Ruby."

chapter 8

VISITING CHRIS IN the hospital daily for the first two months after his accident, Ainsley struggled with whether he would want to live the kind of life that lay ahead of him, one overflowing with limitations, if he was conscious and could choose. She'd given up predicting when he would wake up, instead settling for the hope that it would happen when someone he knew was with him, to help him cope with discovering his condition.

Her speculation ended one afternoon in late July, after weeks of setbacks and small improvements, as she sat in a corner of his room, writing a letter to her parents. She paused her writing to smooth her white, sleeveless dress, the coolest thing she could find in her closet. After that, she moved on to the task of adjusting the strap of her sandal, which had been bothering her all day. Holding the sandal in her hand, she inspected its tiny ankle buckle. She thought she felt someone's eyes on her and looked at the doorway. No one was there, but Chris was moving his right hand and his eyes were open.

She ran to him, tripping over her feet, wearing one sandal. "Oh, my God! Chris!"

His eyes were empty.

"Can you see?" she asked. "It's me, Ainsley!" she shouted, leaning over the bed rail.

"Ains—Ainsley?" The words came out slowly, slurred. "Did I... fall off the roof?" he asked. Most of his facial wounds had healed, but the right side of his face bore a thin diagonal scar, temple to jaw, from striking the dashboard of the Mustang as it completed several full revolutions after swerving off the Williamsburg road. His emergency room crew cut had given way to short, soft curls, darker than she was accustomed to seeing, because he'd been out of the sun for months.

Ainsley saw bewilderment in Chris' eyes as they darted back and forth. "No," she said. "That was years ago. You've been in a coma. You were in an accident about two months ago. A car accident."

"Two months? Months?" He struggled with the words, and the effort caused his heart rate and blood pressure to escalate. A monitor beeped loudly and a nurse flew into the room.

"What's going on here?" she asked. It took her only seconds to assess the situation. "Well, all right young man. Welcome back." She ran through a list of questions to determine his level of orientation as she checked his vital signs. "I'll notify Doctor Kanter immediately," she said, before stepping outside the room to use the phone.

Chris scanned the room as he took in his surroundings, repeatedly touching his face with his hand.

"You're lucky, Chris. Everything's still there," Ainsley said. "Do you remember me—us?"

"Ainsley," he said again. "Yes." He tried to shift in the bed. "I can't get my legs...." The words came out slowly at first, "My legs won't—my legs—Jesus, no!" he yelled. Ainsley jumped back from his bedside. "My legs!" he shrieked, his voice rising as he thrashed his upper body on the bed. "Oh, Jesus Christ! No!"

The nurse reappeared, unruffled and kind. "Let's take it slow and easy, Mr. Bohan, okay?" she said politely, opening up the drip in his IV.

"What's wrong with my legs!" he screamed.

"Mr. Bohan, your wife is here with you, and Dr. Kanter is on his way." She patted Ainsley on the back, and reached for the sandal she was clutching in her hand. "Honey, let me help you with that."

"Oh, God..." Chris' crying diminished to a whimper and he drifted off.

The nurse ushered Ainsley back to her chair and helped her with her sandal. "I'm Martha," she said.

"Thank you, Martha," Ainsley said, her voice barely audible. She looked back at Chris, now peacefully at rest. "Is he...all right?"

"He's safe. We have to do this, Mrs. Bohan, to *keep* him safe, to prevent him from hurting himself. He'll probably sleep on and off through the night now. Why don't you go home—get some rest? I'll talk with his doctor when he arrives. Fill him in on what's happening."

"Are you're sure?"

"I'll call you with any updates. It takes some time for patients to come to terms with this. It's always tough going in the beginning. With most, it gets a little better each time they wake up."

"Thank you." She felt dizzy and nauseated as she stood there watching him. "I'll be near a phone—if he wakes up tonight." She gathered her belongings and left for home.

Being in her own bed quelled Ainsley's headache and nausea, but not her anxiety. The months of maintaining a daily hospital vigil, holding down a fulltime job, and uncertainty about her marriage had combined to sap her strength. She knew Chris' emergence from the coma would present yet another set of obstacles, but she had no idea what those obstacles would be, or how to meet them.

Sick again the next week, and worried about infecting Chris, she skipped a visitation day. And, then another. In her absence, Chris' parents and his sister, Amy, drove in from Richmond to sit at his bedside and endure alternating bouts of weeping and spewed expletives, directed at whomever was in front of him. When Ainsley missed a second menstrual period—she'd ignored the first, attributing it to the stress of John's death—a drugstore pregnancy test confirmed her suspicions.

"Mom, it's me," she said, when her mother answered the phone. Before making the overseas call, she had carried a cup of tea up to her bedroom, set it on the nightstand, and plopped an old desk phone on her lap. It was a few minutes past two-thirty in the morning.

There was apprehension in Julie Plante's voice. "Honey, isn't it the middle of the night over there? Is something wrong?"

"Nothing bad, but I need to talk," Ainsley said, playing with the phone cord.

"Sure, honey. Is it Chris? Has something changed?"

"No. They've got him on some new medication. The doctor says depression and rage are the norm with his type of injury. It's a difficult adjustment—for everyone." She dropped the facade. "Oh, Mom, it's horrible...."

"Ainsley—"

I'm pregnant," Ainsley blurted out.

"What? Oh, my God! Honey! Are you...happy about it—him—her?"

"I'm scared, and sick. But, I'm keeping the baby, if that's what you mean. And, I don't know if it's a boy or girl."

"Are you still planning to separate? I mean, with what Chris did the night of the accident, everything that's happened...."

"We were having problems for some time before that, Mom. I didn't want to tell you when you were here for John's funeral. It would have been too much to deal with."

"Don't worry. Dad and I will help you. Why don't I come home?"

"Not yet, Mom. I'm barely three months along, and Chris still has months in the hospital. That gives me time to work through what I'm going to do, about him, about us."

"What about his parents? Maybe they could...take over...the visits, you know. Until you figure out how you want to proceed."

"They were here for several days, but Amy starts her sophomore year in high school in a week, and they had to get back to Richmond. There really isn't a lot they can do from two hours away."

"I just thought that under the circumstances, they should be more involved. Perhaps even...take over his care."

"Mom, despite our problems, legally I'm still Chris' wife, his next of kin, his advocate. I have to make decisions regarding his treatment—especially if his condition changes for the worse. It still could. He has a long way to go."

"We can come back," Julie repeated. "God, I wish...John was there with you...to help you with all of this."

"Me, too, Mom, but he isn't. He won't be," she sighed. "Remember Dad's cancer scare? You said it made you stronger, it was your test. Well, it's my turn to get some guts about my own life, regardless of what's going to happen with Chris."

"Do you mind if I'm a little excited about the baby?"

"Please, don't we all need something to be happy about right now?" Ainsley asked. "As soon as I get over being sick twenty-four hours a day, I'll be excited, too."

"I'm proud of you Ainsley. So is your dad. You've grown into a fine person. I mean that."

"Thanks, Mom." she said, dismissing the compliment. "I'll let you get on with your day now. I'm going to try to get some sleep. Goodnight." She sipped some tea, and then ran to the bathroom to throw up.

chapter 9

AINSLEY SAT NEXT to Chris' hospital bed in late August. "Dr. Kanter says you've made tremendous progress," she told him.

Chris stared past her to the white hospital room wall. "Ainsley, if you care," he begged, starting to weep, "please...help me. I want to go to sleep, and not wake up."

It wasn't the first time he asked her to help him commit suicide, and while the request no longer surprised her, it was disturbing all the same.

"I thought we were past this, Chris."

"We? Ainsley, you don't know what it's like. Please, bring me some of that Xanax you take for flying. Please! No pain, I go to sleep, it's over."

She shook her head. "I can't do it, Chris." Out of desperation, she spoke sooner than she expected. "You need to hang on. You have more than yourself to think about now." She put a hand on her flat stomach and smiled self-consciously.

"What do you mean?" he asked.

"There may be one less empty room—bedroom in the house."

It hit him. "You're...pregnant? Are you sure?"

"Yes," she said. It was strange to be talking about a baby in the midst of the chaotic situation, but she forged ahead. "If everything goes okay, by next spring, there'll be a new Bohan in town."

He remained fixated on her stomach.

"No more talk about death, Chris. We can get you through this—together." With that simple statement, she'd set their futures in motion, indicated that she would stay with him, and they would raise their baby together.

His surprise turned to self-pity. "What kind of father can I be, like this?" he asked.

"As good a father as you want to be," she answered bluntly. "It's not over. Your life's not over. You will leave this hospital, sooner or later, and you will continue to recover. Don't leave our child without a father."

By November, Chris' condition had improved enough for him to enter New Bridges Rehabilitation Center, an in-patient facility two miles from the hospital and a few miles closer to home. Through intensive physical therapy, he progressed to the point of feeding himself and writing simple words. As Ainsley's belly expanded with the developing baby they now knew was a girl, the suicidal depression that had plagued Chris since his accident beat a slow but steady retreat.

The Christmas holidays passed quietly and winter faded into a warm, rainy spring. Ten minutes before midnight on Saturday, March 26, 1987, Ruby Bohan made her way into the world, following twenty hours of painful labor. Julie coached Ainsley through the exhausting delivery as Don paced the floor and made phone calls to their family and a list of friends. Chris listened to the final hour of labor and birth over an open phone line from his room at New Bridges.

"Who does she look like?" he asked Ainsley, as she cradled her daughter on her chest.

"Me, I'm afraid. A rubber stamp of me as a baby."

"Blue eyes, too?"

"Yes...blue," she repeated, groggily. "But, most babies have blue eyes."

"I'm sure they'll stay that way. Thank God," he sighed, "a third generation of excellence." He sounded upbeat. "Let's hope she'll inherent other traits of yours, as well."

Ainsley didn't hear him; she'd fallen asleep before she transferred out of the labor and delivery room.

At four-thirty the next morning, a nurse brought Ainsley's newborn daughter, swaddled in a pink and white blanket, into her small, private room.

"Here she is," the nurse cooed, as she passed Ainsley the sleeping baby. "Do you have a name for her yet?"

"Ruby."

"Ruby? That's a pretty name. Do you want me to stay while you try to nurse—to make sure that she's latching on correctly?"

"No, thanks," she answered, preferring to maintain some privacy. "I'll call if I have problems."

The previous day's lengthy and grueling labor left Ainsley with only hazy memories of her baby's birth. Now, she took some time to look at her with clear eyes. Ruby's translucent, pliable toes and fingers were no bigger around than the stem of a rose, her skin soft and poreless. A fine sprinkling of chestnut hair crowned her round head. Somehow, that recessive Spencer family gene seemed to have surfaced in her blue eyes, which mirrored her mother's.

Ainsley put Ruby to her breast. The pain was sharp and fleeting, followed by pins and needles, and finally vague but tolerable pressure. Ruby squirmed and Ainsley repositioned her higher across her chest, slipping one hand under the top of the baby's diaper in the process. The adhesive tab stuck to Ainsley's thumb, and she laughed out loud as it adhered in turn to each successive finger she used to free the last. Finally, she managed to push away the plastic and free her hand.

The world stopped.

"No," she said. Her hands began to shake. She looked around the room, paranoid—terrified a nurse might have come in. There was no mistaking the small mark inside Ruby's right hipbone. It was identical to the one Blaine had. She had seen it clearly that night on the boat. Nine months ago, she had convinced herself that her feelings for Blaine and their subsequent ill-fated encounter wasn't love, but an extreme reaction to grief and betrayal. She prayed that, wherever he was, he had found some form of reconciliation that would allow him to continue in the church. Then, she tried to forget him and focus on her new family. She prayed for forgiveness and the strength to continue on the path she'd forged for herself, Ruby and Chris. And, it had almost worked.

Blinded by panic, she rang for a nurse. In seconds, one appeared in the doorway.

"How did it go, Mrs. Bohan?"

"Uh, fine," she choked out. "I think I need some rest. It must be the pain medication. Could you take my baby to the nursery—for a little while?"

The nurse took Ruby out of Ainsley's arms. "Okay, we'll be back at seven. Sweet dreams."

Ainsley shut her eyes tight and buried her face in the bed pillow, sobbing silently.

chapter 10

FROM ITS PERCH atop the kitchen's stone fireplace mantle, the Bohan's Ansonia clock rang in the ten o'clock hour.

"So?" Ruby asked, sitting cross-legged on her chair, arms crossed in front of her chest. She wiped at her eyes with her t-shirt. "The day after I was born, you discovered that I was Blaine's. You had no suspicions before then?"

Ainsley picked up a fork up from the table and twirled it in her hand. "Ruby, your dad and I were trying to get pregnant before I left for Michigan—before I found out about his—affair. Losing my brother devastated me. I hadn't had time to grieve. Your dad's accident—days and nights in the hospital. He was barely hanging on, physically or emotionally. Then I found out that I was pregnant. Just the thought of you inspired your dad, and I was excited about bringing you into the world, meeting you. You gave both of us hope. I'd convinced myself that what happened with Blaine was a tragic mistake—that I couldn't have fallen in love with him after the brief period of time we spent together. It wasn't until after you were born, when I saw the birthmark—suddenly, nothing was as I thought. But, your dad already loved you, and I couldn't bear to take that from him—I couldn't stop what I had started. Time passed so quickly. Before I knew it, you were a year old."

By June 1988, it was time to go back up north. Ruby was nearly sixteen months old, and Chris had another three months of round-the-clock, inpatient care at New Bridges ahead of him. Ainsley was burned out from her role as his cheerleader and life-coach, and desperate for a break from her grant writing job, consisting lately of long hours of research and writing, and less than fruitful results for her clients.

"It's fine, Ainsley. Go up north," Chris told her, as Ruby napped next to him in his bed, clutching a stuffed kangaroo Julie and Don had sent from Australia.

"It's been two years...and the house needs some attention. I think I need some time to regroup, and some time—"

"Away from me?" he asked, frowning.

"Come on, Chris," she argued, not up for one of his mood swings so early in the day. They looked at each other for a moment.

"It's okay," he said. "If I were you, I'd want some time way from me, too. From this." He looked around the room, filled with medical paraphernalia.

"My mom can come down from Richmond for some of the time you're gone. Can she...stay at the house?"

"Of course."

"Go, then. I swear that place is in your blood. It's part of who you are. You need to keep that part of you alive, and you should show it to Ruby."

"You're sure?" she asked.

"I'm sure."

She looked at him, perplexed.

"What?" he asked.

"Well," she hesitated, uncertain whether his improved mood would hold, "in all the years I've known you, I've never known you to be that...insightful."

"So, maybe I gained something from the accident," he remarked, "to make up for all of the things that I lost."

Before dawn a week later, Ainsley, Ruby and Attila, now the size of a small pony, set out from Water's Edge Lane and drove thirteen hours to Frankenmuth, Michigan. Ainsley remembered her parents' ritual of stopping off in the small village, known as the "Christmas town," on their way to the U.P. First, it was a chicken lunch or dinner at Zehnder's Restaurant. Then, on to purchasing handmade ornaments from Bronner's Christmas Wonderland Factory and Store for their own tree, and an extra dozen or so to give as holiday gifts. Ainsley decided to keep the tradition alive for her daughter.

Bronner's factory tour and store displays thrilled Ruby, who shrieked with delight at the giant nutcrackers, snowmen and twinkling lights intermingled with handcrafted decorations. After dinner, Ainsley found a pet-friendly hotel and they settled in for an overnight stay.

The final leg of the trip was routine until Ainsley crossed the Pointe Aux Chenes River and approached Mark MacGearailt's roadside shrine. The cross and silk flowers remained unchanged from two years ago, when she stumbled upon it for the first time, but the weatherproof photo and typed tribute were new, a little larger and more substantial than the original, probably professionally mounted and framed. She debated for a moment before stopping the car. Sitting there, eyes closed, she wished she could go back. Back to when the Upper Peninsula was her sanctuary—wild, unspoiled, beautiful. A safe place. Her place. *I've got to get back to that*, she thought. *I need it to stay the way it was—before Blaine.*

Two hours later, Ainsley's Bronco sat in the driveway of the Makwa Point house. A full assessment would have to wait until morning, but from what she could see in the dusk, the house had weathered another two years unscathed, thanks to Janice and Ren. After half an hour of crimeless, regional news highlighted by the next day's fishing and boating forecast, she locked up the house against non-existent intruders, and turned off all but the front and back porch lights. She and Ruby slept in the front bedroom, lulled by a steady, cool breeze that skimmed over them like delicate incense.

"Hel-luuu, you two. Welcome back," Janice Mercer called from Ainsley's front porch at a little before seven o'clock the next day. Attila answered her early morning knock with a glass-shattering bark. Janice was undeterred. "I know ya got in late, so I brought ya some wild blueberry muffins. Can't make 'em as good as your grandma, now, but I hope ya like 'em."

"They smell wonderful," Ainsley told her, still sleepy, as she opened the door in shorts and a Led Zeppelin t-shirt. A bright, floral scarf covered Janice's rolled hair, and she had gone to the trouble of applying a smear of geranium red lipstick and a thick layer of beige face powder. She carried a foiled-wrapped plate in her hands.

"Oh! Is that her?" Janice peered into the living room and spotted Ruby holding onto the side of the living room sofa. "Your new addition?" She was begging for an invitation to come in.

"Janice, please have some coffee with me." Ainsley said, stepping back from the door.

"My, she turned out to be a big one," Janice gasped, watching Attila pace the floor with giant paws, a domestic lion in a cage. "You won't have to worry about any trouble with her!" She turned her attention back to Ruby. "Well, your daughter is the spitting image of you and your husband. She'll be a beauty, too."

Ainsley scooped up Ruby and carried her out the kitchen. Janice followed behind, and they all sat down at the round oak table in front of the unlit corner fireplace.

"Eddie Roleau came by and took your boat in for an overhaul last week," Janice said, as she broke a muffin into a dozen bite-sized pieces to avoid messing her lipstick. They'll drop off the invoice when they bring it back—should be today or tomorrow. I hope the storm windows Ren put in held up okay. Let's see...how's your husband, Chris, doin' these days then, Ainsley?" she asked, a look of maternal concern on her face.

"He's making progress—getting better," Ainsley answered. "It's slow going, Janice. A lot of hard work."

"Will he be coming home soon, then?"

"In the fall, if all goes well."

"Well, I know you'll be glad to have things back to normal—I mean—to have him back home again."

"Right," Ainsley replied absently. Janice didn't know her circumstances outside of visits to Makwa Point. She didn't understand that Ainsley was content without Chris in the house, living the past two years as a single parent.

Janice's curiosity got the better of her. "Dear, what exactly was it—happened to him?"

Ainsley recited the version of the story she and Chris decided upon when they realized that Ruby would eventually want to know about his condition. "He lost control of his car, Janice, driving home late one evening, overly tired from law school exams. He sustained serious head and spinal cord injuries."

"Will he walk again, do ya think?"

"His doctors say no." She was tired of the subject.

"Oh, how sad. It'll get better, now. Time is a healer. That's what my priest says."

Ainsley nodded.

"I'll let ya get settled, then. I'm right across the street if you need me. If you don't find me home, now, I'm most likely up at the church."

Her last sentence got Ainsley's attention. "Are you and Ren still going up to that church in Escanaba? That's a long drive."

"Oh, no, Ainsley, right here. We're havin' services at St. Mary's again. Wednesday nights."

"Really? How are you managing that? St. Mary's has been boarded up since I was a teenager."

"Funny thing. There's a new priest 'round here, willing to come into the old parish towns, even for a handful of us. About six months ago, he got Ren and some of the other men around here to help him clean out St. Mary's and fix it up. Now, all we do is maintain the church and parish grounds, and keep a treasury. Take a peek up the street and see how beautiful it looks!"

"I will," Ainsley promised her. "Have you got someone coming down from Marquette to conduct services?"

"No, from right here, in Manistique. A new priest—name's Father Blaine MacGearailt. He's the one whose relative—brother—was killed up here a couple of years ago. Remember, you asked me about that memorial last time you were here? That was Father Blaine's brother."

Ainsley listened, dumbfounded.

"Ya know, dear," Janice continued, "I have the vestry—it's just Father Blaine, me, Ren, and Eddie and Carol Roleau—over to the house for dinner after the weekly Wednesday-night service. I know you're not Catholic, but why don't ya come over and join us, eh? Since Father Blaine lost his brother, you two have something in common. And, the...problem with your husband? Maybe he could help."

Ainsley responded with a quick, "thanks," mumbled through a cloud of disbelief. She hadn't anticipated Blaine staying in the area. She assumed that in the last two years he had moved on to another parish, or perhaps another diocese, somewhere—anywhere—else. Her heart was in her throat as she saw Janice to the door and paced the side yard with Ruby and Attila. In daylight, the newly painted steeple of St. Mary's Catholic Church was clearly visible at the end of Bay Street, a ship's figurehead parting a sea of lush-leaved maple trees. In three days, Blaine would be at the altar of that church, conducting Wednesday Mass. It would be a question of when, not if, she would see him again. There was no escaping that.

Back inside, she slid into a kitchen chair. Ruby waddled in and stood next to her, holding the chair back for support. Ainsley watched her for several minutes, agonizing, before she picked up the phone. "Forgive me, Ruby," she said, "but I think it's time to meet your father."

Short of breath, she dialed the rectory at St. John's Catholic Church in Manistique. With her eyes closed, she could have been sitting on an airplane, seatbelt fastened, waiting for it to take off.

"Father Blaine MacGearailt here," the voice on the other end of the phone said. "Hello?"

She couldn't find her voice.

"Is someone there?" he asked, sounding older than she remembered. "Hello?"

"Blaine, it's Ainsley. Ainsley Bohan." Her palms sweated as she waited for an awkward response.

"Ainsley? Yes, of course." He was pleasant but distant—wholly composed. "Makwa Point. Mark's watch. Your late brother, the pilot. I remember you."

"Blaine," she swallowed reflexively, her stomach in knots, "I'm up here for a month at my family's house." Her words led her thoughts. "Can I talk with you?"

He took a moment to answer. "Ainsley, it's great to hear from you, and it would be good to see you again. I'd be happy to talk with you."

"How about tomorrow, Blaine? We could meet at Stone Beach, maybe go for a walk." It seemed like a neutral setting, quiet and private, even in the middle of summer.

"I...take my meetings here—at the rectory. I have paperwork to finish this morning, and then a counseling session, but I have some time this afternoon. Okay?"

"Okay," she said, hurt that he treated her like a stranger, and knowing she had no right to feel that way. "I'll be there at two."

"God bless you," he said. "I'll see you at two."

Before leaving for the rectory, Ainsley tried on and cast off a pile of clothes, finally overdressing for the warm day in jeans, boots, and a yellow, snap-front corduroy shirt. The heavy clothes served as armor, disguising her figure, her sexuality, and, she hoped, granting her a degree of invulnerability to Blaine's reaction to news that would surely stun and alarm him, and potentially destroy his life's work. She wore no makeup, and pulled her hair into a ponytail. She dressed Ruby in a pair of denim overalls.

"Play?" Ruby asked as Ainsley put the toddler's feet into tan suede moccasins, which fit in the palm of her hands.

"Visit," Ainsley replied. "Visit a friend."

St. John's Catholic Church and its attached rectory emerged from behind a wall of sand dunes at the end of a lakeside road, about three miles outside of Manistique. In the architectural style common to turn-of-the-century seafaring buildings, both the A-frame church and its diminutive rectory featured brown shake siding with white window and door trim. Acres of six-foot high, wild grasses surrounded both structures, as well as the church's empty, sand-strewn parking lot.

Ainsley released Ruby from her car seat, deposited her on her hip, and walked to the rectory's front door. It had a brass doorknocker in the shape of an anchor, which Ainsley studied intently while she waited for Blaine to answer. A rush of nerves hit her as the door opened and he appeared, in full vestments, including a green stole. *His armor*, she thought.

"Well, hello, Ainsley. What a surprise hearing from you after all this time." Blaine looked back and forth at Ainsley and Ruby. "Is this your—daughter?" he asked, tilting his head to get a better look at Ruby, who was half-asleep and shyly leaning into Ainsley's shoulder, her chin-length hair obscuring her face. "I think," he said, "she looks exactly like you."

"Yes, she does...Blaine," Ainsley said, wondering if he might have forgotten her. "Am I still allowed to call you that?"

"Yes, of course you are," he insisted. "Everybody calls me Blaine. I'm not much on formality."

They remained in place in the doorway, the tension between them becoming palpable.

"A lot changes in two years, doesn't it?" he said, stepping back from the door and motioning them inside. "Come in, please."

Ainsley sat down on an old maroon sofa in the corner of the room. She positioned Ruby next to her and waited for a small gesture from Blaine, some show of her significance to him. What she received was a benign smile, as he sat down in a straight-backed chair, swathed in brocade and muslin.

"Blaine, it's only the three of us here, isn't it?" she asked, her voice lowered.

"Yes, it's just us." The vein on his temple was pulsing visibly. "I appreciate you thinking of me," he said, measuring out the words evenly, "and calling on me to say hello."

She couldn't stand the pretense any longer. "Blaine, stop treating me like I'm some...kindly neighbor, or something. It's me, for God's sake!"

"What is it that you want from me, Ainsley?" he asked, pursing his lips.

"I want you to stop this. Stop it, Blaine."

"Stop what?" he asked.

He peeled off his stole, alb and cincture, revealing black pants and a blue t-shirt beneath. When he sat back down on the chair, he was physically familiar again. A surge of adrenaline coursed through her. She wanted to grab onto him, shake him into the person she'd left two years ago.

"I'm not sure what's going on here," he said.

"Blaine," she started, "I know this is uncomfortable—"

He talked over her. "Ainsley, that was two years ago. Since then, we've both matured, found a way to put our lives back in order—obviously."

"So, you want to forget what happened."

He seized the arms of his chair in frustration. "Forget what happened? How could I forget—what we did?" he demanded. "You come up here for one month a year, and then return to your world. I don't leave, Ainsley. My whole life is here. Do you have any idea what it's been like for me the last two years? After that night on the boat, you left town without a word. Nothing. For the first year, every time I drove through Makwa Point, I looked for any sign that you might be up here. I found excuses to spend time at St. Mary's, at the Mercer's, hoping to see your car in the driveway, all the while knowing it was wrong. Eventually, I gave up—stopped myself from thinking about you. I had to find a way to go on with my work, to feel worthy of setting foot in church or counseling my parishioners." He straightened up in his chair. "I went through Hell, as I should have. In time, with faith, work and prayer, I put it...to the side. Or, I thought I had," he said bitterly. He paused, and his resentment shifted to contrition. "Ainsley, that night two years ago—what happened between us was my fault. I failed God. I failed the church. I failed you." He looked at

Ruby. "You and your husband found a way back to each other. I found my way back to God's grace."

"Blaine, listen to me," she said. "That night, after I left you at the marina, I got home to a phone call from Virginia. My husband had nearly died in a car accident. He was with another woman when it happened—another of his affairs. She died and he was critically injured. Chris is a paraplegic."

Blaine looked sympathetic. "Ainsley, I'm not sure what to say. You and your family have gone through so much pain and loss. But, thank God, your husband did survive, and you have your beautiful daughter. Why would you want to bring our mistake back to life now?"

Ainsley leaned toward him, pressing her elbows into her thighs until it hurt, her shoulders hunched forward. "Blaine, Chris and I are legally married, but we're not—together—in the way you're suggesting. I've had to two years to think about what happened between us. It's haunted me—"

"Both of us," he agreed.

"We were both in denial back then, about our feelings for each other. I know that night on the boat was more than mutual grief or misguided emotion."

"What are you saying?"

"It was love. We both know that. I tried to forget it. I can't. Can you at least say it—acknowledge it—if only to me?"

Blaine rubbed his temples. "Ainsley, I'm so sorry about your husband, and about your feelings, but listen to yourself," he said gently. "I can't fill the void in your life. I'm not available, I'm not viable, to you or any other woman...in that way." He looked at the floor, carefully contemplating his next words. "Can you honestly say that you love me, when we hardly know each other? I'm committed to the church, and that commitment must come before everything and everyone else. It prohibits me from having any relationship with you, other than that of a good friend. We both know that I've already strayed—horribly—from my sacred vows. I will never deny that to you—of all people. But, I can't succumb to temptation and break my vows like an experimenting adolescent, and then run back to the altar and pray for forgiveness. That's not the way of the church. That's not my way." He saw the pain in her eyes. "Two years ago, you saw a side of me that belonged in the past. Time is a healer, Ainsley. Time and prayer. I've learned from our mistake. I don't want to hurt you, to cause you any more pain than you've already endured. Ainsley, I know having a baby is difficult, a big adjustment. It can leave you...out of sorts, emotional. I've seen it with some of my younger parishioners. Add to that what's happened with your husband. It takes a tremendous toll—"

She bolted from the sofa and stood in front of his chair. "Do you honestly think that I came here today because I'm some lonely, new mother with emotional problems?"

He stood up and put his hand on her arm. "I didn't mean to suggest that. I'm saying that sometimes, we confuse our feelings—"

"I can't stand your rationalizing any longer!" Ainsley roared. "She's yours!" Her shouting roused Ruby from her nap.

"What?"

"She's your child, Blaine! Ruby's yours!"

He fell back into his chair.

"Blaine, I didn't plan to tell you this way," she said. "I thought you had moved on, left for another assignment by now. Then, I got up here, and found out that you were still in the area, and working with the church in Makwa Point. I knew I would see you again, and with Ruby—"

"Are you absolutely certain," he asked, still shaken, "about Ruby?"

"Yes, I'm certain," she replied, unsnapping Ruby's overalls and exposing the birthmark.

"But, we stopped—"

"Not before we conceived Ruby."

"My God...." He scrutinized his daughter, unblinking. "Why? Why did you wait two years to tell me?"

"Blaine, I didn't know—until the day after she was born. By then it was too late."

"What do you mean, too late?" he asked, angry. "The last two years were purgatory, Ainsley. Didn't you think I had a right to know?"

"Blaine, I made a commitment to Chris, when he was at his lowest point—before I knew about Ruby. He was suicidal, Blaine. He needed something to hold onto—he needed hope."

"Ainsley, I worked so hard to get away from wanting you." He picked up Ruby without asking to, cradling her in his arms as he sat down on the floor in front of the sofa. Silent tears rolled down his cheeks. They were infectious. Ainsley hurt with him, for him, for all three of them. She sat down next to him and leaned her head on his shoulder. Ruby drifted back to sleep.

"I think I probably started falling in love with you the day I met you," he admitted. "Every day I spent with you, I fell a little more. Yet, we both know that I can't love you. Not that way. And, now this. A baby—our baby." He turned and tucked Ruby into an afghan on the sofa. "There is no way to reconcile this to a life in the church." He smiled sadly, and reached back behind Ainsley's head. She felt a fleeting beat of fear. He pulled the band from her ponytail, and arranged her hair around her face.

"What are you doing?" she asked.

"That's how I remember you from that summer," he said, before he kissed her. She ran a hand through his hair and pressed herself against his body to get the feel of him. They rolled onto the floor and made love there, still dressed. There were moments she felt like he hated her—that he wanted to wipe the love out of her through force. She didn't care.

They kissed once more, with finality, still damp with sweat. He smelled her perfume, released by the warmth of her skin, and wanted to drown in it.

"I crave you, Ainsley. I can't get you out of my system. I was foolish to think that I could." He sat up. "But, take a good look at me. Look at what I am. Why would you love this? How could you want this? Lying and cheating—words you used to describe your husband. Well, I lie everyday I don't confess what we've done, and I've cheated God. Is there anything worse?"

"I'm jealous of God," she said, resentfully, pulling her clothes together.

He recoiled from her. "What are you saying? You're a Christian. If you're casting blame, don't look at God. Blame me."

"I'm jealous that God called you before I found you. I know it's wrong to feel that way."

"Committing to the priesthood doesn't include picking and choosing which vows I break. I can't live that way. What we've done, even the conversations we've had, it's forbidden. I suppose none of that matters anymore. It's done, finished. I've made my choice by being with you here, today." He stared at a large crucifix, mounted to the wall across from where they were sitting. "I'm leaving the priesthood, Ainsley. It's what's right for the church and what's fair to Ruby."

"No, it's not fair, Blaine. It would destroy Chris, and scandalize Ruby...and our families."

"Then, what do you want?"

"I don't know. I don't know." She moved to the sofa and picked up Ruby without waking her. "I had to tell you about Ruby. I had to tell you how I feel. I needed to hear that you loved me." She brushed a strand of hair from Ruby's face. "Leaving the church and acknowledging her won't change that fact that she is the illegitimate child of a Roman Catholic priest. If you make this public, she'll carry that stigma forever. Is that what you want for her?"

"No."

"I made a decision two years ago, and I'm not changing things now. I'll raise her with Chris as her father."

He stood up and paced the floor. "Where does your decision leave me?" he asked.

"Blaine, I need you to be there for her, someone who can teach her the things that Chris can't anymore. I have to know you're accessible, present in some way, just between us."

Ruby opened her eyes and lifted her head. Blaine stopped in his tracks.

He whispered, "If either of them find out...."

"We have to make certain they don't, Blaine." She took out her car keys and handed them to Ruby to play with.

"Ainsley, I can't keep doing this—being with you—like this."

"This will never happen again. We have to keep our distance... from situations like this one. You'll be in my life, and our daughter's life. I'm not even sure what form that will take yet, but you have to promise me." She waited for his answer.

"I promise. Nevertheless, I have to leave the church, Ainsley. Staying is impossible. What you're proposing—it's sacrilege, blasphemy."

"Other priests have done things that are worse. You have too much work left to do here. These people need you. You've made a difference, given them hope, a sense of community. You have to continue your work."

"But...your husband Chris. You're staying with him—after everything he's done?"

"Years ago, you made a promise to the church. Before Ruby was born, I made a promise to Chris. He isn't keeping me from happiness, fate is." She went to the door. "I have to go now."

"Will I see you—before you leave for Virginia?"

"I'm not sure. I need some time—to think about things." She left him standing in the doorway. He was still there long after her taillights vanished beyond the sea grass.

❦

Ainsley was busy the entire month she and Ruby stayed on in Makwa Point. The Queen Mary returned from Garden Boatworks fully refurbished, and Janice and Ren joined Ainsley and Ruby on a short voyage inside the bay to test the repairs.

"Glad to have you back up here, Ainsley," Ren said, as they launched the boat into the Makwa River. "So, you'll be startin' up your summer visits again regular, eh?"

"I hope so," she answered. "It's good to be back, with you and Janice, doing the things we used to do. This is the one place, the one thing, in my life that's always here, always the same."

"You can pretty much count on that, eh?" Janice said. "And, we'll be here for ya, until the day comes when God takes us."

After a week of painting the summer home's white window trim and picket fence, Ainsley revived her grandmother's perennial garden. Kneeling in the rich, black soil, she vigorously hacked away at weeds and pruned wayward flower stalks, until neat sections of day lilies, sunflowers and gladiolus craned their blossoms to the sun.

Ainsley heard the familiar sound of Janice crunching a piece of hard candy between her dentures before she saw her. Janice had wandered over to her yard with a Kleenex in one hand and a cookie tin full of fresh doughnuts in the other.

"You sure do love your flowers, don't ya?" Janice observed. "Now listen, Ainsley. Why don't I take some pictures of the flowers once they bloom? I'll send them down to you in Virginia, eh?"

"That would be great, Janice, if it's no trouble. Feel free to cut as many of them as you like. No point in wasting them," she said, sensing that Janice had more on her mind than gardening.

"Will do, dear. Thought you might want these for the road," Janice said, pushing the tissue up her sleeve and passing Ainsley the doughnuts.

"Thanks," Ainsley said, putting the tin in her wheelbarrow.

"Now, you know it's Wednesday again...."

For the three previous Wednesday evenings, Ainsley managed to find somewhere else to be between five-thirty and eight o'clock, but today Janice caught her without an excuse. On her last night in Makwa Point, Ainsley caved into Janice's invitation to attend St. Mary's vestry supper. She and Blaine shuffled through the two-hour trial with mixed results.

"Ainsley, I'm not sure I can do this," he said over the phone early the next morning.

"You've got Ruby to think about, Blaine. If you love her, you'll find a way, like I will."

"So you're leaving today?" He sounded solemn.

"Yes. I'll let you know how Ruby's doing," Ainsley promised.

"And you, too. I want to know how you are—if you need anything. When will I see you? When will you be up here again?"

"I intend to continue my summer visits."

"So I go back to my life as a priest, and you go back to yours as Chris' wife?"

"No, Blaine we go on, not back. Somehow, we'll navigate forward—with God's help. Isn't that what you would say?"

"I'm not sure anymore," he answered. "I don't know that God has much charity for people like me."

"You'll hear from me—soon." She hung up the phone.

"You're saying that you and Blaine struck a deal to hide the truth about me," Ruby said.

"That's not how it was," Ainsley countered. "Let's get out of here before everyone comes back from breakfast. We'll go to the beach and talk some more."

They left a note for the others, and drove fifteen minutes to Sandbridge Beach in Ainsley's old Bronco, finding a quiet spot away from sunning vacationers. Ruby sat in the sand, staring into the Atlantic Ocean. "Mom, I'm trying to understand what you did—put myself in your place. I really am. There's no way around the fact that I was—I still am—a dirty little secret."

"No, you're not," Ainsley said sharply. "You're a gift, the best thing that ever happened to me, and to your dad—to Chris. You saved his life."

chapter 11

Back home in Virginia Beach after Ruby's first visit to Michigan, Ainsley devoted most of her free time to readying the first floor of the house for Chris' September release from New Bridges. She rearranged each piece of furniture and household item to ensure its accessibility and safety, rolling from room to room in a borrowed wheelchair, maneuvering between tables and chairs, behind sofas and in the newly adaptive bathroom. Some nights, she dropped Ruby off at the Horner's house to play with Jill's son Robin, and then drove to New Bridges for meetings with an endless stream of Chris' physicians and therapists, each of whom appeared to hold an individual agenda for his recovery.

There was his attending physician, Dr. Beegle: "Mrs. Bohan, I think we're ready to transition your husband out of here, and back home and into the real world. We'll need you to come in during August for some orientation and training, meet with some of his team members. No time to waste on this."

And, the head of orthopedics, Dr. Richards: "We'll go over some hands-on ADL work, so you'll know what to do at home. You're going to be his therapist for a while, you know."

Chris' psychologist, Christine Rocco, had her own set of concerns. "Mrs. Bohan, we'll schedule an appointment to discuss issues related to your...personal life." She half-whispered the last few words. "Specifically about what you can and can't expect from each other in your future relationship. With no sensation below the chest, Chris could possibly father a child, but there will be other challenges to overcome to restore an intimate relationship. We can help you transition."

Ainsley answered curtly. "Let's wait for that. Chris has other hurdles to clear right now,"

Dr. Rocco returned a look of slight disapproval. "Is there something we should talk about?"

"No, *we* don't have to talk about anything," Ainsley answered. "My husband and I will work through things."

During Chris' eighteen months of hospitalization, Ainsley was a generic, concerned loved one, who left her unstable, troubled marriage at the door of New Bridges each night. She had created a workable balance by splitting her life down the middle—devoting herself to Chris and his issues while she was at the hospital, and retreating to her own life with Ruby at Water's Edge Lane. With his homecoming, they would be husband and wife again, with their ugly past, all of which she remembered, much of which he couldn't recall, revived by the return to familiar surroundings.

"Ruby, you know Daddy's coming home in a week?" Ainsley asked Ruby, as she positioned the toddler squarely on her lap. They were sitting on the stone wall of Ainsley's rose garden, enjoying a late summer evening.

"Daddy!" Ruby shouted proudly.

"Right, honey." She turned Ruby around to face her. "Ruby, your Daddy's coming home, to live with us, in a week."

"Daddy's home?" Ruby repeated, grabbing Ainsley's hair.

"Almost. Daddy's coming home very soon." Ainsley hugged her. "Let's look at his room now," she said, carrying Ruby into the house, and making one final inspection of the library before closing it off. "All set," she said.

"All set," Ruby mimicked, "for Daddy!"

Despite several successful trial visits, Chris' mid-September arrival home was awkward. Ainsley had tried to think of everything; his new bedroom featured an adjustable, hospital-grade bed, an oxygen delivery system for his bouts with respiratory distress, assorted mobility assistance devices, and a pharmacopoeia of medications for chronic pain, paralysis-related muscle spasms, blood clots and other side effects of his condition. He would never return to the second floor, or their shared bedroom, so she emptied his upstairs closet and dresser, and relocated his belongings to accessible furniture in the library.

Whether out of consideration or pride, Chris had elected to undergo a permanent colostomy and insertion of an in-line catheter to self-manage his personal hygiene before leaving New Bridges. "I couldn't tolerate losing that level of dignity," he explained to Ainsley when she questioned the risk of complications during the operation. "Besides, you have enough diapers to change already." Although the surgery was technically successful, he was struggling with managing the equipment-dependent functions independently. Until he was stronger and more coordinated, he would be dependent upon Ainsley for help.

Within weeks of his return, Chris recovered from the physical exhaustion of transitioning back home, but his emotional adjustment to everyday life lagged noticeably behind. New Bridges was not a microcosm of the real world. The days of twenty-four hour attention from medical staff and a specially-designed environment were gone. He had to adjust to making his way in a world ill-equipped to accommodate him. He vacillated between two mood extremes: sullenness and agitation. Ainsley never knew which of them to expect—sometimes they came at her simultaneously.

"How did we meet?" he asked her, clumsily propelling himself into the kitchen one Saturday afternoon. She sat at the kitchen table, hunched over a stack of unpaid hospital bills. Attila lay stretched out on an old Oriental rug and Ruby slept in a wind-up swing next to the fireplace.

"Thank God, we don't have a house payment," Ainsley said, deflecting the question. She understood that his memory had gaps. She just didn't want to go back to that place in their relationship. Once was enough.

"Ainsley, tell me about the first time we met," he repeated.

She straightened up and answered tersely. "At William and Mary. My first year—your third. At The Cheese Shop." She put her head back into the stack of bills.

"The Cheese Shop," he repeated, as though he'd never heard of the place. "Give me details."

"You offered to buy me lunch. Afterward, you reminded me that there's no such thing as a free lunch."

"And, the price was?" he asked, his hands shaking.

"The price was dinner at the Trellis. I said yes."

On that first date, they sat in the restaurant, eating almost nothing before rushing to Chris' apartment. Ainsley's well-guarded virginity was a memory within five minutes, but she omitted this information from her narrative. Chris was a stranger to her now, and intimate details of their young love and lust were out of bounds.

"Ainsley, I know something was going on the night of my accident. We had problems, didn't we?"

She hesitated before answering. "Chris, do we have to go into this now? Let's wait until you're a little stronger—better oriented to things."

"You haven't once touched me, kissed me—in almost two years. I'm not an idiot," he said, short of breath. "Where were we in our relationship when this—" he gesticulated, indicating his legs, "—happened? I heard some of the staff at New Bridges gossiping from time to time—about a woman—the woman who was with me in the car. Who was she? Where is she now? I can't remember...."

"We've been through a lot, Chris. Look, I'm here now, aren't I?"

"And, I'm grateful. I am, Ainsley. Without you, I wouldn't have survived. Now, what happened?" His voice rose to a shout. "Goddamn, tell me what happened!"

Ainsley was glad he couldn't get up out of the chair. "Stop yelling at me, Chris" she said, glaring at him. "You'll wake Ruby."

"Okay, okay," he answered, fidgeting in his wheelchair.

She went to the kitchen window. "Look Chris, there's a reason I took John's ashes to Michigan alone, a week before your accident."

"Do you mean...the woman in the car?" he asked defensively. "Because John and I—we were close."

"Chris, I took John's ashes to Michigan alone because the day before we were supposed to leave, I confronted you about an affair—your third in less than two years—that I knew of," she said, trying to hold onto her composure.

"Were you sure about the affair? I honestly don't remember."

"Yes, Chris, I was positive." She was thoroughly exasperated. "I found the condom wrapper in your pants pocket. If you don't remember—and I'm sure you don't—we were trying to start a family. I wasn't using birth control. That was your idea, by the way. Are you satisfied?"

"Ainsley, I'm sorry. It was a ridiculous mistake. I know how much I must have hurt you."

She resented having to relive the event, but opted to finish what she had started. "The night of the accident, I was still away. Classes were over, but you drove all the way up to Williamsburg to drink with your buddies. You ended up with a student—Karen Knight. You were both roaring drunk and you let her drive your car, probably on your way to her place. She died, Chris."

He looked horrified. "Oh, my God. Why didn't anyone tell me sooner—that she died?"

"You weren't ready—to face them."

"Face who?"

"The Knight family, Chris." Ainsley looked over at Ruby. "Their daughter's gone forever. At some point, you owe it to her to try to make peace with them for what you did. If they'll let you."

"I don't understand why you stayed with me—let me come back here."

"Because I'd seen enough death. First my brother John, and then your accident. I wasn't prepared to watch you die, too. And, when Ruby came along...."

"You're right," he said. "We shouldn't have talked about this now. I'm really tired."

"I'm tired, too," she replied. The ugly truth was back between them, a sturdy wall.

"Ainsley," he said, humbled for a moment, "can you help me out of this chair? I think I need to get some rest."

They made their way to the library, where she helped him into bed. "Chris, your doctors tell me that you should be a candidate for a motorized chair once you've made some more progress with your coordination and balance."

His faced turned glum. "Progress? Yeah, maybe someday I'll be able to sign my own fucking name again," he sulked. "Maybe even hold my own child."

She'd reached her breaking point. "Damn it, Chris, where did that come from?" she huffed. "I'll help you any way that I can, but only if you stop wallowing in self-pity and do some of the work yourself." She picked up some dirty clothes from the foot of his bed and helped him pull a blanket over his legs. "I'm going to look at adaptive cars this week. You should come with me."

He stared past her out the window, where a pair of sparrows were hopping along the porch floor in search of stray seeds and insects. "I'll think about it," he said, crossing his arms over his chest.

"Talk into the baby monitor if you need me." Ainsley closed the door most of the way before leaving the room.

Back in the kitchen, Ruby slept on in her swing, and Attila twitched and jerked her way through a silent doggy dream. Ainsley sat down at the table again, reached for the stack of bills she'd abandoned half an hour earlier, and began sorting through them. Only the ticking of the old clock on the mantle cut into the quiet of the room. Chris had probably fallen asleep. Over the last two years, she had grown adept at crying in silence. She put her head in her hands and let the tears flow.

chapter 12

ANOTHER SIX MONTHS of intensive physical and occupational therapy had the welcome side effect of improving Chris' sense of self-esteem and independence. He came around slowly at first—a few less tantrums, a handful of helpful gestures. He answered the phone, fed Attila, tried to keep his room organized. Then Ainsley noticed him showing an active interest in fatherhood.

She had persuaded her boss to allow her to work fulltime from a home office, and set up shop in an empty, second-floor bedroom directly above the library. A functional dumbwaiter ran between the rooms—she and John had played in it as children. Ruby discovered it one day, and seeing her sitting in it with one of her toys gave Ainsley an idea: she and Chris could transport Ruby between floors throughout the day. Ruby loved the ride, and Chris developed a fascination with watching her as she played next to him with blocks and dolls. He began to assist her in feeding and grooming her dolls, improving his own fine motor skills in the process. Ainsley took his accomplishments at home as a sign that he was capable of much more.

"When are you going to finish your last year of law school and take the bar?" she asked him on a dreary March day in 1989, as they sat on the front porch, planning Ruby's second birthday.

"Take the bar? Oh, I don't know," he said. "I don't know if I remember enough—if I'm capable of passing it."

"What's stopping you from finding out?" Ainsley asked. She had to push him to do most things now. The overly confident, demanding man she had married was no longer anywhere to be found. "There's a free handicap bus service from here to Williamsburg, and I can help get you there when I'm not working," she offered.

"Honestly...I'm afraid," he admitted. "I don't think I could handle going from top of my class to...incompetent. I don't want to fail."

"You're not going to fail, Chris. Besides, this isn't a contest. Get back in there and complete your law degree. Even if it doesn't work out, at least you tried."

He looked pensive. "This is new to me, Ainsley."

"What's new?" she asked.

"This life of constantly fighting against failure. Knowing that now, because of my actions, I'll never have many of the things I want in life."

"I think all that you can do is learn from your mistakes, endure their consequences and—" she cut herself off.

"And, what?"

"And, accept that perhaps you weren't meant to have some of the things you want."

In September 1989, Chris returned to William and Mary as a part-time student. Weeks into the semester, he questioned his previous plan of pursuing a career in criminal law with a large law firm.

"I found some courses on disability and bioethics on the fall schedule," he said to Ainsley from across the dinner table.

"What are you thinking of doing?" she asked.

"It's an underrepresented area. With everything that's happened to me, I want to change my focus. I'm thinking of private practice, disability issues—if I can get through the course work. I know there are other people out there, struggling with permanent injury, trying to make their way through the world. We're a silent minority, and I want to do my part to change that. What do you think?"

"I think you should pursue it. Of course, that brings up another important decision."

"Okay, sure," he said earnestly.

"Where on the house are we going to hang your shingle?"

chapter 13

THE WATER'S EDGE Lane house was irrefutably beautiful, and as spacious as a hotel, but it was four walls, all the same, and by June 1990, Chris believed he had conquered it. The first floor, at least. Other than twice-weekly law classes and time outside with Ruby, he felt out of touch with the rest of the world. He loved the outdoors and had always enjoyed making the trip to Michigan with Ainsley before and after they were married, so it was inevitable that he would want to go back again. The Bohan's black conversion van made getting around easier, and while Chris couldn't drive, his progress with respiratory therapy and his upper body fitness regimen gave him the confidence to insist upon accompanying Ainsley and Ruby on their summer trip to the U.P. They were leaving in five days.

"I'm finished with classes until fall, and there's nothing else on my agenda," Chris said, incessantly tapping the arm of his wheelchair with his wedding ring. He was wound up—hyper. "I already called my mom, and told her to hold off on her visit here—and I cancelled the home health companion."

"What? You've blindsided me, Chris," Ainsley said. She had endured fewer of his manic episodes lately, but this one promised to make up for lost time. "Your doctor says that we should make any changes to your routine *gradually*. With your cardiac issues, I'm not comfortable with you traveling to any area without a level-one trauma unit nearby. That trip we took to D.C. last winter was a close call. Why don't we try a trip to Wintergreen first? Something with access to a major medical center, in case anything...happens."

"Like what?" he shot back. "I've been doing great lately."

"Chris, why didn't you say something sooner? The U.P. is so remote, especially Makwa Point...and my grandparent's house isn't equipped to accommodate you yet."

"What do you mean?"

"To begin with, there's no way to get you into the house," Ainsley told him. "We need time to make some modifications. And, even if we get you inside, in that old house, there may be problems with your wheelchair clearing the hallways, fitting in the bathroom, things like that."

"I hadn't thought about that. How about a hotel?"

"Chris, the closest hotel is twenty-five miles away, and with one income, we can't afford it. I don't want to ask our parents for help." She was resentful of his last-minute invasion of her annual respite, and had to remind herself that staying in the marriage was her choice.

"Oh, come on," he said. "It's easy for you. You specialize in persuading people to do things."

"I'll try to work something out, maybe with Ren and Janice."

"I remember them," he said. "They live across the street, right?"

"Right," she answered in a lifeless tone.

"It's settled then. And, away we go!"

Ainsley grudgingly placed a call to Janice Mercer about last-minute help with access to the house.

"Don't worry about it, dear," Janice said soothingly. "We'll try to rig up something, hopefully before you get here. And, I'll measure the doorways and get back to you if there's a problem inside the house. Safe trip now, eh?"

"Thank you, Janice. You're a Godsend."

It took three miserable days for the Bohan's to reach Makwa Point. Ainsley drove no more than six hours a day to minimize Chris' fatigue and discomfort, stopping for hour-long breaks. He angered without warning: "That dog of yours is driving me nuts." He succumbed to frequent attacks of fatigue and sleepiness: "Pull over. I have to rest—now!" Muscle spasms struck at all hours: "This van sucks. We need to stop so I can stretch. I can't travel like this again."

Ainsley made no stops at Frankenmuth for Christmas ornaments, Mackinac City for a walk in the sand, or Totem Village to buy moccasins, but she held her ground against Chris' insistence that they bypass Lehto's in order to reach Makwa Point faster.

"Can we just get there, please?" he whined. "We got started too late this morning. We won't hit town until seven."

"No way, Chris. I'm keeping one tradition on this trip. If you don't like it, walk the rest of the way."

"I would if I could," he said scornfully. She left him in the van and made her way to the line of customers queued at the entrance of the pasty stand. Moments later, he had second thoughts and stuck his head out of the van window. "Since you're stopping anyway," he called after her, "would you pick up one for me?"

Returning to the van, it took every ounce of self-control she could muster not to throw the bag of food at him. She set the car's tripometer and counted down each one of the final one hundred and thirteen miles of the trip.

By the time Ainsley entered the driveway at the Makwa Point house, she longed for nothing more than a bedroom door to close behind her. As she came to a stop by the garage, her headlights met with a welcome sight—a new wheelchair ramp, complete with an artificial turf floor and wood safety railings, painted red to match the house.

"Thank God," she said, under her breath.

Chris smiled for the first time that day. "I guess they knew we were coming."

"Yes, they did," Ainsley said. She could have cried with relief, since she had no alternative for getting him in and out of the house. "Let's go inside and get some sleep." She opened the van door and lowered the wheelchair ramp. Attila bounded out, followed by Chris. Ainsley reached back in for Ruby.

When Chris reached the top of the ramp, he took an exaggerated lungful of air and rubbed his chest. "I'd like to go out on the boat tomorrow," he said with a sigh. "It's been too long."

"Chris, why don't we give it a day or two?" Ainsley asked, struggling with all of their suitcases.

"I can't stay cooped up forever," he complained.

"I understand, but I've got to have some help along."

"You mean for me?"

Fatigue ate at her civility. "For you—for Ruby. I refuse to go out in the open water with a baby and you—without help. It's not safe."

"Oh, now I'm in the same class as our three-year-old daughter?"

"Chris, please. That's not what I meant."

"I'll be fine."

"Let me see if Ren and Janice want to go. They built your ramp. We'll bring lunch along, as a thank you."

"Okay, then," he said, sarcastically, "get a babysitter for me."

"Stop blaming me...for doing the best I can," she said. "Now, can we please get some sleep?"

❧

The next morning, Ren and Blaine—not Janice—met the three Bohan's in their driveway. Janice had mournfully passed on the invitation because of standing plans with three other women for their monthly grocery-shopping expedition to Escanaba, an outing which involved coupons, coolers, and a leisurely lunch at the Stone House Restaurant, and usually lasted most of the day. Ainsley tried to hide her excitement at seeing Blaine by staying busy, milling around the boat trailer and loading up the van with supplies.

"Morning," Ren said. "I brought along Father Blaine—the man who did most of the work on that ramp of yours."

"You're the guy—excuse me—the priest who helped Ainsley with my brother-in-law," Chris said as Blaine approached the van. "Good to meet you, Blaine," he said.

"Blaine MacGearailt," Blaine confirmed, extending his hand to Chris. "Thanks for having me along." His eyes went straight to Ruby, another year older, more independent, even more like her mother. He saw nothing of himself in her. "Good morning, Ruby," he said.

"Hi," she answered shyly.

Chris turned to Ren Mercer. "Ren, good to see you again. Let's get going."

They set out for the boat slips at the end of Bay Street, where decades before, the SchoolGrounds' lumberyard deliveries arrived by boat. Back then, the boat slips were hot ponds, filled from fall until winter with massive pine logs, awaiting extrication from their icy traps by pressurized steam. From there, they were hewn into boards, and finally, crafted into playground components. When the plant closed, several townspeople descended upon the slips, constructing half a dozen small docks and a roughly poured, concrete launching ramp.

After releasing the Queen Mary from her trailer, Blaine and Ren lifted Chris out of his chair and onto the boat. Next, Blaine helped Ruby, who was disappearing into her life vest, climb aboard.

"Whew, it's a cool one today, eh?" Ren said, buttoning up his flannel shirt. Won't even hit sixty-five degrees at high noon. "Glad you got some layers on, everyone."

"Chris, let me help you with your vest," Ainsley offered, reaching for the buckles.

"I'm fine. I'll do it myself," Chris snarled.

Ren and Blaine stopped what they were doing while Chris and Ainsley bickered.

"Are you sure?" she asked. "You've got limited dexterity in your hands."

"Can we not broadcast to the world all of my limitations?" he grumbled. "You take care of Ruby. I'll take care of myself."

Ren tried to change the subject. "I love this old girl. I remember when your granddad built her," he said fondly, re-lighting a stubby cigar.

"Why don't you take us out today, Ren?" Ainsley asked, embarrassed by her sour exchange with Chris.

"Are you sure?" Ren asked.

"Absolutely," she confirmed. "Let's go."

"Father?" Ren asked. "How about a quick blessing...for a safe voyage today?"

Blaine hopped into the boat and led them all in an informal prayer. As soon as he finished, Ren fired up the engine. The water in the boat slip was the color of brown glass, sliced open by the Queen Mary's red bow. Gliding by the old burner, a bullet-shaped, rusty cylinder standing forty feet high, Ainsley remembered exploring its base with John and their summer friends, crawling in the rubble, pretending it was a castle. They would stick their heads in a side opening as far as they could, gazing up at the kaleidoscope of open metalwork overhead.

"There's been some talk of taking down the burner," Ren said.

"Why?" Ainsley asked, downcast.

"They say it's because there's no use for it anymore," he replied.

"Why does it have to serve a purpose now other than standing?" she asked. "It's a landmark."

"Well, dear, don't fret now. Change comes slow up here. We'll give it ten years, see if anyone mentions tearing it down again, and then start worrying, eh?"

They passed through the quiet of the inlet through a shallow labyrinth of bright green reeds and headed east to Stone Beach. After evading a sprawling sandbar dressed with whitecaps, they hit the deeper water of the bay. Two-foot wave crests elevated the boat's hull for a moment, releasing it just as fast with a soft thud into the trough of the wave below. Sitting next to Chris on the portside bench seat, Ruby held out her small hands to snatch at the spray.

"Daddy," she giggled, her hair wet from the mist, "it's cold!"

"Look Ruby, my hand disappears into the water," Chris said, leaning his upper body against the side of the boat.

"Chris, please be careful," Ainsley said. "Your balance—"

"I'm fine," he argued.

"You haven't been in a boat for years, since...before the accident."

Chris continued to lean over the side of the boat, playing with the waves. Blaine settled on the starboard bench next to Ainsley, across from Chris and Ruby. Ren remained in the helm's tiny seat, his hands never leaving the steering wheel.

She's a real beauty, eh?" Ren said, craning his neck toward Blaine for a second. "Ainsley's Grandpa Ray made her by hand, he sure did."

Blaine agreed. "It's a gift, to able to create something like this by your own hand, Ren. No question about it."

"Wheee! Look Ruby," Chris said animatedly, hoisting himself up higher onto the gunwale with his arms, using his hands to splash the fresh water at Ruby. "Like a fish's fin, Ruby. See?" he said.

He made Ainsley uneasy. "Chris, please!" she pleaded. "Keep your eye on Ruby."

He ignored her.

"Anybody want a drink?" she asked, trying to quash her worry through distraction. "We've got coffee and sodas."

"Coffee for me," Ren requested. "With sugar, if ya could."

"Me, too," Blaine added. "Black, please." His eyes followed Chris and Ruby's every move.

"I'm fine," Chris said.

Ainsley slid along the seat to the stern of the boat and opened up her grandmother's well-worn Thermos. Ren made a subtle direction change to bring the boat closer to Stone Beach, allowing them all to scan the woods behind the beach for deer or moose.

Blaine faced the bow and peered out over the boat's windshield, perusing the beach line. "This was a great idea. Thanks for having me."

The boat rose above a whitecap and Chris reached out with both hands to splash Ruby. "Yaaay!" she shrieked.

As the Queen Mary curled in the water, Chris reached deeper over the gunwale to scoop up a wave. He reached too far, shifting his weight out of balance. Ainsley watched, disbelieving, as he arched into the water headfirst, his lower body unable to react or fight gravity. He reminded her of a slinky sliding down a step in slow motion; it took several seconds for her brain to register what she'd seen.

"Ren! Ren!" she screamed above the noise of the boat motor, pulling at Ren's shoulder and lunging across the boat for Ruby.

"Daddy!" Ruby cried. "Daddy fell!"

Blaine looked back at her, incredulous. Ren's cigar fell out of his gaping mouth; he picked it up and threw it into the water. Blaine ripped off his sweater and shoes as Chris' vest exploded onto the surface, empty. He threw the vest to Ainsley. "Tie this to a line and have it ready!"

"Hurry!" Ainsley yelled, knowing Chris could be anywhere below the boat's lengthening wake line, weighed down by heavy, water-soaked clothes and shoes.

Blaine dove into the water. Ren cranked the steering wheel hard to port, turning the boat completely around. He cut the engine but didn't drop anchor for fear it might hit Chris. One minute had elapsed. Ainsley began crying hysterically.

"Hang on now, honey," Ren said, squeezing her trembling hand in his. "We've got one of God's best men on our side."

Another fifteen seconds crept by. The silent boat drifted in the waves.

"Give me the baby, Ainsley," Ren said, reaching his thick arms out for Ruby. "You watch starboard side, I'll watch port." Ruby screamed and grabbed at Ren's balding head. Ainsley tied two life vests together and secured the rope line to the boat's engine mount. She clenched her fists until they hurt, trying to hold herself together for Ruby's sake.

Twenty-five more agonizing seconds passed. *Please God, don't take them*, Ainsley prayed. She strained to see any sign of Chris or Blaine in the water. Nothing was there.

At a minute and thirty-five seconds, the water's surface broke starboard, and Blaine and Chris' heads appeared. Ainsley cast out the vests and a life ring. Blaine grabbed at the boat with one arm, still holding Chris in a rescue chokehold with the other. Chris was conscious, choking and gasping for air. Ainsley took back Ruby and sat at the helm. Ren held onto Chris while Blaine swam to the boat's transom. Once Blaine got a foot back onboard, he and Ren dragged Chris into the boat.

"I'm startin' 'er up to get us back to shore," Ren said calmly. "Try to stay warm everybody, eh?"

Ainsley found a throw inside one of the waterproof bench seats and tucked it tight around Chris body, propping his head up with a seat cushion. Blaine put on his sweater over his wet t-shirt and collapsed onto a seat, chilled and out of breath.

"Thank you, Blaine, thank you," Ainsley said in a faltering voice. She rocked Ruby on her lap to keep both of them calm. Chris laid motionless, eyes closed, in the center of the boat hull until they reached shore. Ren and Blaine carried him to the van, and positioned him across the back seat.

"Ainsley, should we drive straight to the hospital?" Blaine asked.

"Oh, yah, I think we better," Ren added. "Quicker than waitin' for an ambulance."

"No," Chris murmured. "No. Take me home."

Ainsley, Ren and Blaine looked at one another.

"Please," Chris repeated, "get me home."

Ainsley briefly debated his request and then nodded. "It's only a few minutes to the house. Let's try that first."

"I'll bring the trailer and van back for the boat after we get all of you dropped off at home, eh?" Ren volunteered.

"Thank you, Ren." Ainsley started up the van for their two-minute trip up Bay Street. As soon as they got in the house, she checked Chris' temperature, blood pressure and pulse. All were within the normal range. Blaine carried Chris to his room and helped him change his clothes and get into bed, while Ainsley gave Ruby a quick bath and talked to her about Chris' accident.

There was a knock on the front door.

"Hello, there," Janice shouted. "Why don't I take Ruby across the street for an hour or so, 'til you get things calmed down? I can even give her lunch if you like."

"Janice, are you sure?" Ainsley asked, motioning her into the house.

"Oh, yah, no trouble at all. She can play with Ren's new kitten. I'm just glad I got home from town early today."

Ruby clapped her hands. "Mommy, can I?"

Too tired to resist Janice's offer, Ainsley watched her lead Ruby, in pink flowered pajamas and carrying a baby doll, across the deserted street. Back in the house, she met Blaine in the kitchen. He was lighting a fire in the fireplace, still wearing the same saturated clothes he'd had on in the boat. She could hear the water squishing around in his shoes when he walked.

"Blaine, let me get you some dry clothes and I'll run yours through the dryer," she said, before going into Chris' room with a cup of soup. She found him close to drifting off, covered with a white chenille bedspread and an electric blanket.

"Can I get you anything?" she asked him.

"Blaine took care of everything. Please thank him for me," he answered.

She pulled some shorts and a sweatshirt from his dresser. "I'll check on you in a little while," she whispered to him before closing the door and going into the living room.

"You can use my room to change," she told Blaine, passing him the dry clothes. "There's a towel and hairbrush on the dresser. Use whatever you need."

She heard him move around her room for several minutes before he came out to the living room and handed over his clothes. As she carried them back to the utility room, she caught his scent in the warm, damp shirt collar. She plunged her face in it as though she was leaning into his shoulder, then wiped her own tears with it and threw it in the dryer with the rest of his things. When she returned to the living room, Blaine was waiting for her. He had put cups of tea out for both of them.

She sank into one corner of the sofa. "I'm sorry," she said softly. "All of this—"

Blaine cut in. "Those scuba diving lessons my parents gave me years ago came in handy today. Why don't we leave it at that?" He took a gulp of tea.

She didn't try to apologize again. Instead, they shared the sofa in silence for an hour, drinking tea and listening to Blaine's shoes and clothes tumble and snap in the dryer's drum.

By four o'clock, Blaine's clothes were dry, and he left Ainsley's house for St. John's rectory. Janice met Ren in the driveway and they walked up Ainsley's porch steps together, presenting Ruby, well fed and sleeping, in Janice's arms.

"One less thing to worry about, eh?" Ren said, churning a dead stogie in his mouth.

"Thanks, you two, for everything," Ainsley said, her voice wavering.

"Oh, honey, don't give it a thought," Janice said. "So, Father Blaine headed out, then, eh?"

"About ten minutes ago," Ainsley answered.

Janice didn't hide her disappointment. "Oh, darn, I was going to have him over for supper...."

"Something tells me that he may have had enough excitement for today, Janice," Ainsley said. "How many people go to bed at night knowing that they saved a life?"

"Oh, yah, that's true Ainsley," Janice said. "He is a funny young man."

Ainsley wasn't sure what she meant. "How do you mean 'funny,' Janice?"

"Well, he's so good looking and all, I don't know how he does it—stays true to the church, in this day and age. There must be a lot of temptation...."

"Now, Janice, you shouldn't talk about him like that. It's not our place...to question," Ren chided. "And don't look a gift horse in the mouth. It's our blessing that he came our way."

"Janice," Ainsley said, "I think Father Blaine knows that God has chosen him to perform his work, and performing that work well requires sacrificing some of the earthly pleasures the rest of us spend our lives chasing."

"Why Ainsley, that sounds like something he might say. I swear, you two...maybe...well...."

"What, Janice?" she asked, nervous.

"Well, maybe he'll take up where John left off. He can, you know, be like a brother to you...." Janice said.

Ainsley relaxed. "That's a nice thought, Janice."

"Well, you know, Ainsley, it could be John's watching out for you now, especially with your husband...uh," she dropped her voice to a whisper, "limited."

"Could be. Thanks again." Ainsley said goodbye, and put Ruby in the front bedroom's double bed, flanked by an embankment of pillows and rolled blankets. Attila followed Ainsley out to the back porch, and jumped up on the chaise where she was sitting, dangling her giant paws over the edge. Within minutes, they were both asleep.

Chris woke up at dinnertime, in turn awakening Ainsley with his calls. "Ainsley, can you help me? Ainsley, where are you?"

She shook herself awake and went into his room to help him into his wheelchair.

"How are you feeling?" she asked as she checked his vital signs again.

"I'm alive," he rasped, "and I wish I was capable of crawling under a rock."

She saw no point in vilifying his behavior, and ignored the sarcastic remark. "You got some water in your lungs today, Chris. I've put in a call to Dr. Woods. We're going tomorrow. Pneumonia would be, well—let's play it safe." She sat down on the bed.

"Dr. Woods...Dr. Woods," Chris recited. "Isn't he your grandpa Ray's old doctor?"

"Yes, and I trust him. We have to make sure you're okay."

"Ainsley...."

"Yes?" She expected a refusal, but he surprised her.

"I was an idiot out there today, beyond reckless, trying to prove...that I'm still the same. I put Ruby and everyone else on the boat in danger. It was stupid and selfish." His hands trembled as he used them to push tangled blond hair out of his eyes. "I thought I was going to die out there today, Ainsley." He started to cry. "I was less than ten feet under water. I could see the surface, but I could do *nothing* to save myself. I gave up."

She grabbed his hand. "What do you mean?"

"I was ready to—to take in water—purposely," he whispered. "I wanted to get it over with. And, then Blaine..."

"It's over, Chris. You're okay," Ainsley said.

They went into the living room and sat across from each other. "Ainsley, what if something had happened to Ruby? I wasn't even thinking of her—of *her* safety."

"Thank God, it didn't."

"I'm not the man I was, Ainsley. Am I even a man? I don't know anymore."

She found Chris' struggle with his devastated physical condition heart wrenching. "Chris, I know it's rough—this transition. And, I'm not going to tell you that I know how you feel, because I don't. But, I do know pain, and fear, and disappointment."

"I'm responsible for teaching you some of those things."

"That's not my point. You have to take it slowly, and dwell on each accomplishment, however small—not the failures. No one's keeping score. You have the rest of your life ahead of you. There's a lot for you to make of it—if you can find the strength to move on."

"Speaking of lives, Blaine saved mine. I like him—I owe him. And, he helped you with John...."

"He's been there for both of us now."

"He has a connection with us, Ainsley," Chris said, using her words, the same words she had spoken to Blaine years before on Presque Isle. "Can we do something for him before we leave?" he asked.

"I'll talk to Janice," Ainsley said, blindsided again. She hadn't anticipated a convergence of the two men. "I'm sure that we can come up with something."

She woke up Ruby and brought her out to the living room to play. "Let's try some small steps for the rest of the trip. Oncc Dr. Woods clears you, let's restrict ourselves to land-based sightseeing."

"Agreed," Chris answered wryly.

Their last week in Makwa Point, Ainsley and Chris held a community barbecue on the lawn of St. Mary's Church. Sixty people happily stuffed themselves with fried perch, potato salad, blueberry cobbler, and homemade maple candy, made from local syrup.

As neighbors cleared picnic tables and crumpled up paper tablecloths, Chris made his way over to Blaine. Ainsley watched them as they sat together, talking. After a few minutes, they approached her together.

"Ainsley," Chris began, "Blaine says he has to get back to the rectory, so we won't see him before we leave."

Her heart sank. She needed more time around him. "Well, I guess we'll...see you next year?" she said, trying to hold a neutral expression.

Chris smiled. "Not necessarily. I had a thought. Why doesn't Blaine come to Virginia Beach for a week or two this December?"

Blaine and Ainsley exchanged a furtive glance.

"He can spend some time with us, get to know us," Chris went on. "Have a change of scenery, see the east coast, hang out with some people his own age."

"I'm sure you've got commitments—with the church," Ainsley said, searching for a way out of what seemed to her to be a risky situation. "It's Christmas, after all."

"Blaine told me that the diocese takes pity on its little parishes during the holiday and brings in the big guns to conduct services," Chris said. "Come on, Blaine, it's a free vacation for you, and we have an enormous place. I'm sure Ainsley's told you about our house."

"She mentioned that it's her family's home—and an old house," Blaine said. "I don't want to put Ainsley on the spot."

"I'll wear you down. Wait and see," Chris said.

Blaine was touched and uncomfortable at the same time. "It's a tempting offer, Chris. Let me look at my calendar and see what downtime I have at the end of the year."

"I'm going to keep checking back in with you, Blaine. I'm determined," Chris said with a laugh, "to bring you into this family of ours—one way or another."

chapter 14

SIX MONTHS LATER, Blaine appeared on the front doorstep of 313 Water's Edge Lane, suitcases in hand.

"Come on in!" Chris said enthusiastically. Appearing out of nowhere, Attila lumbered over to Blaine and greeted him with a silent tail wag as he entered the hallway with his luggage. Her lack of a reaction perplexed Chris. "Now that's a first. Attila must be losing her edge—or her hearing. She barks at everyone." He shook his head. "Oh, well, how was your flight, or should I say flights?"

"Yes, flights. And all three were long but successful," Blaine answered, eager to put the solid day of travel behind him. "I have to adjust to leaving behind three feet of snow for a balmy sixty-five degrees, though."

Ruby skipped her way down the hall to Chris, nearly colliding with his wheelchair. In the six months since Blaine had seen her last, she had grown another inch. Her round baby face and belly were diminishing as she continued her evolution into a smaller version of Ainsley.

"Hi, Father Bl-a-a-a-ine," Ruby said as she curtsied, obviously coached by her parents. She grinned and retreated to Chris' side.

"Hi, Ruby," Blaine answered, wishing he could scoop her up in his arms and hug her. He extended his hand, enveloping her damp palm and rubbery fingers in his grip as he surveyed her face. "Aren't you something?"

"They're all like that—all of the women in the family," Chris said resignedly, as Ruby climbed onto his lap and put her arms around his neck. "Born heartbreakers. The neighbor boy has already announced to his mother that he's going to marry Ruby when they grow up."

"I'm not surprised one bit," Blaine remarked. "I hope he's worthy."

"Are any of us worthy?" Chris asked. "Ruby, honey, do you think you can show Father Blaine the room he's staying in—like we talked about earlier?"

She hopped off Chris' lap and led Blaine upstairs to the second floor. He was awestruck by the architectural details in every alcove, doorway, and window of the house. It was the antithesis of his parents' enormous neo-Tudor eyesore, filled with all of the gadgets and design trends the market had to offer.

They came to a stop on the second-floor landing, confronting four heavy, four-panel doors. "Which one, Ruby?" Blaine asked.

"One, two," she answered as she pointed at the second door from the right and disappeared inside.

Blaine picked up his luggage and followed her. Yellow and gray floral wallpaper covered the walls of the room, broken up by shuttered windows cloaked in heavy, purple velvet drapes. Furnished with a pewter-stained oak sleigh bed, black-plaid upholstered wing chair and two mirrored, dark cherry dressers, the room had ample space to move around in and relax. He put his suitcases down by the bed as Ruby pounced on its gray-and-white-striped linen comforter.

"You like it? I helped Mommy fix it for you," she said proudly.

"It's beautiful, Ruby," he replied. "Do you think it would be okay if we looked around at some more of the house? It's so pretty."

"Okay," she said. "Daddy's on the phone. He lives down there." She pointed at the staircase.

Ruby took Blaine's hand in hers and stopped in front of the door to the left of his room. "That's where you go potty. Do you wash your hands?" she asked. They moved on to the next door. "This is my room. It's pink!" Ruby opened the door and they walked into a bright room brimming with childhood whimsy: dolls, stuffed animals; a tea table and chairs; and, a bookcase crammed full of collections by Beatrix Potter and Dr. Seuss, along with Meindert De Jong's *Hurry Home Candy*.

"Oh my," Blaine said, as he picked up the brown book, "I love this story."

"Mommy does too, but she cries when she tries to read it to me." Ruby looked disappointed as she spoke. "Is the story good?"

"Yes! A little dog...has to search for someone to love him—the right way. He goes through a lot of...sadness and loneliness before he finds his destiny—the place where he's meant to be and the person he's meant to be with. It's different than he thought it would be when he started, but he ends up safe, happy and loved." Blaine realized the description was probably beyond a three-and-a-half-year-old's comprehension.

"He finds a—family?" Ruby guessed, scrunching up her face.

"You're something special, Ruby, " he said, taking the book with him. "You're right, and we can start reading the book tonight, if you like."

"And you won't cry?"

"No."

"Okay, 'cause Mommy cries a lot. It's a secret."

"You mean when she reads to you, right?"

"And when she gets papers...."

"Papers?"

"From the mail. They look scribbly. She reads them and cries. I say, 'Mommy what's wrong?' She says the papers hurt her eyes and she cries. She puts the papers in her table."

It saddened Blaine to think that reading his letters caused Ainsley pain. She asked him to write to her. He did it as much for her as for himself.

Beaming, Ruby turned on her white, lace-cuffed sock heel, and led him back into the hallway. She pointed to a closed door on the far right, shrugging her shoulders. "That's Mommy's office room. She works a lot. Daddy says he's trying to work, but he says it's Mommy who keeps us floating."

Ruby's earnest attempt at playing the informative hostess distracted Blaine from his concern over the letters. He bit his lip to keep from chuckling, opting not to correct her.

She tugged at his sleeve. "Do you wanna see Mommy's room?"

"Sure," he replied, smiling, "if you think she wouldn't mind."

What sounded like a grandfather clock tolled ominously from an unknown location as they walked down a long, wide hallway lined with framed photos, on their way to Ainsley's room. It was clear that a majority of the house remained unseen.

Ruby opened Ainsley's door, revealing the palest of aqua walls. Here and there, delicate hairline cracks appeared in the plaster, the result of more than a century of the home settling and resettling on its stone and mortar foundation. They were the veins and arteries of the place, which seemed to Blaine to have a life of its own, independent of its mortal inhabitants.

Between two large, rectangular windows sat a king-sized four-poster bed covered with a gold quilt and several pillows in striped, teal shams. Well-worn, mahogany furniture reached out from the pastel background. A heavy crystal vase filled with red roses sat on Ainsley's dresser, along with several framed photos of her family and friends, one of which included Blaine. He pictured her in the space, there on the bed, the silk of her skin touched by the sheets. The image mesmerized him. The fact that he conjured it disturbed him. He needed a distraction.

"Why don't you show me some more rooms?" he asked Ruby.

They made their way back to the staircase.

"Come on—Grandma and Grandpa's house is here," Ruby explained, stomping upwards to the third floor before winding him through a three-room suite that looked like it belonged in a hotel.

She grinned. "Grandma brings toys when she comes on the plane. She comes here soon." She fidgeted, gathering her dress in her fists. "I wanna see my daddy now, okay?"

Back downstairs again, Blaine found Chris in the living room. "Chris, this house...I wasn't expecting something of this...magnitude."

"Ainsley's the queen of the understatement, isn't she? Her mother Julie started it, and Ainsley picked up where she left off. You know," Chris continued, "this place has been as much a part of my recovery as all of the surgeries and the endless therapy—really."

"How so?"

"When I first came home, I was hell to live with—I'm sure I still am. Anyway, I couldn't do anything for myself—I spent my time indoors. All of the open space, the natural light, the high ceilings, helped lift my depression. As I got stronger and more mobile, I started to explore it. I've photographed all of the first floor rooms, and researched the architectural elements, as a sort of...history project. Yeah, I swear it was this house, and my girls...that's the reason I'm still around. I wouldn't have made it otherwise."

Blaine hated Chris' use of the possessive term "my girls," although he knew he had no claim to either of them. "Well, Hallelujah to that!" he said, putting on his best paternal front.

"Amen, Father," Chris agreed, attempting an Irish brogue. "Come on, I'll give you a proper tour of the first floor." He rolled through the rooms, touching on interesting features as they went along. The tour ended in the converted library.

"So this is the famous dumbwaiter," Blaine said, laughing, "The Ruby Express."

"Yeah, this is it," Chris replied, puzzled. "How'd you find out about the dumbwaiter?"

"Oh, Ruby said something about it upstairs—when she showed me Ainsley's office...."

"Really?" Chris asked. "I'm surprised she remembers—she was two years old when we did all of that. Well, smart girl. It was a sad day when she outgrew it."

I'm a hypocrite and a liar, Blaine thought. Ruby hadn't shown him Ainsley's office. Ainsley had told him about the dumbwaiter during one of their twice-weekly phone calls. Calls she'd made for years, usually late at night when Chris and Ruby were asleep. If Chris asked Ruby about the dumbwaiter, it could prove disastrous. Blaine's carelessness had brought the flimsy little boat of secrets they were all clinging to a stroke closer to a dash against the rocks.

They returned to the dining room, lined with green toile wallpaper and crowned by an ornate rococo chandelier.

"How about a drink?" Chris asked. "You do drink?"

Blaine could have swigged from the bottle right then. "Yes," he said. "Whatever you're having is fine."

"Oh, I don't drink these days," Chris said. "And, the world's a better place for it, trust me. I knocked back enough for two when I was younger, with tragic consequences. You want ice?"

Blaine nodded no.

Chris was pouring him a neat bourbon when Ruby burst into the room with Attila hulking along beside her. "Mommy's home! Mommy's home!" The words shouted out, she was gone.

Somewhere in the distance, a door opened and closed, followed by Attila's yowling, some scuffling noises, and finally, Ainsley's voice. "Okay, okay, honey, let me put my things down," she said.

A knot of excitement and anxiety formed in Blaine's stomach. Suddenly, she was in the dining room doorway, wearing a belted, sleeveless black dress and high-heeled black-and-white Mary Janes. A thick pearl bracelet encircled her wrist. She had gathered her hair loosely at the nape of her neck in a black barrette, and her lips were cherry red. Blaine almost dropped his glass at the sight of her. In Michigan, she dressed in casual, summer clothes. He had never seen this side of her life, the one she had the love-hate relationship with, the one she escaped from when she went up north.

He drained his bourbon and walked toward her to deliver a platonic hug. "Ainsley, it's so good to see you," he said. As their bodies met briefly, he smelled a soft, floral fragrance in the curve of her neck and felt her breasts press against his chest. It brought back the memory of exploring every surface of her body. He wanted more of her. He hated himself for wanting her.

She pulled back from his embrace, breaking the spell. "Glad you made it safely," she said. "I see the welcoming committee has gotten to you already."

"Oh, yeah. Ruby's run him ragged all over the house," Chris said.

Blaine smiled. "I told Chris, I feel I should pay to stay here."

"Trust me, you may wish you *had* paid for a hotel after a week in our house, between the noise and the non-stop chaos," Chris assured him. "However, if you absolutely insist upon earning your keep, we can always put you to work. There are some chores around here that I can't accomplish anymore."

"Sure. I'd be happy to help," Blaine said.

"You can help me ride my bike!" Ruby screamed, jumping up and down.

"Ruby, let Father Blaine unpack first," Ainsley lectured. "Remember, this is supposed to be his vacation."

The next morning, after the sun had melted the December frost from the grass, Blaine helped Chris with winter household chores, including gutter cleaning, checking the home's vast red roof for loose shingles, and rounding up the pride of rescued cats who now called Chris and Ainsley's three-story carriage house their home. The two men paused from their work for a few minutes outside one of the carriage house's three bay doors.

"Okay, I've saved the toughest chore for last," Chris said.

"What's that?" Blaine asked.

"The head count. See that can over there?" Chris pointed to a large, silver trashcan. "Would you mind getting some food and filling those silver food dishes over there on the floor?" He pointed again, this time to five large dog bowls, lined up against the inside wall of the bay.

As Blaine dispensed the food, the sound of it hitting the stainless steel bowls produced a silent stampede of multicolored housecats. "How many are there?" he asked, trying to count the squirming mass of fur rubbing against his legs and now meowing in unison.

Chris sighed. "Depends on what day of the week it is. Originally, there were a dozen or so, but things are in constant flux. We should have about twenty today."

"Why is that?"

"Let's see. Last week, Ainsley went for a run and saw a female cat, injured, on the side of the road. The cat had four kittens. Look around. You'll find all five of them running around here somewhere. We're trying to limit the population as best we can, but Ainsley won't call animal control because she's afraid the adults won't be adopted. She and her friend Jill find new homes for them on their own—sometimes." He lowered his voice. "When you get to know Ainsley better, you'll discover how sensitive she is. She can't even sleep at night if she knows one of them is missing."

Blaine changed the subject. "This carriage house is fantastic."

"I love it, too. It was built to house the original owner's carriages, horses and for additional storage. A lot of the harnesses and equipment are still in here. Have a look around." Chris put his hand on Blaine's arm. "Listen, before things get too hectic, I want to thank you for all that you've done while you've been here. It's like you're part of our family."

"Glad to help. I'm not close to my parents, and you know my only brother's gone. I'm a priest all of the time, but it's good to have a place to go—without all of the expectations of my parish. It's an informal sabbatical, a much appreciated respite, Chris."

"I understand completely," Chris said. "That's what Michigan is for my wife."

They lingered in the carriage house.

"Hey, see that tarp over there—in the corner?" Chris asked.

Blaine pointed at a canvas-wrapped mass. "That one?"

"Yeah. Take it off."

Blaine pulled at the tarp, unveiling a pristine, Brittany Blue 1965 T-bird convertible. "Wow," he exclaimed as he stepped back from the car. "Where'd you get this beauty?"

"My parents," Chris answered, watching Blaine circle the car, admiring its lines. "I had my eye on it from age five, and my dad finally broke down and gave it to me as a wedding gift. I used to be addicted to speed, among other vices. I'm strictly in the passenger seat now."

"I consider myself a boat fanatic, but this has the potential to send me over to the other side," Blaine said.

"We'll get the girls and take it out before you leave. I promise, it won't be like the infamous boat ride at the summer house," Chris said, taking on a rueful expression.

"Chris, I've yet to meet a near-perfect human being."

"I don't know. I think you come pretty close, Blaine."

They returned to the house, where Ainsley and Ruby were working in the kitchen. Blaine showered and changed clothes. Alone on the second floor, he lay on his bed contemplating what he was starting by coming to Virginia. He had chosen to remain in the church. Ainsley had chosen to stay in her marriage. The man her husband, Chris, was becoming was impossible to dislike. Stepping into the middle of the reconfigured Bohan family would be an exhausting, delicate balance to keep, with everyone poised on the edge of disaster. He tried but couldn't make sense of the situation. He broke from the attempt and got dressed.

The minute dinner was over, Ruby pushed her chair back from the table with all of her might. "I want Blaine to be my new uncle," she commanded.

Ainsley had no comeback. "Um, Ruby...."

"Gee, honey," Chris said gently, "why don't we let Father Blaine relax and enjoy his vacation? We can talk about that later, okay?"

"Uncle Johnny lives in Heaven. *Uncle* Blaine lives where I can see him!" Ruby wailed.

Blaine jumped in. "How about if I help your dad teach you how to ride your bike like you asked me to? He can instruct and I'll I do the legwork."

Ruby's eyes lit up. "Yaay! Tomorrow? Please?"

Chris tsked. "It never ends," he groaned. "Blaine, be glad you don't have any children."

❦

When the front door opened two days before the start of 1991, Blaine confronted a more mature Ainsley, but with slightly shorter hair. "Julie Plante...and Don, right?" he guessed.

"Yes," Don said, extending his strong, tan hand, "that's us." He looked as though he was in his late forties, although Blaine knew he was ten years older.

"Father Blaine, isn't it?" Julie asked. "Our daughter's friend, our son-in-law's guardian angel...any other roles you're fulfilling that we haven't heard about yet?"

"None so far."

"Well," she said warmly, "glad you could come down from the Great White North to see us and spend the holidays." She took his hand in her two, one of which was laden with a pearl bracelet similar to the one Ainsley wore. The handshake sent a shudder through him. She shared Ainsley's touch.

"I want to thank you, personally, for helping Ainsley with John—with John's ashes," she said. "We are grateful."

"I was in the right place at right time, I guess."

"It's too quiet. Where is everyone?" Don asked.

"In the living room, worshipping the tree before it comes down," Blaine answered.

"Don and I have to get here before Christmas from now on," Julie said, as she smiled and attempted to take back her hand. "Well, let's get inside and unload our treasures."

"Yes," Don said. "Let's unpack and settle in before that cold front they're talking about hits." He started up the stairs with their luggage. "Hello?" he shouted out playfully. "Ruby! Where's my precious gem, Ruby?"

They heard loud barking and clattering footsteps coming in their direction. Julie looked to the heavens. "Here we go."

It began snowing some time in the middle of the night. When Ainsley woke up at five o'clock to let Attila outside, she couldn't believe what she saw. A thin, white carpet of snow covered the yard and roof. A mere dusting by northern standards, it was cause for celebration in temperate Virginia Beach. Excitement infused the entire household by breakfast time.

"Let's get out there and build a snowman, guys, before the snow melts," Ainsley said. "It'll be a while before we see this kind of weather again."

"I'm in charge of the hot chocolate!" Julie called out.

"Come on Ruby, time to get bundled up," Chris shouted.

Each person had a job. Ruby rolled and packed the snowman's head. Don and Blaine worked on the base. Ainsley searched for a hat, eyes, nose and scarf. Chris packed the middle snowball and acted as photographer.

True to her word, Julie stayed inside and manned the cocoa station. "I've been in Fiji too long," she confessed. "It's freezing out there."

"This is fun!" Ruby yelled, running around the slushy yard, throwing tiny, icy snowballs at everyone. "Can we build a snowman tomorrow, too? To keep this one company?"

"Now, Ruby, the snow is going to melt, and so is the snowman," Chris said.

"Why, Daddy?" she asked, upset.

"Because, it's getting warmer. We'll build another one the next time it snows."

"When will it snow again, Daddy?"

He looked at Blaine. "Umm, when God decides we need more."

Blaine gave him the thumbs up.

Chris set the camera on automatic and took several pictures of the entire family group in front of their rapidly liquefying work of art. Afterwards, they all tramped into the house, shed their jackets and gloves, and carried cups of hot chocolate into the music room. While Don stoked the fire, Blaine and Julie recounted stories of school snow days and white Christmases from their midwestern childhoods.

"Blaine, we'd find it difficult, missing Christmas with our children—" Julie stumbled over the words, "I mean with our daughter—and Chris and Ruby."

Don was blunt but sincere. "Your family must be devastated that you don't go home for the holidays."

Blaine responded truthfully. "Not even members of the clergy are immune to family discord," he said. "Family holidays in my house were always strained. I don't think any of us even knows why. It's been worse since my brother's death. My parents and I tried again a few years ago, but all we did was tiptoe around talking about anything that was potentially painful, which didn't leave much else. We do see each other once or twice during the year...."

The room fell silent.

"Well, we can understand that," Don said. "It's hard to get past the grieving, and feeling guilty when you have a great day, or feel happy. It takes some people longer than others. You're always welcome here, with us. Not to speak for Chris and Ainsley." He held up his hands, still holding the fireplace poker. "Oops, I guess I just did...."

They all finished their hot chocolate quietly, huddled together in front of the hearth, as the crackling fire faded to a mound of dark orange embers.

chapter 15

SUNBATHERS STREAMED ONTO Sandbridge beach in droves, pulling carts filled with umbrellas, food, drinks, and small children. Ruby paused briefly from gnawing her right thumbnail down to the quick and turned to Ainsley. "After that first Christmas, that's when Uncle Blaine started visiting every year?"

"Yes. Strangely as it started out, things...fell into place. It sounds hard to believe, I know, but it worked—for everyone."

"It worked?" Ruby asked.

It hurt Ainsley to see her daughter's beautiful face riddled with pain. All she could do was continue with her confession, hoping that honesty—finally—might lead to some sort of resolution. "Yes. We felt like...a family again. It was your father's idea, Ruby."

"I can't believe Grandma didn't know, that she didn't sense something."

"I never told a soul, no one, even though I desperately wanted to. So many times, I think my mother wondered what was going on, but it never surfaced. If my parents had been living here, maybe they would have seen more, but when they visited, we had every minute accounted for. There wasn't time for scrutiny." She stared off into the surf for a minute. "Let's walk for a while."

The water was cold on their feet as they waded along the surf line. "Ruby, you know how close your dad and Blaine are," Ainsley said. "They've been that way since they first met. Almost like brothers."

Ruby didn't believe her. "If everything was okay when Uncle Blaine left after his first Christmas visit, why did Dad stop going up to the U.P. with us?"

"It was entirely his decision, based on the difficulty he had getting around up there, the toll the trip took on his health, and...."

"And, what?"

"He knew it served as a break from my job and taking care of him. Remember, until you were in school, and until your dad's practice started turning a profit, I put in twelve-hour days most of the time. I worked mainly from home, I had some flexibility, but it was still exhausting."

"Dad simply informed you one day that he wanted to stop making the trip?" Ruby asked, sounding unconvinced.

"That's exactly what he did."

Ainsley's church had no formal confession of sins, so she wasn't able to cast off her guilt into a dark screened box, releasing it to a clergyman whose identity was known but undisclosed, in exchange for prescribed penance. Most Sundays, she sat alone in Atlantic Episcopal Church, in her white pew, the small one behind the soundboard, while Ruby attended Sunday school across the covered walkway. Chris was never much for attending church, sitting out most Sunday services at home.

Before each communion, Ainsley knelt in her pew, silently confessed her sins, and prayed that what she perceived as God's responsive guidance was indeed that, and not merely a guilt-driven inner dialogue. In the quiet building that had stood in various stages of construction and renovation for nearly four hundred years, she found a sense of being home, of pervasive calm. It was the one place where she was free of all secrets.

Easter Sunday 1991, all three Bohans went first to Easter services and immediately afterward to the local Ruritan Club's Annual Easter Egg Hunt. Ainsley and Chris positioned themselves at the edge of the club building's lawn, watching four-year-old Ruby, in a yellow-and-white eyelet dress, run after dozens of brightly-colored plastic eggs. Grown men, mostly farmers and contractors with giant, weathered hands, had painstakingly fumbled over filling and taping the eggs tightly shut before nestling them conspicuously in the mowed grass, ensuring that no child was deprived of his or her fair ration of jelly beans and chocolate candy. Ruby placed each egg that she found in a green wicker basket.

"Ainsley," Chris said, as his eyes tracked Ruby's zigzag trip across the grass, "I think...unless it's a special occasion...that I'll leave the Michigan trip to you."

"Where did that come from, Chris?" Ainsley asked.

"Because, I know you, and I know it's the time of year that you start planning for the trip. We don't talk about it these days, but we both know last year's trip nearly did me in. It took a toll on you, too—having me along, my accident. For now, let's leave it as your time—your place—with Ruby. Explore it with her unfettered and unburdened."

Ruby ran up to them, breathless, an orange egg in her flailing hand. They grinned and waved at her. Seconds later, she flew away again, her green basket swinging from her arm as if it were a pendulum.

"Are you sure—about staying home?" Ainsley asked.

"Yeah. We both know that my strength now lies in my intellect, not my physical prowess. I'll have my mom come down from Richmond to stay with me while you're gone, instead of a home health nurse. She needs something to do now that my sister Amy's in college."

"I don't know, Chris."

"I have to start reaching toward my limits, see what I can and can't do for myself, by myself. I love it up there, but Michigan is really your place, your family's place. For now, I'm fine where I am. I wish it wasn't such a punishing trip, with only you driving. Maybe you should fly up there, when it's only you and Ruby."

"As long as I can break up the trip, I'm okay. If I fly, we miss the scenery. And, I'll have Attila, unless you want me to leave her here—"

He laughed. "God, no, you can't forgo your co-pilot! Attila should be with you when you travel alone. I'd be worried sick otherwise."

Ainsley smiled faintly. "All right, then."

"Puffy Creek," Chris said. "Take Ruby to Puffy Creek this summer. If you find any good arrowheads, I'll teach her how to display them when you get back."

He had surprised her. "You remember Puffy Creek?" she asked.

"Yeah. Small things come back to me at the strangest times, Ainsley. I hid your engagement ring in the sand there and you dug it up, right?"

"Yes." She had buried the memory, as he had buried the ring.

"We were in a different place then," he said.

"Yes, we were," she replied.

Ruby marched toward them with her basket of eggs, bursting with pride over her sugary cache. "Can we go home now?" she asked, standing between them and holding each of their hands. "I'm hungry!"

"So," Chris said, "plan that trip of yours, so you and Ruby have some adventures to tell me about when you get back."

chapter 16

THIN WHITE CLOUDS broke up the Robin's Egg Blue sky, on a fall day in 1992. Tightly woven ropes of century-old Forsythia branches, covered with green leaves, walled in the borders of 313 Water's Edge Lane. Farm trucks and mini-vans cruised slowly by, their passengers admiring the Bohan's picturesque residence and rose garden. Ruby sat on the edge of her sandbox, pouring buckets of sand on Attila, who had dug up a cool pit for herself in the box's center. Chris hunched over a folding table on the porch, typing into a portable word processor that Ainsley had set up for him. He looked better than he had in years, with color in his face, and life in his green eyes. He kept his blonde hair shorter these days; it was easier for him to manage. He had worked hard to reach a level of independence that required minimal assistance from Ainsley, or anyone else. Unless struck by fatigue or occasional breathing problems, he could hold his own in and around the house. That included trailing Attila around the yard with a pooper-scooper and caring for five-year-old Ruby when she got home from morning kindergarten. While his home-based practice had yet to yield a significant income, he had saved one Desert Storm veteran's job at a local chainsaw manufacturer and enabled an amputee to gain access to a museum with a previously archaic public entrance. He found these small victories a more than adequate reward for his freshman efforts at practicing law.

A jogger passed by the front of the driveway and waved. Attila barked and Chris greeted the man with a hello. Ruby watched the jogger disappear around the bend, and then left the sandbox and ran to Chris.

"Daddy, why can't *you* run?" She looked up at him, waiting for an answer.

He always knew the question would surface. He stopped typing. "Come up here with me," he said, extending his arms out in front of him. Ruby stepped onto the footrest of his wheelchair. Between the two of them, they managed to get her into his lap.

"Years ago, before you were born, I was in an accident—in my car," Chris explained.

"Our car, Daddy?" she asked.

"No, honey. It was a car I used to drive before you were born."

"Where's the car now, Daddy?"

"It's gone, honey."

"Did somebody crash into you?"

"No. I—we—were alone." As he said it, he felt a shudder. He saw the face of the woman he was with that night. Blonde, pretty, a sweet smile. He saw Karen Knight's face.

"Did you put on your seatbelt, Daddy?"

"No, Ruby, I didn't. That was a terrible mistake. My friend didn't, either...." He remembered sitting in a bar on Henry Street with a group of students he'd just met, all in varying stages of drunkenness. Ainsley was in Michigan alone, heartsick over her brother John's death. He hated seeing her sad, beautiful face, staring past him, looking for something she could never find again. Or, listening to her muffled sobs in the middle of the night. He wasn't sure what she wanted from him, and at that time, he was too selfish to understand how to give of himself with no easy reward. He'd fucked around again, with another student, and Ainsley found out. She was dead set on not taking him back one last time.

The beers kept coming, and Karen Knight was hot for him, groping him under the table, whispering in his ear what she wanted him to do to her. Lots of women were attracted to him, and he liked it. It was his weakness. And, he was on his own for three more long weeks.

"Daddy? Daddy?" Ruby tugged on his sleeve. "What happened to your legs?"

"Well, my...friends and I were tired from...studying," he continued, "and it was late. I offered one of them a ride home."

Chris learned only recently from an acquaintance at William and Mary the details of that night that he would never remember on his own. He and Karen were going to her apartment, but never made it. He told everyone at the bar that he was going to teach her to drive his five-speed Mustang, because they both thought she was less drunk than he was. Karen had only driven a manual transmission once or twice and probably got confused with which pedal she was pressing. The car left Ironbound Road and rolled several times, tossing both of them around as if they were dice on a Las Vegas craps table. The impact broke her neck. She died instantly.

"Where was Mommy?" Ruby asked.

"Mommy was at the summer house in Michigan—alone." He felt a fresh dose of shame and remorse welling up inside as he said it. "I guess I didn't drive very well, and our car went off the road." Karen wasn't a friend. He barely knew her name, and he threw away his marriage for a drunken one-night stand that ended in a tragedy.

"Can she still walk?"

"Honey, she died in the accident."

"Oh. Are her mommy and daddy sad?"

"Yes, they are." His eyes clouded with tears. "Your mommy told me I need to go see them, and I think I should—soon."

"Don't cry Daddy," Ruby said, putting her hand on his cheek. "When will you get all better again?"

"I'll never walk again, Ruby. In other ways, though, I'm better now than I was before the accident—because of you and Mommy. You'll understand more about that when you're older."

"You mean you love us!" she shrieked.

"Yes, that's exactly right. Now let's go get Attila and look for birds in the yard. We may find some new ones today."

They went inside to gather their equipment and some drinks, and stuffed everything into a backpack that Chris slung over the back of his new electric wheelchair. The chair enabled him to travel easily over gravel and grass and be more involved with Ruby's outdoor activities.

He started what was, for him, the unlikely hobby of bird watching when he first came home from New Bridges. Initially, he was in bed more than out of it, still weak and somewhat confused, his body an alien that he fought to control. It wasn't that Ainsley didn't try to help. No one could have done more. But, she couldn't suffer through rehabilitation for him.

Some days, seeing a bird or two outside the library window was the only enjoyable part of Chris' day. When Ainsley discovered his interest in birds, she installed a feeder in front of the porch railing, in full view of his window, and bought him a bird book. He started documenting what he saw and heard, and his fascination proved therapeutic. It was years later that he learned of a form of psychotherapy based on rapid back and forth eye movement with origins in bird watching. He believed in its validity. His own ornithological pastime, rooted in desperation, helped him claw his way out of a deep depression.

Chris made his way to the kitchen door. "Okay, Ruby, I think we're set now," he said. "Attila, lead the way!"

They crossed the yard, ducking down between the overhanging branches of the Forsythia hedge. Attila plopped down underneath it in the soft, sandy dirt and Ruby squatted next to her, trying her hardest to be quiet, despite her rapid, audible breathing.

"What are we going to see, Daddy?" she whispered, her voice louder than if she had spoken.

"I have no idea. That's what makes it fun."

They stayed outside for an hour and spotted Eastern Bluebirds, House Finches and a stray Cattle Egret that mistook their expansive, two-acre lawn for a pasture. As Chris watched Ruby struggle to concentrate and remain quiet, he wondered what he could contribute to her upbringing, what memories she would have of him, independent of Ainsley.

"You know what I've learned since I hurt my legs, Ruby?" he said softly. "To be patient, to look more closely at things than I used to, to take in everything I see around me. You can do that too, Ruby. Really look to see all that's around you, even the people you're with."

"Like what I see when I look at Attila, Daddy?" Ruby asked.

"What do you mean, honey?"

"Look, Daddy. I think she has to go to the bathroom. See her eyes? She's crying inside—like Mommy does."

"Like Mommy?" he asked.

"Yes, Daddy. Like when Mommy cries but no water comes out."

"When does she do that?"

"Oh, sometimes upstairs...."

Attila nudged Chris' hand with her giant nose.

"Daddy! Attila has to pee-pee."

"Well, let's help her out," he said.

They left the hedge and traveled back across the lawn to the house, leaving Attila to roam freely for a few minutes. Ainsley came home unexpectedly from a client meeting in time for lunch.

"I remembered some more today," Chris said, as he watched her crumple onto the living room sofa.

She put her feet on an ottoman and closed her eyes. "What do you mean?"

"I remembered what Karen Knight looked like. And, being in the bar...."

"What do you think triggered that?"

"Something Ruby asked me."

"Where is Ruby?"

As if cued, Ruby flew into the room and hugged Ainsley's legs.

"Mommy, Mommy! Since Daddy can't walk, he's going to tell me how to see better and be a patient!"

"What?"

"I'll explain," Chris said. "Do you want some lunch, Ains?"

"What did you call me?

"Uh, I don't know. It just came out."

"You haven't called me that in years."

"Do you mind?"

"No."

"Okay then, let's have some lunch. You look a little thin these days."

"Come and look, Mommy!" Ruby took Ainsley by the hand and led her to the kitchen. They settled in at the table for a lunch of cheese, bread and fruit that Ruby had helped Chris to prepare.

"Ains—Ainsley, I've learned so much about life, myself, these last few years," Chris confessed, his voice faltering. "After my talk with Ruby, I think I'm overdue...."

"Overdue for what?" Ainsley asked, bewildered.

"Doing the right thing for Karen Knight."

"What do you mean, Chris?"

"I can't change the past, but I want to do something positive—for her parents. I'm going to talk to the development department at William and Mary about setting up a small scholarship fund in her name."

chapter 17

ONE DAY IN September of 1997, Attila didn't come when Ainsley repeatedly called her name. At eleven years old, the dog slept much of the day, her trips outside reduced to those that were physically essential, unless a car ride was involved. At the sound of jingling car keys, Attila begged like a puppy to go along, regardless of the length of the trip. Ainsley would pull the van or the Bronco up to the porch and remove a section of Chris' wheelchair ramp railing, enabling her to walk halfway down the ramp and over a carpet-covered crate into the vehicle. After struggling onto the backseat, she would hang her wrinkled, graying muzzle out the window, and sniff the air outside. Minutes into the trip, she was sprawled on the seat, where she remained until returning home. Other than these occasional automobile adventures, Attila's retirement was pleasantly soporific.

It was late morning. Ten-year-old Ruby was in school and Chris had dozed off at his desk in the library. Ainsley broke from working in her home office, intending to run an errand. With no response to her calls, she shook her car keys as she began a search of the first floor; Attila had long ago abandoned attempts to conquer the stairs and visit the upper stories of the house. It was in the last room Ainsley searched—the sun-filled living room—that she found Attila. Lying on her side, unable to lift her head, she thumped her tail up and down against the rug as she watched Ainsley pass through the door.

"Hey, big girl," Ainsley said in a soft voice, listening to Attila's loud swallowing, which alternated with panting breaths. Ainsley dropped to the floor next to her.

"Ainsley? Ainsley?" Chris' voice called out from another room.

"In the living room," she croaked back, barely able to form the words.

The whirr of his wheelchair motor grew louder until he appeared in the doorway and stopped abruptly. Attila responded to his arrival with several more thudding wags of her tail. Chris saw the silent tears streaming down Ainsley's face.

"Oh, no," he said, maneuvering his chair as close to her and Attila as possible. "I wish I could get out of this chair right now," he said. " I'll call the vet."

"No—not—now," Ainsley stammered. "There isn't anything they can do. I don't want her taken from here or...traumatized." She stayed next to her dog, petting her head and ears. "It's okay, girl. Good girl."

Attila's breathing slowed and she blinked her eyes less and less, until finally not at all. She was still. Ainsley held onto her body, sobbing. Chris cried, too, managing to reach down and touch Attila's shoulder.

"It was good that she was here. At home. Peaceful," he said.

Ainsley was beside herself. "I don't know if I can let her go."

"You don't have to." Chris reached out his hand to her. "She'll stay with you, Ains. With all of us. She was family."

Ainsley covered Attila with a blanket while Chris called the pet crematorium their vet had recommended, arranging for someone to pick up Attila at the end of the day. Two hours later, they tried to figure out the best way to tell Ruby what had happened.

"I...I don't want to upset her," Ainsley said, emotional again.

"Ainsley, there's no way to avoid that," Chris said.

"She should know what happened, not have Attila just...disappear. I'm not sure what to do here...." She started to cry.

"We'll...give her the option of saying goodbye," he said firmly, placing his hand on her arm. "I'll handle it. Let me do this for you."

Chris met Ruby at the kitchen door, and told her about Attila as the three of them sat around the kitchen table.

"We know you're upset," Ainsley said, searching Ruby's face for some show of grief.

"I'm okay, Mom," she said coolly. "Now Attila won't have to go to the veterinarian and be put to sleep."

Ruby left the table and came back a few minutes later. It was obvious she'd been crying. "I want to see her," she said. Chris took her by the hand and they made their way to the living room.

"Is that...her?" Ruby asked, pointing to the blanket on the floor.

"Yes. Do you want me to help you?" Chris asked.

"No, Dad, I'm okay. Uncle Blaine talked to me at Grandpa Ray's funeral about what happens after we die. I know she's going to Heaven. Do you think she's there yet?"

"I'm certain she is," he answered.

Ruby sat next to Attila and pulled back the blanket. Reaching in her pocket, she pulled out one of her prized possessions: a silver locket Blaine had given her for her sixth birthday. She removed Attila's black leather collar, replacing it with the locket.

"Now, we each have something of the other's to keep with us forever," she said to Chris as she kissed Attila's head and pulled the blanket back up. "Dad, I'm gonna miss her so much." She ran to him and hugged him, crying in his arms.

"I'm so proud of you, Ruby," he told her. "Should we go check on your mom? This is hardest for her."

Ruby nodded her head in agreement, fingering the collar. "Dad?"

"Yeah?"

"Maybe I should give the collar to Mom. You know, to remember Attila by."

"Good idea, Ruby," he said, as they left the room.

Three weeks passed, and the Bohan house resumed a normal, but quieter rhythm. Ainsley cleaned and stored Attila's bowls and dog bed in the laundry room, pulled the straight, tan hairs from her dog brush, and gave up listening for her heavy paws on the wood floor or her wailing baritone howls whenever a siren sounded in the distance. Ainsley couldn't help it—she had pangs of loneliness. She missed her companion, her silent witness, the one being in the world who shared her unedited life story without blame or judgment. She had spread Attila's ashes in the rose garden, but couldn't give up her collar. She kept it on her nightstand.

"Jill's coming by to take Ruby and me over to Bender's Bookstore in Phoebus," Chris said, as he rolled through the house looking for his wallet.

"Really Chris, I don't see why you won't let me take you," Ainsley protested. "You'll have to ride in her car for an hour, and it's going to be hard for you to get in and out. What if something happens? If you need something?"

"I'll be fine," he argued. "I can lift myself up completely with my arms." Chris raised himself off the seat of his wheelchair with muscular arms. "Ruby and I can bond over old comic books and search for that monster cat that lives in the store."

"All right," Ainsley said, feeling shut out and a bit sorry for herself. "Have fun."

Chris and Ruby left with Jill, allowing Ainsley some time to check for email, a new computer program she had yet to master. Blaine also had email, and being able to send messages that he responded to the same or next day seemed to shrink the twelve-hundred-mile distance that separated them. She had emailed him the day after Attila died, and he emailed back that he would look for another locket to replace the one Ruby gave up. Ainsley dialed in and straightened up her desk while she waited for a connection. After logging on, she checked her mailbox for new mail. There it was: a new email from Blaine. He wrote that he found a new locket for Ruby while on a trip to Chicago, and had it mailed to her for an early Christmas present. Ainsley re-read the email and then reluctantly deleted it, triggering her internal countdown of the days until the week after Christmas, when Blaine would visit for two weeks. She tried not to do it, but it happened every year, midway between returning from her month-long trip to Michigan and his annual arrival in Virginia Beach. She scanned the desk calendar. He would arrive in exactly one hundred and eighteen days.

Ainsley walked through the second floor of the house straightening up and collecting laundry. It was dead quiet. On her way to her bedroom, she heard the front door open, and then muffled bumping and shuffling downstairs. "Hello?" she called, wishing she had armed the alarm after Chris and Ruby left. She missed Attila's reassuring presence.

"Shhh!" someone hissed.

Ainsley's heart pounded as she tiptoed toward the front staircase, debating whether to run up the stairs to the third floor or hit the alarm's panic button. The control panel was across the landing by her bedroom door, in full view of anyone looking up from the foyer below. She held her breath.

"Oh, no!" she heard from downstairs. "Dad, look out!"

"What's going on?" Ainsley called down the stairs, relieved to recognize Ruby's voice. "Was Bender's closed? Did you two forget something?"

"Look out, Mom!" Ruby yelled as she appeared at the foot of the stairs with a tan bundle. Just as Ainsley was about to ask Ruby what she was holding, the bundle sprang to life.

"You didn't!" Ainsley said.

"Oh, yes, we did!" Ruby squealed, sending the Mastiff puppy up the stairs.

"Isn't it a bit...soon?" Ainsley asked, cringing. The puppy stood below her, barking excitedly. She dismissed her apprehension and bent down to pick up the dog.

"Oh, my God," she said, laughing as the dog wriggled in her arms.

"We haven't heard you laugh in too long," Chris said. "It was a joint decision—and we can't return her. She was flown here all the way from Massachusetts."

"But, that's where we got Attila," Ainsley said.

"The puppy's aunt *is* Attila," Chris said.

"What? Oh, thank you both, so much," Ainsley struggled over the words. Still carrying the puppy, she walked with Ruby down the stairs to Chris, who was waiting in the foyer.

"What are you going to call her?" Ruby asked excitedly.

"Well...Attila is a man's name, but Attila was as big and strong as a male, and I thought the name would fit her." Ainsley looked to confirm that the fat, tan and black puppy was a female. "Who are you, sweetie?" she asked the dog, before it scrambled to the floor. "I'm not sure about a name...."

"Mom, I have a name," Ruby suggested.

"What is it, honey?"

"Pilot. Can we call her Pilot, after Uncle John? And, she'll be kind of be a pilot, when we're in the car—like Attila was...."

"Sold," Ainsley said. "Ruby, I believe you just named our new dog."

chapter 18

"IN TWENTY YEARS, you never thought of leaving Dad?" Ruby asked, as she picked up a shell and threw it into the waves. "He had to know something was missing from your relationship."

"Ruby, a lot was missing from our relationship—before the accident. Most marriages aren't like the one your grandparents have," she replied. "For me, you came first, your dad's health and well-being, second. I didn't even put myself on the list. You were happy. Your dad told me he was. I've gone through every emotion imaginable over the years. Questioned myself. Done some things right and a lot of things wrong." She thought back for a moment about the hours she spent with Tyler Richardson. Was that right or wrong? She was still uncertain.

Until 1998, Ainsley somehow managed to fulfill her continuing education credits through local conferences. She would attend classes during the day, skip the socials, and drive home in time to help Chris with his nighttime routine and Ruby with hers. 1998 was an exception. The closest course she could find was in Washington, D.C., and it required an overnight trip. The one-day conference ran from eight in the morning until after six at night, and several hungry attendees staying at the same hotel decided to have dinner and drinks together. Seven of them—three men, four women—all of them married except for Tyler Richardson, who drove in from Philadelphia, enjoyed good food, conversation and several bottles of wine. As they ate, each took a turn volunteering their professional bio and tidbits about their families and life at home.

Later that night, Ainsley went to the lounge on her floor to get some decaffeinated coffee before turning in. Tyler Richardson was sitting on a sofa in the corner of the lounge, reading the paper, tall and lean in jeans and a teal sweater. At dinner earlier, he told everyone that he was thirty-two and newly "disengaged" from his fiancé of four years. "I think when you move past the four-year point and can't seem to set a date, something's wrong," he said. They all concurred.

"Can't sleep, either?" Tyler looked up at Ainsley from *The Washington Post* and squinted his hazel eyes.

"Separation anxiety. I don't leave my daughter behind very often—ever." She pursed her lips as she said it, suppressing the emotion in her voice. "I'm not accustomed to having downtime. I don't quite know what to do with myself."

"Now, she's with your husband, right?" He ran his fingers through his straight, dark blonde hair. "He's a...lawyer? As a breed, they're pretty self-sufficient, aren't they?" he asked.

"Yes, but he's...disabled." Ainsley turned to the refreshment counter and stirred some cream and sugar into her coffee, imagining Tyler's chagrin and trying to spare him a face-to-face apology. "Do you want anything?" she asked, without turning around.

If he was fazed, he didn't show it. "From the kitchen? No thanks."

She thought for a moment that he might be flirting, but quickly dismissed the thought as ridiculous.

"His disability—is it severe?" he asked. "You didn't mention it at dinner."

"Chris is a paraplegic. He's very independent, but I still worry that something could happen...." She walked to the sofa and sat next to him, leaning forward and resting her chin on her hand.

"Then, why don't you give him a call," he suggested, "so you can relax—enjoy a few hours of time to yourself?"

"I did—earlier." She sipped her coffee. "I'm sure they're at the neighbor's house for dinner, or walking the dog, and I'm being overprotective. They're fine."

Tyler leaned back into the sofa cushion, putting his arm behind Ainsley's back. "You're welcome to wait out the suspense here. Here's half of the paper," he said, holding it over her lap with his other hand. She felt a jolt of electricity sitting there next to him. It seemed like a lifetime since she had been alone with a man she found attractive, in a situation that could actually lead to intimacy. They sat and talked while she finished her coffee. He saw the emptiness in her eyes.

"Do you want to come to my room?" he asked without warning, standing up and extending his hand.

She was immediately offended, but found herself nodding and following him down the hall. Once they were inside his room, he closed and bolted the door, and led her to the bed. He watched her sit down but remained standing.

"Do I seem...desperate?" she asked, questioning what she was doing. "We both know...this is wrong."

He smiled. "I'm sure this sounds like a line, but I've never done this before—with someone married. There's something about you—aside from the fact that you're a glorious creature." He looked down at her and ran his hand along her cheek. "Whether it's wrong or not, I can't say. Something about it feels right to me. Are you sure you want to be here?"

"Yes," she whispered, aching for the touch of a man's hands.

At first, Tyler simply held her, fully clothed, as they lay on the bed together. "How long has it been for you?" he asked.

"Years," she said, visibly trembling from more than a decade of pent-up emotion and futile desire. "Ten years."

"That's a crime—for a woman like you." He traced her collarbone with his fingers and unbuttoned the top button of her blouse.

"Like me?" she asked, her heart racing from anticipation and excitement. "I've heard that before."

"Well, you're the kind of woman men should fight over—fight for. Isn't there some way that your husband—"

At the mention of Chris, the mood was lost. "It's—not solely because of my husband's disability. We had serious problems in our marriage...before his accident." She pulled away from him.

He propped himself up on one elbow. "God, Ainsley, then why do you stay? You're only thirty-six, right? Is it for your daughter?"

"Tyler, it would take more time than we have to explain it all. I made a choice years ago, and I'm living with it. Don't do this because you feel sorry for me. I don't deserve it."

"Are you going to spend your life like this?" he asked, concern in his voice.

She sensed she was drawing him in, that he wanted to help her solve her problems. "Tyler, I'm taking a chance that this will be a private memory for us. Not the start of anything, not a beginning." She sat up on the bed, ready to leave. "If you want to analyze my life, I have to go—now."

Tyler pulled her back down on the bed so she faced him. "I understand the rules," he said, smiling at her again. He took a lock of her hair in his hand and inhaled its fragrance. "It's getting late. Let's make the most of what's left of the night."

When they awoke at eight o'clock the next morning, after a scant hour's rest, Tyler Richardson was love-struck. "Will I ever see you again?" he asked, staring longingly at her as she slid out of bed.

"Not like this," she said gently, dressing in the previous night's clothes. "Tyler, please don't try to get in touch with me." She kissed his soft, beautiful mouth and walked to the door of his hotel room. "Thank you."

He jumped out of bed and followed her with his eyes as she disappeared down the hall and out of his life, a waft of intoxicating perfume slipping through his fingers. He was afraid that she had been an incredible dream.

Driving home to Virginia Beach, Ainsley was heady from the sleepless night filled with Tyler's sweet touch and insatiable demands. Their hours together left her feeling as if she was an adored object, one lovingly toyed with until its novelty was worn away.

Each passing year since Ruby's arrival deepened her hunger for a feeling of belonging to someone—all of her, not just bits and pieces. Blaine had her love, sterile and unrequited. Chris had her respect and companionship. Between the two fractured relationships, she remained unfulfilled, yet committed to her situation. And, she couldn't rationalize searching out another Tyler here and there to quell her transient emptiness.

Her cell phone rang. She flipped it open, supporting it against her shoulder as she drove. "Hello?"

It was Ruby. "Hi, Mom. Dad said I should call to let you know I'm leaving for school now."

"Is everything there okay?" Ainsley asked. The high from her encounter with Tyler was fading fast. It was a feather cradled in a dying breeze—one too weak to suspend it above the ground.

"Yeah," Ruby replied. "Pilot and I slept downstairs in the music room, in case—you know." She almost whispered the words.

"But...everyone's good?" Ainsley asked. With one last push, she felt the feather spiral downward until it grazed the ground and landed somewhere far in the back in her mind. "I'll be home in a few hours. I love you. See you after school."

"How was it?" Chris asked when Ainsley arrived home at noon, wheeling her suitcase behind her.

"It was all right. Nothing much to talk about," she answered.

"Well, you sure look great," Chris said. "I made us some lunch. I've got a client call in an hour, but until then, we can talk about the holidays, get some things planned. Oh, and Blaine called this morning."

"Really?"

"Yeah, he has some date changes or something for his December trip. Do you mind calling him back?"

"Uh, sure. I'll call him back," she mumbled.

Chris took his phone call in the library and Ainsley unpacked her overnight bag. She sat at her desk and dialed the rectory at St. John's Catholic Church. Blaine answered on the third ring. Her heart lurched as it always did when she heard his voice. Then she felt a surge of hatred toward him.

"Hello?" he repeated. His voice sounded deeper than when she spoke to him a week earlier. He covered the phone and suppressed a chest cough.

"Blaine, it's Ainsley. Chris said you called this morning."

"Yes. How are you doing?"

"I'm okay." Her voice was flat.

"Is this a bad time to talk?" he asked, coughing again.

"No, go ahead...." she answered, ignoring his obvious illness.

"I'm definitely planning to visit over the holidays, but I need to move the date forward a week if that's okay with everyone—"

"Fine," she interrupted. "Is that all?"

"Ainsley, what's going on? Is everything okay there?" Her repellent attitude bewildered him. "Has something happened, Ainsley? Please, tell me."

"Do you want to know? Really?" she hissed at him.

"Of course I do. Whatever you want to tell me—"

"I had an affair."

The phone went dead for a moment.

"Ainsley, what—"

"It's not as though I was unfaithful to you!" she cut in. "How could I be?"

"I didn't say that!" Blaine answered, flustered and less than clear-headed from a dose of prescription cough medicine. "What about Chris?"

"What about him?"

"Your marriage."

"That didn't stop you, did it?" she ranted. "And, Chris? Screwing around got him where he is today! That's what landed him in that chair! Can't you feel jealous? Can't you feel something?" she demanded.

Blaine was lost. "What are you talking about? Of course—"

"I know—you're a *priest*," she said sarcastically.

"Ainsley, why are you doing this? Don't punish me for the decision we made—together."

"You don't love me," she said, backing down from her attack.

"I do love you, and I love Ruby. And I care about Chris, too. It's a house of cards, Ainsley. We can't pick and choose who falls in this. It's all or nothing."

"Hypocritical bastard!" she screamed, crying. "I hate you, Blaine MacGearailt."

"No, you don't," he said. "You wish you could. I know the feeling. It would be easier that way. I'm sorry, but I have to go now. I have an afternoon funeral. I'll give you a call tomorrow." He hung up the phone, exhausted.

As Ainsley moved to her bed, Pilot hulked through the doorway, a solemn look in her brown, heavy-lidded eyes. She pounced on Ainsley's bed and stretched out next to her, releasing a low groan.

"I suppose you'll take up where Attila left off," Ainsley said sullenly, "keeping the family secrets."

Pilot wagged her tail and closed her eyes.

"Mom? Hello?" Ruby demanded as they stood in place on the hot sand. "What are you looking at out there in the ocean? Europe, for God's sake?"

Ainsley snapped back to Ruby and their surroundings. "Sorry."

"What where you thinking about?" Ruby asked.

"Just old friends. Nothing related to...today. Telling you all of this—it stirs up all kinds of memories, that's all."

"We've been standing here forever. Let's go back to our place on the beach."

chapter 19

In 1999, Chris simply pushed himself too far, too fast. Having his law practice located in the house meant that client meetings sometimes spilled over into mealtimes, Ainsley was happy to set another place at the table so that he could mix business with a little relaxation. Over dinner one February night, Jack Johns, a disabled veteran, relayed his experience at the 1996 Paralympics.

"Man, when I came back from the Gulf minus my right leg, I thought the rush of competing, at any level, was over for me. A friend of my wife's—a woman with cerebral palsy—said she was going to ride in the 1992 Paralympics. I assumed I heard her wrong and she meant she was going to fly over to Spain to *watch* the games. She was actually doing some special horse competition—dressage I think they call it—in the fricking Olympics!"

"No kidding," Chris said, fascinated by the conversation.

"Brother, I kid you not," Jack continued, shoveling a forkful of asparagus into his mouth. "She didn't medal, but she loved the experience. Came back and wouldn't shut up about it! I started thinking about it. I tell ya, I was a beast on the rugby field in college. We even scrimmaged over in Afghanistan, before—before I was hit. So I thought, why not try? Why not try to get into the competition?"

"Did you do it?" Chris asked, enthralled.

"Hell, yeah! There's a process to it. I had to find a trainer—each sport has a federation. You have to get yourself into the system and all of that. These competitions, and competitors, are serious—hardcore!"

"And it was worth it?"

"Absolutely! I barely made the team, and I rode the bench, but I loved it. I'm going to do it again. Sydney in 2000. I'm telling you, you should do it, Chris."

"Sydney's only a year and a half away."

"Yeah, but you played basketball and ran track at William and Mary, didn't you? I saw the pictures in your office. "

"A long time ago," Chris said wistfully.

"Pick your poison, man," Jack said enthusiastically. "You can compete in either sport."

Chris was too excited to eat the rest of his dinner. Ainsley was too worried to finish hers.

❧

There was only one Paralympic sport that Chris would consider—wheelchair racing.

"I've missed the adrenaline rush of running for too long," he told Ainsley. "I want to—I need to—do this."

She detected a long-absent but familiar, manic energy in his voice. "Please pace yourself, Chris," she said.

He started out slowly and sensibly enough, working with a local college coach at a nearby high school track. By the two-month mark, sensibility gave way to obsession. His bi-weekly training sessions evolved into strenuous daily road runs on a special chair. He fueled his efforts with a highly restrictive, vegan diet and exotic performance supplements that Ainsley had never heard of. His extreme regimen concerned her.

"Chris, you're losing too much weight," she told him one day as he warmed up for a practice run. "You have no protection. What if you get sick or injured?"

"The less weight on me, the faster I go," he said, rationalizing the changes to his physique. As he talked, the old facial scar from his accident moved back and forth over his right cheek, noticeable for the first time in years against his newly gaunt, pale face. "Don't be negative about this. I've got a plan."

Weeks later, Ainsley woke in the middle of the night to the sound of what that she thought was Pilot's barking. She turned on the light. Pilot was lying at the foot of her bed, silent. The barking sound was traveling from the library to Ainsley's room through the baby monitor she kept Velcroed to the side of her beside table. By the time Ainsley reached Chris' room, he was nearly unconscious from spasmodic coughing and a high fever. The paramedics responded in less than five minutes and packed him up into a waiting ambulance. Jill sent Robin over on his bike to stay downstairs at the house in case Ruby woke up, so that Ainsley could follow the ambulance to the hospital.

The ER doctor was straightforward as he stood with Ainsley outside Chris' cubicle. "Okay, so here's the lowdown. Pneumonia. Full-blown. We'll keep him here for a couple of days."

"A couple of days," she repeated, running through her internal calendar. "And after that?"

"Home and bed rest for as long as it takes, I'm afraid." He saw her troubled look. "Is something wrong?"

"Oh, I'm scheduled to travel for work the day after tomorrow," she said. "It's pretty important, but I'll figure something out."

Ainsley had no idea what to do about the situation. To her largest client, a women's shelter desperately in need of a new residential building, her pending trip to Ohio was worth half a million dollars in grant money. As an independent consultant, she had no one to call on to cover her meeting with the Grentle Corporate Foundation. The foundation required applicants to defend their funding requests, in person, at the corporate headquarters in Cincinnati. Once a nonprofit made it to the hard-won presentation stage, rescheduling the presentation was not an option. It was Ainsley—or no meeting.

Blaine's weekly phone call to the Bohan's house came at an opportune time. "What's going on down there?" he asked Ruby, when she answered the phone.

"Hi, Uncle Blaine. Mom's losing it," she told him, chomping on gum.

"Details, please, Ruby?"

"Let's see, Dad's in the hospital. Mom's freaking out because she's supposed to go to Ohio or someplace for this huge grant thing—"

"Hold on, honey. Is your dad okay? What happened?"

Ruby explained as well as a preoccupied twelve-year-old could, in between blowing bubbles. "He trained too hard for the wheelchair Olympics. He's got pneumonia, and last night they took him to Beach General Hospital in an ambulance. He'll be okay, though. I've seen him. Mom's over there visiting him right now."

"When's your mom's trip?"

"Tomorrow or the next day, but I think she's canceling it."

"Tell her not to cancel anything—I'll see what I can do. I'm scheduled to leave for my month's studying sabbatical in Colorado, but maybe I can move some things around."

"Your what?"

"I'll explain that when I get there. Tell your mom to call me as soon as possible. Love you, Ruby."

Love you, too, 'Unc.' Bye."

Ainsley took her trip to Ohio and Blaine stayed with Chris and Ruby, changing Chris' colostomy and catheter bags, giving him his medication and cooking meals. He drove Ruby to school and riding lessons, and walked Pilot three times a day. Robin, or Rob as he now preferred to be called, visited every day after school under the guise of checking on things, but everyone in the house knew he was there to quietly worship Ruby, who was a year or two away from being interested in him—or any other boy. Even so, his adoration was as steadfast as it was unreciprocated.

Blaine left for Colorado the day Ainsley returned from Cincinnati with her client's grant awarded. Chris gave up the idea of training for the wheelchair competition, but not the Paralympics themselves.

"We've been here before, haven't we, Ainsley?" he said, a month later, when he was fully recovered. "Me pushing myself too hard and dragging everyone else down with me. I've got to accept that I can't realize every dream I have."

"True. But, we all need some dreams. You shouldn't give up."

"I'm glad to hear you say that. So do you want to hear my dream Plan B?"

She was afraid of what he had in mind. "What do you mean, Plan B?"

"This may sound crazy, Ains."

She waited.

"Archery."

"Archery?

"Yes. You know I used to crossbow hunt with my dad. I was good. I can train right here. We'll set up a range in the side field. I promise you, I won't starve myself or run myself into the ground. And, there's one more thing...."

"What?"

"We go to Sydney next year."

"But you're not competing...."

"I know. We can go anyway, check out the competition itself. Meet some of the people involved. Go on to your parents' place. You have my word—no repeats of that crazy Michigan trip. We have our own money now. We don't have to ask your parents for help. We can even surprise them. Why not?"

"Deal," she said, relieved. "I'm sorry, Chris—that you didn't make it into the competition."

"No biggie. I've got years to prepare for the next one."

Fortified with sedatives, buckled into Air Pacific's fully reclining leather seats, and visited regularly by considerate flight attendants bearing food, drink and distracting small talk, Ainsley almost forgot she was airborne in October 2000. Until she and her family left Australia and changed planes in Nadi, Fiji. Chris' wheelchair cleared the aircraft's doorway with difficulty, following ten minutes of wrestling by Noni, their male flight attendant, whose other job was as a forward for Fiji's national rugby team. Ainsley gripped the armrests of her constricting seat throughout the two-hour flight, forcing herself to peer out of the tiny window from time to time.

"Whales, Mom! Whales!" thirteen-year-old Ruby screamed. She had been moving around the cabin, looking in the open cockpit door and asking Noni questions about the plane from the time they were airborne. "Check it out, Dad!"

"Humpback Whales," Noni explained, precisely enunciating each word. "A family. See the small form in the middle? That's a whale calf."

A pod of six whales cruised the waters below, leaving faint, white trails in their wake. Ainsley forgot her fear for a moment, lost in Ruby's excitement.

"What other animals will we see on the island?" Ruby asked.

"Actually, not many, except for those introduced by humans. I think bats are the only native mammals. Right, Noni?" Ainsley asked.

"Eeeew, gross," Ruby said, looking sour-faced.

"The bats are harmless," Noni said. "They eat only mangos. The rotten ones. They are simply trying to make their way in *their* world. You are a guest."

Ainsley glared at her daughter.

"Yes, sir," Ruby said.

Ainsley, Chris and Ruby spent their two weeks in Fiji without television, radio, or newspapers, exploring the volcanic base of the Taveuni rainforest in an old van, and basking on the island's palm-tree cooled beaches, which melted into the turquoise Pacific Ocean. Chris and Ruby were inseparable throughout the vacation. Ainsley shadowed Julie as she had when she was a young girl.

"It's good to feel like your mother again, Ainsley. To feel like you need me," Julie said, as they swayed in side-by-side hammocks on the verandah of Julie and Don's bure, eating bowls of fresh mango and pineapple.

"Do you mind me clinging to you a little, Mom?"

"No! I love it," Julie said, bringing her hammock to a halt. "Here it comes, Ainsley, so get ready."

Ainsley sat up in her hammock. "What do you mean?"

Julie placed her bowl of fruit on the verandah's stone floor and clasped her hands together. "The reason you need me to nurture you a bit is because...you assume too much responsibility...for other people's happiness. You've got no soul left for yourself, Ainsley."

"Mom."

"You know I'm right. And I know you won't admit it. So, when you're finished with me, I want you to tag around after your dad for a few days—fill yourself up with unconditional love. That's an order, dear. Okay, I'm finished," Julie said. She and Ainsley picked up their bowls of fruit and set their hammocks in motion again.

"Thank you, Ainsley, for making this trip," Chris said, on the long flight back to Virginia.

"It was good for me, too," she replied, loopy from a requisite dose of Xanax. "I needed some time with my mom and dad."

"Any word on when they're coming back to the States—permanently?"

"They never expected the plantation to be as successful as it is. Now, they have a big decision to make if they want to consider selling. Who knows how long it will be until they're back home?"

"So it's just us, I guess." Chris looked over at Ruby, asleep in her seat. "Our little family of Bohans." He leaned back to nap, a contented smile on his lips. Ainsley closed her eyes, too, heartsick. Hard as she tried, she couldn't will herself to fall back in love with him.

chapter 20

JULIE AND AINSLEY sat on Ainsley's bed on a December day in 2001. Cold rain fell in sheets against the bedroom windows, blurring the view of the trees outside.

"Being away from here, you know what I miss the most, besides you and Ruby, of course?" Julie asked.

Ainsley thought she knew the answer. "This house?"

"That, too. Pie. Good old American pie—with vanilla ice cream. Why don't we go get some?"

Ainsley thought she was joking. "Now? In this monsoon?"

"Yes, now. Right now." Julie went to Ainsley's dresser and brushed her hair, now styled in a flipped bob. "Come on. Before it gets any worse."

"Okay," Ainsley said, starting for the door, "I'll go get Ruby."

"No. The two of us," Julie answered. "Like we used to."

"Sure," Ainsley said, reaching for a sweater from her closet. "I'll bring the car around."

Dripping rainwater from head to toe, they sat at a corner table in the nearby Red Mill Bakery, eating cherry pie with ice cream.

"What's going on, Mom?" Ainsley asked. "It's not Dad—"

"No, he's fine. We both are."

"Mom, I heard it in your voice. We didn't venture out in this torrential rain for nothing. Something's on your mind."

Julie tried her best to tread lightly. "Sweetie, are you sure you want to keep on with this whole thing?"

"By 'thing', you mean the house?" Ainsley answered quickly, then looked at her mother and saw that the response was unsatisfactory. "You mean Chris."

"Yes, Ainsley. I know the whole story, remember? You weren't planning to stay with him before Ruby came along, and it's been more than *fourteen* years now. Every time I ask, you evade the issue, and another year goes by. That time is gone forever, dear. You can't get it back. You can't live it over again."

"Mom, Ruby's doing great and Chris has made tremendous progress in the last few years."

"Where does your happiness fall in this mix of priorities and accomplishments? You're changing Ainsley. I'm afraid that you work so hard at keeping your family together, you're losing yourself in the process. That was glaringly evident when you came to Fiji last year."

"I don't want to break up Ruby and her dad," Ainsley said.

"Are you and Chris...intimate, at all?" Julie asked bluntly. "I know you can't have sex the way you used to, but—if something like that ever happened to your father—there are ways—"

"No, Mom," Ainsley answered abruptly, squirming in her seat. "We're not intimate."

Julie persisted. "Are you...involved...with another man? Quietly having an affair?"

"No!" Ainsley barked. "I'm not having an affair, Mom."

"Ainsley, you're only thirty-nine, and we're long-lived in this family. Are you prepared for another forty or fifty years like this?"

Ainsley pulled her wet raincoat close against her body defensively.

"Ainsley?"

"I'm an adult, Mom."

"Yes you are. You're also my daughter. I only want for you what I have. I'm asking you this out of concern, not judgment."

"You know Mom, I'm sick of what you have. Most people will never love someone like you and Dad love each other. Don't judge other relationships by your own. It's not a fair comparison."

"God, I'm sorry Ainsley. All I meant is, are you thinking of spending the rest of your life alone? Without physical love? It's as though you've...sentenced yourself."

Ainsley looked out the bakery window, watching icy December rain pummel the sidewalk. "I take one day at a time," she said, shifting in her chair. "And, I'm raising Ruby right now." She hated herself for lying to her mother about Blaine and Ruby. She wanted to shed the weight of her secret, to run to her mother for comfort and unconditional love, but fear prevailed. If she spoke the words, everything would be amplified, too real. And telling her mother meant her father would see the agony on Julie's face, and Julie would eventually relent and tell him, because they were that close—no secrets between them. From there, they would try to help Ainsley resolve things, and there wasn't a resolution. Blaine had been right years earlier when he said it was a house of cards. She stayed silent.

"Honey, is there...something else going on here?" Julie probed.

"No, Mom. Nothing."

"Call me any time, day or night, if you need to talk. All your dad and I want is for you to be happy, like you used to be." Her eyes brimmed with tears. "We love you so much."

Ainsley reached for Julie's hand. "Mom, I'm as happy as I can be, right now."

"Right now, I'll have to accept that answer." She leaned around the table and hugged Ainsley tightly. "You know you can come to me with anything—even if you don't want me to share it with your Dad."

"Thanks, Mom. I love you."

They got up to leave, bundling themselves up in preparation for the angry elements outside.

"Let's go see what that daughter of yours is up to," Julie said. She grabbed Ainsley by the hand and they ran to the car. "Is Father Blaine coming in after Christmas this year?" she asked, settling in her seat. "He and Chris have grown close, haven't they?"

"Yes." Ainsley fiddled with her keys, trying to shed some nervous energy.

"I mean, what Blaine did for him on Dad's boat years ago. I guess that's what really started it all…."

"I try not to think about what would have happened if he hadn't been on there with us, Mom," she answered.

"I swear, Ainsley, sometimes I think John had a hand in bringing Blaine into our lives. He has this incredible bond with our family. When you really think about it, he is family."

chapter 21

"Working with Uncle Blaine all of these summers, I know now what I want to do when I get out of school," sixteen-year-old Ruby told Ainsley, as they picked black raspberries along the trail leading from the Makwa Point house to the Makwa River in June 2003. In all directions, locusts and crickets sounded off in the tall grass, which answered back with a shushing rustle, as the wind whipped through its blades, chafing them against one another.

Every summer, during her vacation in Makwa Point, Ruby helped Blaine with the small summer field trip program he had started years earlier for the children in his parish. As a little girl, she went along on the trips to Fayette and Kitch-iti-kipi as a participant. With each passing year, she took on more responsibility, eventually designing the program flyers, coordinating bus transportation, and acting as a guide. Now that most of the parish's children were grown and gone, the "field trip" had evolved into a senior citizen "Wednesday out" to shop, bank, or visit area attractions. Like Blaine, Ruby found working with older adults, many of who had no family in their daily lives, to be particularly rewarding.

"*Mom*," she fished, "do you want to know what I'm going to study or not?"

"Well, unless you plan to break Rob's heart, I know you're not becoming a nun," Ainsley answered.

"Very funny," Ruby replied. "Psychology—social work. I want to work with older people. Be that connection for them. Make a real difference in someone's life. Like Uncle Blaine does up here. I see my youth as a gift—to use to help people. You know, people who've lost the power to wake up in the morning and see the cup half full—to be free to live as they choose. I can make life better for those people."

"I think that's a great choice for you, Ruby," Ainsley said.

"And," Ruby continued, "I want to bring Rob up here next year, if that's okay with you."

"You miss him when you're up here," Ainsley said.

"Yeah," she answered, looking away from her mother. "A month is a long time apart when you, you know, when you—" Her voice broke up with the last few words.

"When you love someone?" Ainsley finished the sentence for her.

Ruby turned around. "Yes, Mom. I—love him," she said, almost wincing.

Ainsley smiled. "Honey, you make it sound painful!" She chuckled.

"Why are you laughing?"

"Don't be defensive, Ruby. Everyone else in the family has known for a while now that you love Rob."

Ruby was relieved. "Well, I also think Rob should come along with us next time, so he can see what it's like up here—before things start to change."

"What 'things' are you referring to?" Ainsley asked.

"You know, like Virginia Beach is now—how what used to be open space is now suburbia."

"I don't think that you have much to worry about, Ruby. I can count on one hand the number of significant changes I've seen up here since you were born."

Ainsley's estimate wasn't far off. A sprinkling of inexpensively constructed casinos, the antithesis of the glamorous high stakes establishments of Las Vegas, crept into the U.P.'s landscape and lifescape starting in the late '80's. These casual, tribe-owned gambling houses offered gaming to tourists and hunters, and infused the local economy with some additional revenue, benefiting local hoteliers, restaurants and retail businesses. A few discount retailers and fast food chains made their way into Marquette, Escanaba, and Manistique in the 1990's, but most of the region remained untouched.

Makwa Point's elderly residents slowly died off, leaving behind a lifetime of knick-knacks and furniture that their children didn't want to inherit, and real estate that fell outside the bounds of a receptive market. Many of the town's once neatly-maintained homes, centerpieces of their late owner's lives, stood empty until they surrendered to the U.P.'s harsh winter climate or the bulldozer's bucket. The little town owed its evolution to attrition.

In Virginia, things *were* changing. Chris' law practice flourished, taking a marked upturn in the mid-2000's, as newly disabled veterans, many of them parents and grandparents, returned from the second Gulf war to an often less-than-supportive society. His caseload was bursting, but he felt a sense of personal responsibility toward his clients, accepting all legitimate cases. Each year, he donated a portion of his income to the College of William and Mary's Law School in memory of Karen Knight.

"Who would have predicted that my law practice would be this busy?" Chris remarked at a 2005 bar association dinner honoring his contributions to the community. "And who could have foreseen that we would be at war twice in ten years?"

Blaine ventured down to Virginia Beach from Michigan most Decembers, and sometimes twice a year. He attended Ruby's confirmation, drove her to her first school dance, and sat with her parents during her high school graduation. He co-officiated at both Grandpa Ray and Grandma Mary's funerals, and fulfilled the roles of doting uncle and spiritual mentor—a constant influence, helping Ruby navigate through issues of life and loss.

It was late afternoon and high tide was coming in, eating away at the Sandbridge coastline. "That's how it's been for twenty-one years, Ruby. That's our story. Our family," Ainsley said. The long day of recollecting left her melancholy.

Ruby rose and stood barefoot in the sand, clutching a beach towel over her shoulders. "But it isn't real—our family isn't real," she said.

"Ruby, I wish that I could take away the pain you're feeling from learning all of this," Ainsley said, fighting to talk over the wind as she stuffed a sandy blanket in her tote bag. They started walking off the beach. "The world can be a cruel place, Ruby. I wanted to protect you from that—give you a normal life."

"The relationship I thought you and Dad shared, that's what I was hoping to have with Rob."

"Don't strip what I have with your father down to nothing. We have a very good relationship, even though it's not typical."

"Did you and Blaine have a plan to handle Dad finding out?"

"No. We weren't calculating about it. We agreed to keep what had happened between us a secret the day I told him about you, the day you met him—my first time up north after you were born."

"You're saying that you were never together after that time when I was a baby? Never in all of these years?"

"That's what I'm saying, because it's true. Blaine would not have continued his life as a priest and engaged in a relationship with me. He was prepared to leave the church the day he met you."

Ruby started toward the beach house, leaving Ainsley standing by the Bronco. "Are you disappearing again tonight, Ruby?" Ainsley asked. "Your grandparents have barely seen you, and Chris—your dad's worried."

"I'm not disappearing, Mom. I'm staying at the Horner's beach house again, that's all. I'll see you tomorrow." She turned back to Ainsley. "It's not fair, you know, you expecting me to live your lie. I guess that's your legacy—my inheritance."

"Ruby, I can't say that I regret you, or Blaine, just as I can't change the impact of what your father did to me years ago. Yes, I lied. And, I've lived with that lie."

"And now you're passing it on to me. I'm cornered Mom. I don't want to destroy Dad, but I can't enter into a marriage with Rob that's based betrayal and secrets. Goodnight, Mom."

Ainsley was running on pure adrenaline. "What should I tell your father?"

Ruby shrugged. "That's up to you. I don't think you have to worry about it tonight, though."

"Why not?"

"I'm sure Dad already went to bed. He's been tired all week. Or, maybe you didn't notice." She walked away.

Ainsley passed a grocery store on her way out of Sandbridge. She wandered the aisles, aimlessly at first, then piled her cart with Ruby's favorite foods. Loading the car, she found a small pink barrette, probably ten years old, tucked into the seatback. She clutched the barrette in her hand the entire drive home.

The sun was setting and the house was quiet. Ainsley put away her unneeded groceries and turned off the most of the first-floor lights. On her way upstairs, she saw a light under the library door and knocked softly. Chris was in bed early, half asleep, a case file on his lap. Pilot was dozing on the sofa. When she heard Ainsley, Pilot stretched, stepped down onto the floor and ambled over to the partly opened doorway.

"Hey, everything okay?" Chris asked. "I'm kind of out of the loop, here."

"Everything's fine. Ruby's at the Horner's beach house for the night." She opened the door all the way and let Pilot out into the hallway.

"What's the deal, Ainsley?" Chris powered up the back of his bed and removed his reading glasses. "Ruby hasn't said three words to me this week. I didn't even see her today."

"I think it's the reality of moving away after the wedding. She has to adjust. We can't do that for her, Chris." Ainsley was steering them all close to those treacherous rocks again. Staying on course required at least another half-truth, perhaps a lie.

"I don't buy it, Ains. She's always been very independent and levelheaded. It doesn't make sense."

"She's twenty-one and getting married in two days, Chris. I think we need to throw the concept of levelheadedness out the window."

He grudgingly accepted her explanation. "Well, if you think that's all it is."

"Trust me on this, Chris. Get some rest. You'll need it for Saturday. Goodnight," she said as she backed out of the doorway. She took Pilot for a walk to the rose garden, and stayed there until dark.

A little before eleven o'clock that night, Blaine broke a cardinal house rule by crossing the expanse of the second floor from his guestroom to Ainsley's bedroom. He heard her parents milling about upstairs, their animated voices drifting down the open stairwell. Then she came into view, passing across her open bedroom door, barefoot, in a knee-length red paisley nightgown. She reached for something on her dresser and the motion of her arm in the bell sleeve of the gown made her look as though she might take flight at any moment.

"Ainsley," he said at her half-open door, "we have to talk."

"What are you doing?" she whispered, a cross look on her face as she backed him into the hallway. "We knew that this day might come with Ruby," she said. Her eyes were lifeless as she spoke. "I never thought it would be at a time like this. I always worried about something coming out when she was a little girl, but we made it through all of those years. I got overconfident. I started to believe things would always be all right. Now this? It's a nightmare. And, it's not over yet."

"Ainsley, please," Blaine said.

"I've talked all day, Blaine. I need some sleep."

Blaine stared at the floor, collecting his thoughts. "I only need you to listen. It's about us...." He said the last few words to himself. She was already behind the closing door.

"Blaine, is that you?" Julie's voice called down the stairs. He froze, thinking of an excuse for being at Ainsley's door.

If Julie suspected anything, she didn't let on. She was charming and nonchalant. "Come up here and have a drink with us. We're on Fiji time. We may be awake all night!"

Blaine loved being with Julie. She was how he hoped Ainsley would be in twenty-five years: beautiful, vibrant, finding the joy in life.

"Come on up," Don roared, leaning over the banister.

Hands in his pockets, Blaine climbed the stairs to the third floor. He was still handsome at fifty; his facial features had gained depth and chiseling from years of love, pain and the burden of safeguarding the dreams and sins of other people. In street clothes, he looked like prime masculine real estate.

"We don't want to corrupt you or anything, but we know you enjoy a good glass of wine or two with us," Julie said, ushering him into the suite.

"Thank you," he said. "I'd love to."

"Great!" Julie was chatty. "I hate to say it, but there is a fair amount of feminine inscrutability around here right now, myself excluded, of course." She laughed softly. "I suppose after all of these years among us, you're accustomed to it."

"I never thought to ask you two this before, but you made a complete life change and moved to Fiji—at what age?" Blaine asked as they drank their wine, sitting in hypnotically comfortable armchairs.

Don looked at Julie for confirmation. "Oh, I was fifty and you were forty-eight, right dear? About Ainsley's age?"

"Yes," she said. "It was in 1985, the year before, right before... John's...John died."

Don and Julie locked eyes, protecting each other from the pain of an old wound that would never heal.

"Yes, that's right. Hold on, you two," Don said, raising his glass. "Here's to our son John. You would have loved him, Blaine. You remind us of him sometimes." They drank to John, and then to life in the South Pacific.

Don spoke from the heart, and from a healthy dose of wine. "It was more than the lure of an island paradise that took us to Fiji. We had the trip all planned out as a vacation. Two weeks before we left, I went in for my yearly physical. I'd had some respiratory issues in the past—I'm a former pack-a-day smoker—so they took a chest x-ray." He emptied his upturned wineglass. "One day, we were talking about arranging our trip, the next day we were deciding how to tell our children I had lung cancer."

"You didn't, though...have cancer?"

"No." He refilled his glass. "There was a mistake on the x-ray. It was like a bad movie, but it happened. During the week we thought I did have cancer, Julie and I went through a total life evaluation."

"Then we took the trip and fell in love with the island," Julie said.

"And I got selfish," Don said firmly. "I wanted time alone with Julie, in that magical place, while we were relatively young and independent, in case the next time, the test results weren't a mistake. Any man loved by one of the women in this family would be insane not to do the same thing, given the chance." His voice quaked as he uttered the last few words.

Julie sat down on the arm of his chair. "Don," she said soothingly, "thank you."

Blaine walked over to the fireplace and perused the pictures on the mantle. "Looks like you have some new ones since I was up here last." He moved in closer to examine a small photo in a white frame. "This is Ruby? No, Ainsley," he said.

"That's Ainsley," Julie confirmed. In the picture, Ainsley sat on the living room sofa in a yellow tutu, looking into the camera pensively, clearly recovering from a big cry. "I found that in a box of pictures up here yesterday, across the hall," she continued, "in John's old room."

"You know how I describe it, Blaine?" Don broke in, his normally commanding demeanor now a casualty of sentimentality and wistful reflection. "When they walk into the room, the feel of the air changes. You know they're there, all three of them, before you see them. Look at Ainsley, even at that young age—"

"For Pete's sake, Don," Julie said, annoyed. "Stop it! Not that siren thing again. The rest of the world does not share your romantic vision of us."

Blaine did, but couldn't acknowledge it.

"You know it's true, Julie," Don kept on. "You all have it. Tell him the story of that picture."

Julie rolled her eyes. "Oh, all right. If it will quiet you down. And, no more wine. I'm cutting you off."

"Really," Blaine said, "I want to hear the story."

Julie picked up the picture and sat down with it in her lap, rubbing her thumb across the glass, as if to help recall the memory. "Well, when Ainsley was, oh I guess, ten or eleven, I dropped her off at dance class. An hour later, I picked her up, as always. She came running down the sidewalk, bawling. As soon as she got in the car, I asked her why she was crying. She told me something was wrong with her teacher. 'Why do you think that?' I asked her. 'Because, Mommy,' Ainsley said, 'Madame Chevreaux looked right at me today and *told* me I was Jenny Sackwaugh.' Then she started crying again. Now, Ainsley had taken ballet lessons from the same teacher for three years. 'What exactly did she say to you?' I asked. Ainsley repeated what she'd heard. I thought about it for a moment and said to her, 'Are you sure that Madame Chevreaux didn't say that you have a certain je ne sais quoi?' Ainsley yelled back at me, 'I told you, that's who she called me!' Of course, I had to explain what her teacher really meant."

Blaine and Don smirked.

"I told her it was a compliment. When we got home, I simply had to take that picture." Julie set the picture back down on the mantle. "It's a sweet memory."

Don sniffled and ran his hand through his gray-and-black hair. "Sorry for the digression. I'd say, it's painfully obvious what, or who, my strength and my weakness is." He stood and jingled some change in his pockets. "Listen to me. It must be my captive audience. I know this particular situation doesn't really apply to you—to your life. But then again, perhaps it's similar to your love of God, isn't it? The most powerful emotion—force in your life. It's what keeps you alive—allows you to go on."

"Yes," Blaine told him, "love does that."

Julie leaned close to Blaine. "We're feeling a pull toward home these days," she said thoughtfully. "We want to get in some time in the U.P.—maybe even in the winters."

"Oh, let's be honest with the man, Julie. We plan to head home for good within the year." Don lowered his voice. "With Ruby getting married, things here are changing around here."

Julie spoke up. "We're worried about Ainsley. We want to be close to her now."

"She's changed," Don explained, his graying brows fused together. "Especially in the last few years. She's become rigid—almost joyless. And, so private...even with us. Sometimes, we feel like we're intruding. Our beautiful, luminous daughter is fading away. You know, when John died, it was as though our hearts stopped for a while. At the same time, it was beyond our control—his accident, his death. Nothing we could have done to prevent it." He stared at the floor.

Julie continued for him. "John's spirit never died, though, Blaine. That helped get us through the loss. With Ainsley, it's as if we're losing her by inches. She's alive, but her spirit is dying...a little more each month, every year."

I'm partly the reason why, Blaine thought.

"John never left us, Blaine," Don said. "We've told Ainsley that. She's spent decades searching for some grand sign of her brother's presence, an affirmation. It's really just here, quietly among us, everyday. In truth, it's Ainsley...the real, Ainsley, who has left us."

"We want her back," Julie said. "And we're willing to fight for her."

chapter 22

THURSDAY MORNING, A convoy of catering and tent rental trucks overtook Ainsley and Chris' driveway and yard. They carried within them an assembly line of workers who heaved poles, sidewalls, tables, chairs, and milk crates loaded with crystal and china across the lawn and into the safety of the canopied reception tent.

Ainsley kept wiping the same spot on the kitchen counter with a sponge, watching the driveway for any sign of Ruby.

"Any word from her yet?" Chris asked, as he rolled up to the coffee maker.

"Not yet. She's probably out and about with Rob."

"Not with Rob. He just called my cell phone looking for her."

"Really? She'll call or turn up, when she's ready."

He turned to face her. "What story are you going to tell me this time, Ains? You're keeping something from me."

"Chris, if I knew of anything that would help, I would tell you." She was telling another thinly-cloaked lie. "I'm going to head outside to check on the tent."

As soon as she hit the porch, Ainsley called Ruby from her cell phone. "Ruby, you can't go AWOL for the next couple of days. You and Rob are getting married in forty-eight hours...aren't you?"

"I can't say, Mom," Ruby answered matter-of-factly.

"Ruby, you can't do this to yourself, or to Rob. I'm coming over—now."

"Mom, I don't want you to."

"We have to finish this. Stay at the beach house. I'll be there in fifteen minutes." Ainsley hung up and turned to her car, almost falling over Blaine. "I—didn't—see you," she stammered.

"Listen, Ainsley, about last night," he said.

"It's okay, Blaine—no one saw us. I've got to go out," she said, rushing past him. "Please tell Chris for me."

From the sand-swept street, Ainsley could see Ruby sitting on the top deck of the beach house, still wearing a white cotton bathrobe.

"Are you going to get dressed today?" she asked, after entering the unlocked house and climbing the stairs to the third floor deck. "It's almost ten. Come home and see if the tent is where you want it, and make sure the rental items are what you ordered."

"How can you talk about tents and flowers like nothing's happened—nothing's wrong?" Ruby retorted.

Ainsley sat down next to her on the wood deck. "Ruby, I don't know how else to handle it. Do you want to cancel the wedding? Do you want me to start calling people? I will. I'll do whatever you want me to, but I can't make the decision for you. This is your wedding, your life. Yours and Rob's."

"Maybe I should." She stared through Ainsley. "Cancel it, I mean. I'm not sure if I should do this now."

"How can you make this decision without Rob? Don't shut him out. Don't punish him, too. You love him. You always have...ever since you were old enough to understand what love is."

"It was the same with you and Dad," she said, examining her nubby fingernails. "You fell in love young. You thought it was forever."

"It wasn't the same, Ruby. There were other factors, warning signs."

"Such as?"

"Such as, whatever we did, it seemed to involve drinking. Your Dad always showed up with wine, beer, or liquor to every event, every date, regardless of the time of day. Or, he'd just...disappear sometimes. I knew something wasn't right, but I didn't dig deep enough to find out what was going on. He said he liked to have a good time.

I thought that marriage would change him. That was my mistake. Ruby, you have to accept the person as they are, not as you want them to be."

"Now you're saying Dad was an alcoholic?"

"I'm certain he was. Your dad can't take all of the blame. I should have known better. He was engaged when I met him. He was unfaithful to his fiancé—with me! She confronted us in a restaurant on our third date. Until that moment, I knew nothing about her."

"That doesn't sound like Dad."

"I know it doesn't. Not the man he is now."

"Why would he do that—hurt both of you like that?"

"He said he thought she was the one, until he met me. I think deep down, your dad was very competitive, addicted to the chase."

"Did you ever love him?"

Ainsley went to the deck railing. "God, yes, Ruby. And, I do love him now, but in a different way. When we got married, I thought that we would end up having a marriage like the one my parents have. I was crazy about him. Otherwise, I never would have gone ahead with the wedding—especially after I found out about the other woman."

Confusion riddled Ruby's face. "Wait. Another woman? Even before you were married?"

"I attributed it to cold feet, even though Chris was the one who pushed to get married."

"Who was she?"

"A student, like the others. I don't know any more than that. I didn't want to know. It would have made it too real. I was naive and in denial."

Ainsley took a deep breath and let it out slowly. "Ruby, the man who rolled his car in Williamsburg twenty-two years ago died that night, in the accident. The father you know and love was born out of the ashes of that event."

"I can be angry at Dad for what he did to you all those years ago, even hate him a little, but as a father he's always been there for me—always. I can't go off and marry Rob on Saturday knowing he'll be alone. I can't do it."

"Ruby, years ago, I made a promise not to abandon Chris, and I've kept that promise, because I know what a good father he is to you."

"You can't leave him alone, Mom."

"I won't."

"What if Blaine wants to...do something, now that I know—now that I'm out of the house. Start a life with you? Go away?"

"That won't happen. He's already taken."

"By God, you mean?" Ruby asked.

"Yes. In twenty-two years, Blaine has never given me any indication that he would consider leaving the church. He's not going to change now."

"Mom, you and Blaine made a choice to live this way. Dad didn't have that option. He didn't get to choose. Neither did I. Are we all supposed to go on like some warped, happy family, never telling Dad the truth?"

"Ruby, I watched your father struggle to regain independence and self-worth, to live a productive life. It took years. I respect him—tremendously—for waging that battle. I honestly don't believe he could have done it without the inspiration and strength he gained from fatherhood. I did not deliberately keep the truth about you from him. Not at first. Until the day after you were born, I thought you were his."

"I'm not his."

"No, you're not. There, I've said it. But, you've had a good life, Ruby. Two strong men who were there for you, no matter what. And, now you have Rob. If you intend to marry him in two days, we've got to go back to the house. People are waiting for us." She stood to leave. "I'll be in the car."

Minutes later, a disheveled Ruby tumbled into Ainsley's car, a change of clothes in her arms. She looked over at her mother as she leaned down to tie her shoes. "What do you want from me, Mom? To forget? Forgiveness? To forgive and forget what you've done?"

"I want us to find...some kind of truth—that we can both accept."

"There's only one kind of truth. It's either the truth—or it isn't. Remember? That's one of the values you and Dad instilled in me."

They started back to Water's Edge Lane.

"Ruby," Ainsley said, "it's not that simple, not for this. I can't change what your father did to me years ago. *His* lies, the way he treated me, led me to Blaine, and my relationship with Blaine gave me you. I believe I've done my penance. I've accepted this way of life, of giving to others, to your dad, to you. I made my mistakes early, and I understand that they'll follow me for the rest of my life. Ruby, you're not me, and Rob isn't Chris. It would be a mistake for you not to marry him."

"So now you're saying that I shouldn't tell him any of this?"

"No. I'm saying that you have to decide what kind of relationship you want to have with him." Ainsley pulled in the driveway and parked the car. "How you choose to proceed from this point, right where you are now, will determine your future."

"Are you playing semantics games with me, Mom?"

"Your future with Rob depends on what and how you tell him about us."

Panic washed over Ruby's face as she glanced at her watch. "Oh, my God...."

"What is it?"

"The fitting," she said. "The damned final fitting. It's in half an hour."

"Do you want me to drive you?" Ainsley asked.

"No. I'll go by myself." She waited for Ainsley to get out of the car and moved into the driver's seat. Ainsley reached in the window and pulled out the shoulder strap, placing the buckle in Ruby's hand.

"I'm still your mother," she reminded her. "Drive carefully."

Ruby stood stoically in front of the three-sided mirror at The Silk Knot Bridal Salon and sipped strong coffee from a paper cup Megan held for her.

"Ruby? Ruby? Are you okay?" Megan asked.

"I'm fine. Let's get this over with," Ruby answered. She remained motionless as the seamstress helped her into her ivory ball gown and pulled the sides of its corseted back together.

"Everything looks perfect. We'll press it tomorrow and have it ready by four. You'll be a beautiful bride."

Megan scrutinized Ruby's vacant expression. "Uh, why don't I pick it up and hold onto it for you, Ruby? Until tomorrow."

"That's fine," Ruby sighed.

"In fact, why don't I bring it with me to the rehearsal?"

"Even better. I've got to go." She stripped off the dress and walked through the store to the dressing room in her thong and strapless bra, leaving her friends and the seamstress slack-jawed.

"She's uninhibited today," Megan said.

"I would be too, if I looked like that," the seamstress added.

Megan and Jan exchanged a skeptical glance as they trailed Ruby out of the store.

"What is going on with this wedding, Ruby?"

"What do you mean?" Ruby shot back.

"Our day at the spa—starting right about now?" Jan asked as she checked her watch. "Remember?"

Ruby stopped at the Bronco and unlocked the driver's side door. "You go ahead. I've got some other things to do." She started the engine.

"Other things? This was your idea. It's supposed to be for you," Megan said.

Ruby waved as she drove away.

"This is insane," Jan said, shaking her head. "Remember Meg—bride brain is alive and well in Virginia Beach."

"Well, someone has to show up at that spa," Megan told her. "Let's get going."

❦

With no word from Ruby by four o'clock, Chris was worried. "Ruby, honey? Where are you?" he asked as soon as she answered her cell phone.

"Dad, I'm staying at the Horner's again tonight. Rob and his mom are picking up his grandmother in Charlottesville. They won't be back until tomorrow morning. I'll have the place to myself until then."

"Do you need anything?" he asked, sitting up in bed.

"Some time to myself, Dad. That's all."

"Goodnight, my little girl."

She felt like a traitor, and tried not to cry. He could always hear it in her voice. She pretended to cough as she said goodbye.

Chris hung up the phone. "It'll be a miracle if this wedding goes off, I think," he told Ainsley. She was leaning her back against the inside of the library door's threshold, and jamming her feet against the opposite side to stay in place. It was where she positioned herself whenever she had something on her mind, or Chris did, and he was too tired to be up and around in the house.

She tapped her lip with her fingers. "You might be overreacting, Chris."

"Me? Admit it. Our daughter is acting bizarre."

"Look, you didn't have to live with me the week before our wedding. I recall plenty of emotional highs and lows. And I'm sure my mother remembers even more than I do."

In truth, Ainsley suffered no such mood swings before their marriage. It was one of the best weeks of her life—until the eve of her wedding, when Chris disappeared following the rehearsal dinner. Ainsley could never prove that he was unfaithful that night, but she was certain that he was. If he recalled that detail at some point during the past two decades, he never said a word. Not to her.

Ainsley returned to an upright position in the library doorway, waiting for Chris to respond.

He yawned. "Okay. I'm trusting you on this one, Ains."

"Thanks. Now, can we call it a night?"

chapter 23

FRIDAY MORNING, AS Ainsley watched the reception tent floor go down, her Bronco appeared in the driveway, drifted to a stop and then stayed there. She stared out the window, but couldn't make out what was going on inside. She walked outside to the car, and leaned in the driver's side door.

"Ruby," she said to her haggard-looking daughter, "Rob's on his way over."

Ruby leaned back in her seat, staring up at the faded upholstery. "What did you tell him, Mom?"

"I didn't tell him anything—yet. You've got to talk to him. You can't shut him out like this."

Ruby didn't respond.

"Ruby, your wedding is tomorrow."

Rob's car arrived in the driveway.

"Oh, God," Ruby moaned.

"*Thank* God," Ainsley said. "Talk to him, Ruby. Go talk to him."

Frantic, Rob ran to the car, and got in on the passenger's side. "Ruby, what's going on here?" he asked, his normally pleasant demeanor hardened by frustration.

"Rob, we have to talk today—right now," Ruby answered. Both of them got out of the Bronco and walked to Rob's car.

"Why do I get the feeling that you're going to leave me before we get to the altar?" he said. He looked back at Ainsley. "Morning, Mrs. Bohan," he mumbled, pleading with his eyes for assurance.

All Ainsley could pass back to him was a friendly wave.

"We're going to the beach house," Ruby called out.

After the two of them drove off, Ainsley walked toward the front porch, where Blaine and Chris were waiting for her. Seeing the expectant look on their faces, she turned around and climbed into the Bronco. "Shit!" she screamed, her truck kicking up dust and gravel as it careened down the drive and onto the road. She had no idea where she was going.

"Who stalled the black cloud over this house?" Chris asked Blaine. The two men stayed on the front porch, in awe of the scene that had just played out before them.

"Can you talk to the man upstairs?" Chris asked. "You've got the inside track."

A woman waved at them from the tent. Blaine shook his head. "Chris, isn't someone supposed to meet with the catering people?" he asked.

Chris shrugged his shoulders. "What do we do?"

"I usually restrict myself to the front end of this wedding biz," Blaine joked.

They looked at each other before they yelled out in unison, "Julie!"

Rob and Ruby endured the ten-minute trip to Sandbridge in silence, with Rob gripping the steering wheel as if it was a lifeline. Once they arrived, Ruby barely cleared the threshold before collapsing on the stairs to the second floor.

"For God's sake, Ruby, what's going on here?" Rob demanded. "This was supposed to be a joyous time for you, me and our families—the best week of our lives. That's how it started, anyway."

Ruby and Rob's wedding week had begun on a joyous note. They pulled airport duty, happily shuttling visiting family members to the house and nearby hotels.

Blaine's plane landed on time, early Sunday evening. Ruby and Rob met him at baggage claim with excited hugs and details of their planned reception and honeymoon in Fiji.

"Be careful now," Blaine warned, as the carousel began a slow rotation of luggage, none of which appeared to be his. "Your grandparents went over there and stayed!"

"Don't worry, I've been there twice and I'm still here. Besides, I would never go that far away from my dad—permanently. It would kill him, and me too."

"How is your dad?" Blaine asked.

"Oh, he's great. He's finishing up some big case. He says he thinks it'll be his swan song, but we all know he'll never retire."

"I heard he made it into the Paralympics again."

"Yes, Sir," Rob said. "He's going to China in twelve weeks."

"That's a tremendous accomplishment," Blaine said. "I'm proud of him."

Ruby beamed. "We're all proud of him."

The next day, Julie and Don stumbled out of the international arrival terminal. "I've got to get my sea legs, dear," Don told Ruby. "Those flights! A plane from LAX, that overnighter from Nadi, our good old island puddle jumper. I'm getting too old for it, I think."

Ruby hugged him. "The third floor's all ready. Mom has wine in your refrigerator, and food for you two up there. Uncle Blaine's already here...so we *know* we'll have the ceremony." She chattered on. "Dad's got him working, detailing his precious T-bird. He must be planning to sell it or something."

Julie jumped in while she had the chance, talking as they walked to the car. "Speaking of details, we've got the honeymoon bure all ready for you, Ruby. You'll love it too, Rob. An outdoor shower, a hammock on the porch. All remodeled, all overlooking the Pacific."

Ruby looked at Rob dreamily.

"Ruby, remember our caretaker, Sataki?" Julie asked, from behind black oval sunglasses. "He's going to be taking care of the two of you—personally. At your beck and call, twenty-four seven. Even though your grandfather and I won't be there for your first few days, you'll be in the best of hands."

They were at the car. "How's your mom doing, Ruby?" Don asked, holding Julie's door.

"You know Mom. She's perfect," Ruby replied. "Like always."

Julie nodded. "We can't wait to see everyone. Let's get going to the house."

The four of them wove their way through airport traffic toward Water's Edge Lane, talking nonstop, happily catching one another up on the last six months of their lives.

Rob was impatient. "Ruby, enough of this," he said. "What is it that you have to say? Just get it over with."

"Rob, I can't marry you—" she said, her eyes brimming, ready to overflow.

"What are you saying?" he jumped in.

"I can't marry you—without telling you what's going on."

"For God's sake, please!" he shouted. "Please tell me what the hell is going on!"

"It's about my past, Rob." She sounded grave. "Things you don't know."

He was incredulous. "Your past? I'm your past! I've known you since you were a baby! The only past you have is with me—isn't it?" He swallowed hard. "Ruby, you didn't...." He grabbed her arm. "Is there someone else? Who is it?"

"Yes, but not in the way you're thinking of. Where we go from there depends on how you feel once you know. You'd better sit down."

He obediently lowered his six-foot, five-inch frame onto the floor in front of the stairs, facing her.

"Rob, I don't know how to move forward with Blaine and my mother, and my dad, but I love you too much to even contemplate starting our life without letting you know the truth."

Rob braced himself for a fall.

"This isn't easy," Ruby started. She held his hand. They talked into the afternoon.

"You know how much I love you, Ruby," Rob said. "And, I would never do anything to destroy the love you've given me." He stretched his legs, and relaxed a bit, grateful that he could continue believing in their relationship.

She pulled away. "I don't understand why you're so...calm. Rob, did you hear anything that I said?" She searched his face for a reaction.

"Yes, Ruby. It's an incredible story, but you're what's most important to me in all of this. As long as we're okay, everything else is—surmountable."

"Are you sure?"

"Yes!" he said emphatically.

"Rob, it's ironic. I used my parents' marriage as an example for us to follow, and it wasn't even real."

"Are you sure about that? From what I've seen, it's as genuine as they come, in its own way."

"Whose side are you on!" she shouted. "How can we get married in two days? Once everything is out in the open, I can't even think about what's going to happen with my dad. This will destroy him."

"Wait a minute. You have your mom and Blaine to think about, too. He's a priest—for God's sake. In this day and age, think of the consequences. Don't hate me, but I can see your mom's reasoning in this."

"I believed in her!"

"Can't you still? I think she acted to protect you and your father, at the expense of her own happiness. I don't know about telling your father...."

"But, it's not fair."

"What's not fair? How about what your dad did to her? Ruby, we'll share many secrets, I hope. As long as we trust each other, love each other, that's what matters. What if this was happening to me?"

"I'd...go along with what ever you chose to do." She said. "Rob, two days ago I loved my mom—trusted her more than anyone in the world. Now, I'm trying my best not to hate her."

"Ruby, if she'd told you when you were young, how could you understand? How could you keep that from your dad? She protected both of you, Ruby. You know, if your father hadn't had that affair, if he had made that trip with your mom—if he'd been faithful—none of this would have happened."

"That's exactly what she said."

"You grew up with two men you know loved you more than anything in the world. Look at my "biological" dad. He wasn't even half a father to me. He taught me nothing. He abandoned my mother. He abandoned me...." Rob stared off for a moment. "So, which way of growing up is worse? I know what my answer is." He sat on the stairs next to Ruby and took her hands in his.

"I know Rob," Ruby said. "I know that the pain I've always seen behind your eyes is from that—from what your father did to you."

"And, your mother spared you all of that. She made it so you grew up happy—and safe. No one and nothing can ever take that from you."

"I don't see this the way you do, Rob, but I think I'm beginning to understand...."

"Understand what?" he asked.

"What people mean when they call their spouse their better half, or their other half. That's what you are to me." She put her hand on his cheek and leaned over to kiss him. "Rob, I love you."

They moved to the thick carpet on the living room floor. She hovered over him, kissing his face and neck.

"Ruby, you're going to have to stop doing that." Rob dropped his arms from around her waist, fighting his arousal.

"I want you now, Rob. I don't want to wait until tomorrow night."

"Are you sure? You always said you wanted to wait. We agreed."

She pulled off her blouse, and unbuttoned the top few buttons of his shirt. "I'm sure. I need to be with you. Here. Make love to me," she whispered, unhooking her bra. "Now."

chapter 24

PANICKY, RUBY STUDIED her watch. "Rob, what are we going to do about the rehearsal? It's in twenty-five minutes." She reached for her blouse and his shirt, lying next to them on the living room floor.

"Well," Rob said, rubbing his eyes, "we're going pull ourselves together, get in the car, and go to the church."

Ruby put her index finger in her mouth, biting what was left of her nail. "Right. We'll get through it together."

"Yes, we will," Rob said, caressing her soft lips with his. "It's official—we've slept together already—technically."

They had managed to stop short of consummating their relationship, holding each other until they dozed off, sleeping for more than two hours.

"Rob, are you disappointed—that we didn't—have sex?"

"Ruby, you know how much I want you, but if we don't wait, we'll never know how special tomorrow can be. Now get some clothes on, before I change my mind."

She smiled and bounded up the stairs to get dressed.

The large church was empty except for the first two rows of pews. Father Thompson stood with Blaine at the altar, perusing the attentive wedding party. "What did you folks do," he boomed, "take a Valium before you got here?"

Everyone laughed.

"Seriously, folks, Father MacGearailt and I are going to walk you through all of this so you can relax and enjoy tomorrow," he continued. "We promise to make it as painless as possible. If you have questions as we go along, speak up." He rubbed his hands together. "Let's get started."

The wedding party configured and reconfigured itself, shuffling about as instructed by Father Thompson. Megan, Ruby's maid of honor, attached a drooping, weathered veil to Ruby's head and handed her a plastic flower arrangement to carry down the aisle. Ainsley and Chris were obedient, sentimental parents throughout the forty-five minute run-through.

"Rob," Ruby asked as they left the chapel and walked through the parish hall to the parking lot, "would you mind bringing the car around, and telling Mom and Dad to go ahead to the restaurant?"

"Uh, sure," he said. "Are you—"

"I'm fine," she said, taking her place inside the kitchen doorway.

"Uncle...Blaine," she called out when he walked by, wiping her sweating hands on her dress.

"Ruby?" He seemed surprised that she asked for him.

"I 'd like to talk to you for a minute."

"Of course."

They ducked into the empty, dark church kitchen. Her heart raced as a few members of the wedding party passed the darkened doorway, talking, their heels clicking along the waxed linoleum floor.

Ruby flipped on the light switch. "Before tomorrow...." she started, but lost her train of thought, intimidated.

"Ruby, I know how difficult this is—"

She held up her hand, determined. "It's my turn to talk. I've been listening all week."

"Fair enough."

"You know, I used to look at my dad, deciding what features of his I'd inherited. I was sure I had my mom's creativity and his tenacity. I'm not the person I thought I was—all of my life."

"Ruby, you haven't changed—"

"What I know about myself, my identity is gone. My relationship with my father will never be the same."

"He never has to know, Ruby. I'll protect him from that, so will your mother."

"I'll know." She crossed her arms over her chest. "I want the truth, Uncle Blaine. Do you love me, do you care at all about my dad, or did you just use us, all of these years, as a way to be near my mother?"

"Ruby, now you know the circumstances of how I met your mother. How our relationship started. I've loved you since the moment I saw you. I love your dad, too. He's like a brother to me."

"A brother?" she huffed, unmoved by his assertion. "You had a brother. Would you lie to your brother—for twenty years?" She started to cry.

"It was to protect you. Both of you." He reached in his pants pocket and pulled out a well-worn but pristine gray handkerchief. "My favorite one," he said as he handed it to Ruby. "I hope that with time, you can find your way back to me. Even though I never said it publicly, you are the most important person in the world to me, and I'll take whatever kind of relationship you want to have with me, whenever you're ready. Or none at all, if that's your wish."

She handed him back his handkerchief. "I have to go."

After the rehearsal, Ruby and Rob's wedding party met at Signature Grill, an elegant golf course restaurant patiently awaiting discovery by the residents of its surrounding neighborhoods. Beneath green-striped awnings on the restaurant's red brick terrace, parents, groomsmen and bridesmaids lounged in white Adirondack chairs around matching slat-topped tables, drinking champagne and martinis, and wolfing down shrimp and local Blue Crab cakes. It was a quiet night at the grill; they had the place to themselves.

Ruby and Rob were the last of the group to arrive. "You're sure you're up to this?" he asked, as they walked through the doors of the restaurant.

"Stay next to me and all will be well," Ruby answered, anxious about being surrounded by Ainsley, Blaine, and Chris.

He leaned in. "I'm not going anywhere."

"If I look like I'm losing it, will you pinch me or something?"

"With pleasure. Any limits on what the 'something' can be?" he asked, as they took their seats.

Chris tapped his water glass with a table knife. "All right, everyone," he announced, "now that the bride and groom have arrived, I have something to say."

More knives clinked against glasses until the group quieted down.

"Thank you all for being here tonight. I want to take a moment to wish my daughter—" he turned to Ainsley, "—*our* daughter Ruby, a life of happiness with Rob—as much happiness as she's brought us. And Rob, we've tried for twenty years to find something wrong with you, and we, and the private detectives, have failed miserably, so...welcome to the family!" He raised his glass of juice, followed by twenty other champagne flutes and martini glasses. More toasts to the couple, rehearsed and spontaneous, followed, along with funny, touching and embarrassing childhood stories, building excitement for the next day's festivities.

As dinner wound down, Don asked for everyone's attention. "Folks, I want to say a little something, before we break up for the night. I'm warning everyone in advance: I'm not a sage. I'm simply an old, tired lawyer."

Guests hushed one another until the noise level was at a murmur.

Ainsley elbowed her mother. "What's going on?" she whispered. "Did he plan this?"

"If he did, he didn't tell me about it," Julie whispered back.

Don stood. "Robin—Rob. Firstly, I want to welcome you to our family, although it seems like you're already a part of it, we've known you for so long."

Rob squeezed Ruby's hand. Ainsley and Jill exchanged a quick smile across the table.

"And now," he continued, "I'd like to impart some wisdom, if I may." He was visibly emotional as he looked at Julie and Ainsley.

Ainsley nudged her mother again. "What is he doing now?"

"Honey, I have no idea. Maybe the emotions of the week have gotten the better of him, or it could be that talk he had with Blaine the other night—"

"Talk?" Ainsley asked. "What talk?"

"Shhh! Let him finish, honey."

"Rob," Don continued to the silent crowd, "you're about to join an exclusive club here. All of us—the men in this family—we're mere mortals—men among sirens." He scanned the table, as though he was in court, reaching out to a jury. "I've lived among them for close to fifty years now. The happiest years of my life. I wouldn't change a thing if I could." He looked at the floor for a moment. "No, that's not true. Time. I'd want more time...and to be here more...especially for my daughter, Ainsley...."

The table of guests maintained an awkward silence. Blaine stared at his plate. Chris smiled absently.

"Do something, Mom," Ainsley begged.

Julie jumped up from her seat stood next to Don. "Come on, everyone. Why don't we drink to the men in our family for once," she said, placing her hand on Don's and raising his glass. The rest of the table joined in, emptying their drinks for the final time that evening.

"We're going now, mom," Ruby told Ainsley as soon as conversation started up again. "Before anyone else in the family feels the need to make any public declarations."

chapter 25

By noon on Saturday, everyone but Ainsley, Ruby and Ruby's bridesmaids had departed 313 Water's Edge Lane for Atlantic Episcopal Church. Ainsley's hairdresser, Ted, set up shop in the second-floor dressing room, and worked his way through Ruby's line of bridesmaids, creating freeform updos, each one adorned with a white rose.

When he finished, he stepped back and assessed the three young women. "Okay, ladies, my work with you is done. Bring on the princess," he said.

"We have to find her first," Megan told him. "Miss Garbo said she needed some time alone—again."

"I'll find her, girls," Ainsley said. She took a slow walk through the second floor, looking at pictures on the walls, reminiscing, finally checking Ruby's room. She walked to the window and looked up at John's old bedroom window, as she had a hundred times before, when she was a girl and Ruby's room was hers. A breeze blew the curtain back from the paned glass. Ainsley guessed Margie had raised all the upstairs windows when she arrived that morning, as she did every week when Ainsley was growing up, before beginning her routine house cleaning. Margie had volunteered to help with Ruby's wedding as soon as she heard about the engagement. Her plan was to give the house a final cleaning after everyone left for the church, making it white-glove ready for guests attending the afternoon wedding reception.

On her way out of the room, Ainsley met Ruby, wearing a white silk robe and burgundy velvet slippers, coming down the stairs from the third floor.

Ruby's eyes looked teary. "I heard you calling me. Is it my turn for hair?" she asked.

"Yes, Ruby," Ainsley said. "Where were you?"

"Upstairs."

"Is everything...okay? Did you sleep all right at Rob's?"

Ruby seemed distracted. "Yes, fine."

Ainsley couldn't tell if she was being genuine or sarcastic. "I think you'd better get in there, Ruby. Ted's waiting for you."

Ainsley leaned in the dressing room doorway, watching Ruby situate herself in an adjustable chair Ted had brought with him from the salon. She saw herself twenty-four years ago, on her wedding day, but with one critical difference. There was an aura of confidence surrounding Ruby today, something Ainsley had lacked in the hours before her own wedding. That day, Ainsley sat in a hairdresser's chair, certain that Chris had been unfaithful the night before. After their rehearsal dinner ended, she called him into the early morning, never getting an answer. The next day, she walked down the aisle uncertain and uneasy, her marriage half over before it even started. Rob would never cause Ruby to confront that kind of pain. They had trust on their side.

"So we're doing the style we tested out last month?" Ted asked Ruby as he placed a caddy full of hairpins, brushes and combs on her lap. She didn't answer, but instead pulled two small photos out of her pocket and handed them to him.

"Hey, that's—your mother? Wow! Okay, I can do that." He took the photo and propped it up on the vanity table. "Let's get this thing started."

Megan, Jan and Rachael rushed over to the table to inspect the photo. "Oh, that'll be beautiful," Rachael said.

"Who's the hottie?" Megan asked.

"That's my Uncle John," Ruby replied. "He died before I was born."

Megan was mortified. "Oh, I'm sorry. I didn't mean anything...."

A wave of emotion hit Ainsley. Ruby threw her a sympathetic look, and then lowered her head so Ted could work on her hair.

"Megan, it's fine," Ainsley assured her, startled by the discovery of the photos. "He *was* a major hottie. And, a great brother, too." She joined Ruby's friends at the vanity table. "Ruby, where did you get those pictures?" she asked.

"In Uncle John's room," Ruby replied. "I guess the wind blew them out of a box on the nightstand. I found these two on the floor by the bed."

"I thought you were wearing your hair down for the wedding," Ainsley said, still puzzled.

"I was, but I saw these pictures in Uncle John's room, and I changed my mind. Is that okay?"

"Yes, of course, Ruby. Ted, I'll tell you how to do the back. I still have the combs and pins. I'll...go get them from my room."

By two o'clock, Ted was gone and Ruby was ready to put on her wedding gown. Margie gingerly crept up the stairs with a tray full of mimosas, a white apron tied tight over her pink duster, and a pink crocheted chignon cover holding her heavily sprayed, pitch-black hair, the result of a weekly color rinse. "These fancy drinks aren't my specialty," she said. "Hopefully, they'll do. Now hurry and drink them, so I can straighten up and get myself to that church."

"Thanks Margie," Ruby said, hugging her as she took the tray. "You take one, too."

"Let's drink a toast to your mom, Ruby," Megan suggested. "She's responsible for all of this." Megan took the tray and handed out glasses.

"To Mrs. Bohan," Jan said.

Margie and the others joined in. "To Mrs. Bohan!"

"To you, Mom," Ruby said, pointedly, raising her glass.

"I'd better get myself dressed, ladies," Ainsley said. "I can't show up at the church in shorts. Ruby, are you all set?"

"We're good. I'll call you when I'm dressed," Ruby said, disappearing into a cloud of crinoline petticoats.

Ainsley intended to go directly to her room to change clothes for the wedding, but detoured back into Ruby's instead. With her daughter's imminent, unsettled exodus from the house, the best chapter in Ainsley's life was ending—without closing. As much as Ainsley chased it, closure seemed to elude her. She sat on the bed and scanned the space. Ruby had already boxed up and mailed the items she would use in her Washington apartment. What remained were mostly outgrown childhood belongings, destined to stay where they were, as they were, indefinitely. Ruby's room, like John's, had the potential to become a lonely shrine for Ainsley to venerate.

Excited voices carried from the other end of the house. Ainsley put her introspection on hold and returned to her room to change clothes.

❦

"Miss Ainsley! Ruby! Your car's here!" Margie shouted.

"We're coming," Ruby answered.

"Oh, Ruby, you're so beautiful," Ainsley said, as she met her daughter on the landing.

"Like you, Mom?" Ruby's voice lacked the irony Ainsley expected to hear.

"Well—yes—" Ainsley could barely mange the words.

Ruby leaned over the stairwell. "Guys, go ahead downstairs. Get the car ready, please. We'll be there in a minute," she ordered politely. They dutifully scurried toward the door.

"Mom," Ruby said.

"Honey, I can drive separately—"

"No. Listen," she went on. "I sat upstairs in Uncle John's room—don't ask me why I went up there—thinking about all of this. There was a moment—I can't explain it—that I realized that there's too much love in this family, to start punishing people now for past mistakes. You asked me to put myself in your place, to think about what I would have done if I were you. I tried, and I don't know. I keep coming back to this: if I can forgive Dad for everything he did to you—his betrayal—I have to forgive you and Blaine, too. This strange family, my family. It will never make sense; it will never be "normal." You once said that every woman in our family has a test. I believe this was mine."

"Ruby, if I thought it would have helped you to know sooner, I would have found a way to tell you."

"I see that now. You never held Dad responsible for the terrible things he's *forgotten* that he did to you."

Ainsley swallowed hard. "So, how do you want us to tell him?"

"Tell him? How would telling him help? We'll steal from him memories of us as his family. He'll have no one to trust. He'll lose faith in what's good in the world. We're his life, Mom."

Ainsley felt weak with relief. "I promised you that I would stay with him. I don't want you to worry about leaving here to start your life with Rob."

"You taught me a lot of good things growing up, Mom. I do love you, but I'm going to need some time away from you, from all of this. Just for a while."

"I understand," she said, stinging from the rejection. "And you're certain—with everything that's happened this week—about the wedding? You don't have to go through with it...."

"I may not be sure of much right now, but there is one thing that I'm certain of, and that is that I want to marry Rob—now—today. You were right about him. He is everything I thought he was. Everything I want. I'm going to spend my life with him."

"What about Blaine conducting the ceremony? I can talk to Father Thompson."

"It would look strange—to Dad—if he didn't. It was always my dream to have Uncle Blaine perform my wedding. It's going to take me some time to figure out how to reshuffle his place in my life, but I'm working on it." She gave Ainsley a thin smile.

"So?" Ainsley said, tentatively.

"So," Ruby answered, taking Ainsley's arm in hers, "let's go marry me off."

chapter 26

RUBY HELD CHRIS' hand and walked beside his wheelchair up the church's center aisle, as one hundred and fifty hushed friends and relatives drank in the sight of her curvaceous body, wrapped securely in an ivory strapless ball gown. She walked tall and proud, not an ounce of her nerves on edge, making eye contact with gawking guests on both sides of the aisle, like royalty out for a walk on the streets, letting the common people feel important for a few moments. Around her neck, gleaming from a new, silver chain, was the locket Blaine had given her as a child.

"I love you, Mom," she whispered as she and Chris approached the altar and her waiting fiancé. The music stopped, and Father Thompson and Blaine began the ceremony.

Ainsley studied Blaine as he faced the congregation and asked them to commit to supporting the new couple. It was a rare opportunity for her to freely indulge the longing she had for him. Everyone focused on Ruby and Rob; no one was watching her. There was no need for her to avert her eyes after a few seconds, or worry about appearing overly familiar with him. She had loved him for so long, nearly all of that time from behind a veil of casual phone calls, letters and family gatherings, yet he knew her more intimately than anyone else did. He shared her deepest secrets, dreams—even her sins.

Blaine asked Ruby and Rob to make their commitments to each other. They took turns reciting their vows, their voices trembling with emotion. Ainsley knew that there was no way to predict with certainty the path Ruby and Rob's relationship would ultimately take, but, if history could in any way, portend the future, theirs was an open, honest love that would last. And, they had Rob's mother, Jill, to thank for it.

❦

One exceptionally frustrating morning in 1989, when Ainsley was out of ideas to simultaneously keep Ruby occupied, maintain a noise level low enough to allow Chris to rest, and get enough work done in order to put food on the table, Jill came to her door, and to her rescue.

She knew almost everything about Ainsley's life, except for one of its most important parts—Blaine's real place in the family. She listened when Ainsley needed her to, without prejudice, to the sleazy details of Chris' affairs and near-fatal car accident. She was a lifeline during the early days of his return back home, stopping by for an hour or so a few times a week, giving Ainsley time to run errands or walk Attila.

"I'm not going to work while my husband's out of the country anymore," she told Ainsley. "I'm taking my son out of daycare and having him at home with me after school. So I was thinking, what's another child? Rob will enjoy a companion."

It was an easy decision. Ainsley got a solid four to five hours of work in at her home office, checking in on Chris when necessary. Ruby was safe in Jill's house, less than a thousand feet away, across the hedge. Unless it was raining, she walked to Jill's house to pick up Ruby, sometimes with Chris. In time, he was able to make the trip alone, wheeling back home with Ruby on his lap.

The arrangement lasted until 1991, when Ruby was four years old, and Chris proposed another idea.

"I want to take care of Ruby," he declared over a simple dinner he had made from scratch.

Ainsley thought she misunderstood him. "Are you serious?"

"Aren't you the sexist?" he quipped.

"Well, it's just that, I mean, you're doing so well. I don't want you to take on too much."

"You and Ruby keep me going, and I want to contribute. You're still home most of the time—in the event of an emergency."

Jill took the change in arrangements well. Her son did not. "You can't take her," six-year-old Robin cried. "She's mine. I'm gonna marry her!"

His firm pronouncement proved accurate. Years later, true to his word, Rob began courting fourteen-year-old Ruby with an invitation to the movies. Jill and Ainsley sat several rows away from the fledgling couple, enabling them to watch *X-Men* with as much privacy as a packed theater and their vigilant mothers would allow.

Ruby and Rob started dating in earnest after Ruby started tenth grade, and both chose The College of William and Mary for their undergraduate degrees. They informed their parents of their intention to marry when Ruby was eighteen.

"We love each other, but we're going to wait until I finish my undergrad degree," Ruby said.

Ainsley was speechless at her announcement.

"Honey, are you sure about this?" Chris asked, concerned.

"Yes, we're sure," Rob said. "We want your blessing."

"Of course, we love you, Robin—Rob," Ainsley said, recovering from the news. "But you two have never dated anyone else. This is a major decision."

Ruby had thought it through. "Grandma and Grandpa were barely older then we'll be and they're still together and happy. Marrying young worked for you two. In our family, we find love early, that's all."

Chris and Ainsley looked at each other. Neither of them had a valid objection.

"Don't worry," Ruby said. "Mom, Dad, you've got four more years to adjust to the idea."

"Ruby, you may want to rethink your plan to be a social worker." Chris said. "With your powers of persuasion, you could have a career in law." It was useless to argue. Chris and Ainsley were bested. The wedding was on.

Ainsley had lost track of time. The ceremony was over. She heard a roar of applause erupting as Ruby and Rob turned to face the congregation.

"I would like to introduce Robin and Ruby Horner," Blaine announced, exchanging a careful smile with Ruby.

"The end of one era, the beginning of another...." Chris said, shaking his head.

After embracing their parents and new in-laws, the new couple glided down the aisle and stole away into the church parlor.

"How are you holding up, Mrs. Horner?"

"I'm fabulous, Mr. Horner!"

"Are you going to make it through the reception?"

"Yes, we are." Ruby gathered the lapels of his jacket in her hands. "Rob, you've always been there for me. I won't forget about us again, no matter how much chaos life throws our way." She brushed his lips with hers. "I feel young again, Rob, the way I should feel."

He hugged her. "I love you, Ruby Horner."

"We need to get this honeymoon started," she said suggestively.

"We have to get through the reception first," he answered.

"Says who?" Ruby said over her shoulder, rushing ahead of him as they made their way to the front of the church. "Come on, young stud. Chase me!"

"Shall we?" Ainsley asked Chris, putting her hand on his shoulder. He moved the control on his wheelchair and they made their way down the aisle for the receiving line and photos.

Blaine walked behind them to the narthex of the church, positioning himself behind Ainsley as guests filed by, one hand briefly pressing into the small of her back, startling her. He hadn't touched her, apart from a brief hug on the occasions that they greeted each other, for years. It was against the rules.

The photographer took her last picture of the wedding party in the church's perennial garden, freeing them to leave for the reception. Ainsley felt a twinge of anxiety watching her daughter and new son-in-law climb into their own limousine, independent, no longer under the watch of doting parents. They appeared relaxed and excited all at once. She envied them their future. Hers scared her.

"Blaine, ride with us," Chris said. "Plenty of room in the car. Champagne, too. We'll share stories about Ruby, you know, get sappy and sentimental." The three of them found their places in the limo and followed Ruby and Rob home.

chapter 27

THE HOT SATURDAY afternoon merged into a close, sweet-smelling early evening as cars streamed into the driveway of 313 Water's Edge Lane. Square, white-clothed tables surrounded by gold bamboo chairs and cooled by a dozen lazy ceiling fans, greeted wedding guests entering the reception tent. At the center of each table sat a clear vase overflowing with red and white roses, each one of them raised and handpicked by Ainsley. Sage green napkins and menus, stark white china, and a sprinkling of small, framed photos of Rob, Ruby and their families made up the place settings. A trio of symphony musicians played cello and violin in one corner, filling the tent with Vivaldi and Fauré, drowning out the sound of popping corks and clinking china. Palladium windows looked out onto the manicured lawn and white-and-red house beyond.

"This is just stunning. I can't believe you planned the whole thing yourself!" Ruby's high school French teacher raved to Ainsley. "And these roses—from your own garden. Magnifique!"

"Thanks. I based it on my own wedding. Ruby used to look at my wedding album, and she wanted the same look." Ainsley smiled at the memory. "It wasn't too hard, since I'd done it all before."

"That is so romantic. Like mother, like daughter."

"I don't know about that," Ainsley answered. "Ruby's definitely her own woman." She made one last inspection of the reception tent, checking every fork, glass and place card, determined to make at least the final phase of her daughter's wedding day as close to perfect as possible.

Looking handsome but tired in the tuxedo Blaine had helped him struggle into early in the day, Chris slumped in his wheelchair. Even from across the lawn, Ainsley could read his body language: full-blown fatigue. "God, these people drink like fish!" she said, approaching him. She estimated he had another hour or so before completely succumbing to exhaustion. "I'm going in the house to get some more wine," she said. "Will you be all right?"

"I'm fine. You go on." He mustered a faint smile and powered his wheelchair away from her and toward his parents.

Inside the house, Ainsley stopped in the kitchen and talked with the caterers before winding her way to the shuttered library. She removed her black evening pumps and climbed behind the sofa in search of a case of Champagne. The library door's spring latch unexpectedly disengaged with a distinctive click, and she poked her head up from behind the sofa to see who it was.

"Ainsley? What are you doing?" Blaine asked from across the room, leaning on the closed door.

"Oh, you know me," she said, flustered, holding the slender line between decorum and intimacy. "The caterers need another case of wine, and of course I have to handpick every bottle myself. I don't really want them back in this section of the house, anyway...with all of Chris' medication and things in here."

Blaine stepped around the furniture and stood in front of her. "Let me help you with those boxes. You're supposed to be celebrating."

"No, Ruby is. It's her day," Ainsley said. She walked over to the window, opening the shutter to let in a thin stream of light from the porch. She was uncomfortable being alone with him in a darkened room. He kept breaking their rules. "Blaine, I'm lucky that I still have a daughter with everything that's happened." She lowered her voice to a whisper. "So are you."

He sat down on the edge of the sofa. "Ainsley, now that things have settled down, we have to talk."

"I think Ruby's going to be okay, if that's what you're worried about," she said, stepping back from the window. "It's going to take some time."

"Ainsley, this isn't about Ruby. It's about me."

"What is it?" she asked. "Is something wrong?"

He crossed his arms over his chest. "I'm—leaving the church."

His words stunned her. "What did you say?"

"Ainsley, I'm transitioning to the lay clergy." He set his jaw, waiting for her response.

"Is it because of what happened with Ruby?" she asked.

"I made the decision two months ago. I can't live like this anymore, Ainsley, committing the same sins over and over again."

"No, Blaine." She kept shaking her head back and forth, trying to block out his words. "When Ruby was born, we agreed—to go on this way. You told me years ago that you'd finally found reconciliation, forgiveness."

"Ainsley, if reconciliation means being able to sleep—fitfully—at night, and passably perform the duties of my parish, then yes, I found reconciliation. But my greatest sin still haunts me. That sin wasn't being with you, that night, all of those years ago. It was staying in the priesthood for the past two decades—when I didn't belong there. As a priest, I should have confessed the sin I committed against you, God and myself and accepted reprimand and counseling. I should have embraced new assignments given to me, without question. Followed the path laid before me by my superiors in the church. Instead, I slid under the radar, used excuse after excuse to stay at my post, my lonely string of dying parishes. I did that to live alongside you, and your family. Any benefit to my church was secondary."

"You didn't have to stay there for us. You could have told me. I couldn't have stopped you from moving on—from moving way."

"Don't you see? I wanted to stay! You became the most important thing to me—you and Ruby. I accepted the loneliness and isolation of the long months alone, in between our visits, as a kind of atonement for what we had done. I may have fooled my superiors, my parishioners, but I couldn't fool God. I'm finished trying." He was near tears. "Ainsley, it's not too late for us, if you still love me."

"Please stop. Stop it, Blaine." Her fragile, secret world was crumbling in her hands. She fumbled her way across the room and sat down on a case of wine next to the sofa, the skirt of her gray cocktail dress spilling over the box. "I thought we'd all gotten through the worst," she said, rubbing her forehead. "I thought—that with time, we could put our family back together."

"Ainsley, I can't go back to the way things were."

"Why not, Blaine?" She was crying.

"Because at some point in every single day I've waged a war against my feelings for you. I did receive God's calling—I'm certain of that—but there's more than one way to answer that call. When I was young, my family firmly indoctrinated me with the philosophy that the only proper way to serve God was as a priest. I think deep down inside, I found the priesthood to be an escape from confronting the issues I saw in my own dysfunctional family. I mean, if I couldn't marry and have a family, I couldn't repeat the same mistakes my father and mother made, right? You made it so easy for me to stay, not coming forward about Ruby."

"I was thinking of her when I made that decision."

"I told you, years ago, that being with you made me feel powerless, that you pulled me from my path—"

"You still blame me—" Ainsley interrupted.

"No. I couldn't admit to myself that I made a mistake and didn't belong in the priesthood. Back then, I didn't know the difference between temptation and real love. God won't punish us for love, not if it's honest and good. You know I love you, Ainsley. Be with me, before it's too late. While we're still young enough to start again."

She couldn't process the words she'd waited so long to hear, and he had waited too long to say. "You're going away?" It was more of a statement than a question.

"I won't be based in Michigan anymore. I'll be somewhere on the east coast for my first assignment. I will keep my house in Manistique, for downtime, in between assignments. You know, most of my parishioners have died off. What I learned from them, I'll use now, in my Hospice work."

Ainsley stood up and leaned against the wall. "I nearly lost Ruby in all of this, and to keep her, I promised that I won't abandon Chris. Now, I'm losing you."

Blaine paced the floor. "Ainsley, you know how much I care about Chris, but he's not a patient or an invalid anymore. Have you noticed? He's a strong, independent man, and you made him that way. When are you going to put yourself first?"

"I'm all he has now, with Ruby gone. I promised her...."

"Chris has a family, too." He took her hand and led her to the sofa. "This isn't about Ruby now. You, me, Chris—one of us has to come away from this hurt. There's isn't any other way."

She was adamant. "Don't ask me to make a choice like this."

"So, you're saying that it's over between us?"

"Us?" she shouted. "We've gone on twenty years. Yearning. Punishing ourselves for the way we feel about each other. Now you think we should just walk off into the sunset together at Ruby and Chris' expense. Why did you have to do this today? A hundred times over the years, I've stood next to you, sat across the table from you, wanting to scream to the world how much I love you, or to simply touch you, but I couldn't—I didn't. I prayed for a phone call, a letter, an email from you, telling me that you changed your mind, that you wanted to be with me, and that we had to find a way to be together. That never arrived. Our indecision forced my choice. I won't break my word to Ruby, not even for you—not even for us, Blaine."

Blaine moved close to her, desperate to touch her again. "So there's no chance?"

Ainsley slid away from him to the other end of the sofa. "Blaine, as painful as it's been, telling Ruby our story has helped me to put things, our past, in perspective. What do we really have, Blaine? Our relationship is about what we can't do, shouldn't say, and mustn't think. Forbidden things. I've done the best I could all of these years, to stay within those boundaries, to hold this family together. Don't question my decision now." She bolted from the library and up the staircase, trying to reach her room without anyone seeing her. Blaine wanted more than anything to follow her, but he couldn't put his feelings before her wishes, her reputation, or her relationship with their daughter. He stayed in place on the sofa.

The library door opened a crack.

“Ainsley?” Blaine asked, standing up.

An older man ducked his head into the library. “Oops, wrong room,” he said.

“We’re conducting a self-guided tour of this incredible house,” the woman with him gushed. “Wonderful service, Father,” she added.

“Thank you,” Blaine said. “See you outside.” He put on his best priestly face for the last time and made his way outside to watch Ruby mingle with her guests.

“Where’ve you been?” Chris asked Ainsley as she found him on the front porch an hour later. “Everyone’s been asking for you.”

“Just a headache,” she told him. “I took something for it, and had to lie down to give it time to work.”

“Well, I think it’s almost the witching hour. Our daughter’s going off to officially start her new life.”

“I think it’s going to throw a small wrench in their idea of making a stealthy getaway, but it was great of you to surprise Ruby and Rob with the T-Bird.”

“Ainsley,” he said, “it’s hard to resist something rare and beautiful, especially when it’s given to you without conditions.” He studied her face intently. “Don’t you think they’ll get a little more use out of it than I will?” He slapped his useless legs hard, unable to feel the impact.

“You never know, Chris. Maybe in our lifetime—”

“Our lifetime is half over. Besides, it doesn’t matter, Ains. I’m okay with things.” He watched Rob and Ruby run the gauntlet of colorfully dressed guests on their way to the convertible. “She looks very happy.”

Ainsley was wistful. “Yes, she does.”

“Now, what about you?” Chris asked.

“I’m happy that she’s happy....” Ainsley answered.

“No,” Chris pressed, “I said, ‘What about you?’”

What could she say? The truth? That she had lived the last twenty years vicariously through Ruby, who was leaving the nest? Blaine's new vocation meant that seeing him in Michigan every summer, and his annual winter visits to her home would end, breaking the delicate strand of hope she harbored for his continued presence in her life, leaving her behind, and unable to follow. She pushed aside her emotions and answered, "I'm good, Chris."

"Ainsley," he said, looking up at her and grasping her arm, "it's my legs I've got no feeling in, not my heart. Don't you think I know that you've been crying? Or, that our relationship hasn't been fulfilling for you all of these years? Our work together is finished. Ruby's leaving. What's next? You retire to your floor of the house and I retire to mine?"

Things were happening too fast. "Where is this coming from?" she asked. "Haven't you been happy, Chris?"

"My happiness wasn't free. It came at your expense."

She felt a surge of emotion and turned away from him. "God, this wedding—why does everyone feel the need to bare their souls?"

"I don't know who else you're referring to, Ainsley, but I know you've given me too much of your life already."

She crossed her arms over her chest and stared at her shoes. "Chris, I told you years ago...that I would be here for you."

"And you have been. You made a life for me when I thought mine was over. You got me through that, allowed me to stay a part of this family. So many times, the only thing that kept me going was watching you with Ruby, or wanting to see Ruby grow up. You gave that to me. I've lived here in this house, among your family's things, taking everything you gave me, questioning nothing, choosing not to tempt fate. I'd be lying if I said I didn't know, all along, that you were living half a life."

No, a double life, she thought. Tears flowed down her cheeks. The love she felt for him when they were young was long gone, but they had somehow survived twenty-four years—they had raised Ruby. Through that journey, she learned a new way to love and respect him. Now, she sensed another change looming.

"Ainsley, don't worry about money or the house," Chris told her.

"What are you talking about?"

"I'm bowing out, Ainsley. It's overdue. The people I love have paid for my sins for too long."

"Are you saying—"

"I'm saying that I'm selling the practice and giving you half. It's sad, really. These two wars have created more clients than I could ever have predicted. More than I can take on. The buy-out offer I've received is outrageous."

"You never told me you were thinking of selling the practice."

He waved at Ruby. "We don't tell each other every little thing, now do we?"

"Where will you go? Who'll take care of you?"

"I guess I'll learn to take care of myself. I want to spend some time with my folks, before they get any older—and my sister Amy and her kids. Don't worry. I'll be less than two hours from Ruby and Rob in D.C., and from here. Who knows? I might finally learn how to drive again."

"Do you know what this means?"

"I blew it with you, Ainsley, years ago. You loved me, and I took that love, and destroyed it. Feeding my adolescent ego came before you. You owe me nothing. It's done. Deep down, I always knew that there was a time limit to this—our life together. My time's up. I'm leaving with my parents tonight."

As many times as she'd wished to be free of him, his leaving now struck her as a loss. "Chris," she said, "I promised Ruby that I'd always be here for you, that I wouldn't leave...."

"You're not leaving me—technically. I'm leaving you. We don't have to break this to Ruby today. I'll talk to her about it when she comes back from the honeymoon."

"I don't know what to say." She felt as though she'd had the wind knocked out of her.

Chris looked her in the eyes. "I do have one thing to ask you, Ainsley, before I go...."

A rush of dread hit her. She managed to hold his gaze. "Of course."

"With Ruby," he asked, "am I—have I been a good father?"

"Yes," she gasped, relieved. "Yes, Chris. She couldn't have asked for a better father."

"Good. Good." He nodded. "Because after what I did to you, I need to know I came close to getting it right with her."

"You did, Chris. Never doubt that. Never doubt how much she loves you."

"Then, it's time for you to get on with the rest of your life." His eyes moved to Blaine, who was exchanging a hug with Ruby. "You've helped everyone around you achieve their dreams, Ainsley. It's time for you to run after a dream or two of your own."

"Chris—" She guessed sometimes that he knew, but in two decades, they had never spoken of it.

He held up his hand. "I'm where I should be. Are you?"

She squeezed his upraised hand, and then leaned down and kissed him lightly on the lips.

Tears welled up in his eyes. "Goodbye, Ainsley. You'd better get on with things." He turned his chair away and rolled down the wheelchair ramp.

Ainsley filled her lungs with the rose-scented evening air, straightened up, and descended the porch steps, unsure of where she was going. The guests' chatter was a foreign language to her, unrecognizable words accompanied by a blur of waving, tissue-clutching hands. She focused ahead and waded through the small crowd.

Across the lawn, Blaine and Ruby stood next to the T-bird while Rob hunched over its open trunk and arranged luggage. A lone FA-18 flew low overhead, drowning out excited voices and laughter. Ainsley braced herself and looked upward to the brilliant blue sky, waiting, but as she tracked the white jet trail toward the horizon, the usual sadness never came. Perhaps John had always been with her, shoring her up through the hard times, and she hadn't known how to recognize his presence. Maybe that was the closure she'd been so desperate to find. She felt lighter, unburdened—free.

"Wait!" she called out to Ruby and Blaine, walking faster in their direction. They looked at her curiously as she took off her shoes. She smiled at them, and started to run.

THE END

Points of Interest & Resources

Lehto's Pasties
2045 West U.S. 2
St. Ignace, Michigan 49781
http://lehtosfamouspasties.com/

Totem Village Museum and Store
http://hunts-upguide.com/u_s__2_from_the_bridge_totem_village_museum.html

Fayette State Park
http://www.michigandnr.com

Kitch-iti-kipi
Indian Lake State Park
Route 2 Box 2500
Manistique, MI 49854
http://www.uppermichiganwaterfalls.com/Kitchitikipi.html

Trenary Home Bakery
E-2914 Highway M-67
P.O. Box 300
Trenary, MI 49891-0300
http://www.trenarytoast.us/

Bronner's Christmas Wonderland
25 Christmas Lane
Frankenmuth, MI 48734
www.bronners.com

Zehnder's Restaurant
730 S. Main
Frankenmuth MI 48734
www.zehnders.com

Mackinac Bridge
http://www.mackinacbridge.org/

Presque Isle Park
Marquette, MI
http://marquette.org/Travel/presqueislepark.htm

Togo's
http://www.upfirst.com/togossubs.htm

Disabled American Veterans
http://www.dav.org/

American Spinal Cord Injury Association
http://www.asia-spinalinjury.org/about/mission.php

City of Virginia Beach
Vbgov.com

Lehto's Original Cornish Pasty Recipe

Makes 8 Pasties
Pastry:
5 Cups Flour
2 cups Vegetable Shortening
1 Tbsp. Salt
2 1/2 Cups Water
(1cup milk for patting on Pasties before baking)

Filling:
5 Medium Potatoes (quartered and thinly sliced)
4 Medium Onions (minced)
1/4 Cup Rutabaga (cut thin) optional
2 lbs Coarse Ground Round Steak (Sirloin)
This meat should include at least 4 oz of beef suet.
Any butcher will prepare this upon request
1 Tbsp Salt
1/2 tsp Pepper
2 tsps Wylers Beef Bouillion, dissolved in 1 cup water

Mix flour and salt in large bowl, and mix in shortening by hand until texture resembles coarse crumbs. Add 2 cups of water all at once and work pastry into a ball. Add remaining water to absorb any dry mixture remaining in bowl. This entire procedure should not take more

then a minute or so before the pastry will be easy to handle. Chill pastry overnight, keep chilled while preparing filling.
Prepare and mix all ingredients for filling.
Preheat oven to 450 degrees.
Spray 2 baking sheets with non-stick cooking spray.

Using chilled pastry, form approximately a 3" ball for each Pasty, and roll out on a slightly floured surface until you have about a 10" round. Place each round (one at a time) on baking sheet with one half of pastry on sheet and the other half off the side of the sheet. Fill the half on the sheet with a generous cup of filling, leaving about a 1" edge. Fold unfilled half over filling and bring the bottom edge up to the top so that the two edges meet with the bottom edge slightly overlapping the top. On each end, (after shaping the Pasty into a half-moon shape) pinch and seal and remove excess pastry. With your hand, pat each pasty with the milk and bake for 15 minutes at 450 degrees. Reduce heat to 350 degrees and bake for 30 more minutes. (Make sure the 4 Pasties on each pan are not touching).

This recipe is protected and registered in the US Patent and Trademark office. Reg. No. 1,167,800. It can only be used for non-commercial use.
Inquiries for commercial or franchising purposes can be made to:
DeRich's Licensing Co., Inc.
2048 West US #2
St. Ignace, MI 49781

Made in the USA